Praise for the works of Laina Villeneuve

The Right Thing Easy

The Right Thing Easy is a well written romance. The writing is clean, the characters are charming, and the story keeps you entertained. Villeneuve wrote the characters with a finesse and grace that I enjoyed, especially when they were struggling with tough choices. Laina Villeneuve writes nicely. The thoughts and feelings the characters had were real...I could not help but understanding what they were going though.

-The Lesbian Review

Kat's Nine Lives

...is a friends-to-lovers romance about putting in the time and energy to figure out who you are rather than accept what others think you should be. ...Villeneuve does a superb job with the pacing of this story. It is clearly a romance novel, but there are elements to it that made me feel like I was reading a mystery. She reveals clues about Kat's past bit by bit. As each new piece of information was revealed I was surprised over and over again. All of these tidbits lead up to a better understanding of Kat's fears and understandings.

-The Lesbian Review

Such Happiness as This

The novel describes Robyn's journey from grief and disappointment, through the joy of new friendships and the uncertainty of potential love. Characters are skillfully drawn, and interweave in a plot with enough realistic problems, local references, and surprising twists to satisfy.

-The L-Word

COWGIRL 101

Other Bella Books by Laina Villeneuve

Kat's Nine Lives
Return to Paradise
The Right Thing Easy
Such Happiness as This
Take Only Pictures

About the Author

Laina Villeneuve spent four summers on horseback in the High Sierras. While working on this book, she had the amazing idea to take her family on a road trip to her old stomping grounds. After pitching the dream, her wife said to imagine their boys and how hard it is to get them to brush their teeth and then put that on horseback. Revised plan: she found a stable closer by and has ridden with the kids one by one. She hopes they fall in love with riding, and one day they'll make it back to Mammoth Lakes for an epic family ride!

COWGIRL 101

LAINA VILLENEUVE

BELLA
BOOKS

2020

Bella Books, Inc.
P.O. Box 10543
Tallahassee, FL 32302

Printed in the United States of America on acid-free paper.

First Bella Books Edition 2020

Editor: Cath Walker
Cover Designer: Pol Robinson

ISBN: 978-1-64247-151-9

Acknowledgments

At the Las Vegas Con, Becky Harmon had a sit-down with me. She told me two important things. One, I write romance. Two, I know horses. Her encouragement woke up these characters who have taken me on the most fun writing experience I've had. For that, I cannot say thank you enough!

I'm super lucky for Jaime Clevenger to have given this story time and consideration to make it better. Heather Coughlin, too, challenged me to think about how to honor the growth of the characters. That early feedback contributed a lot.

Many thanks to my friend George whose status as a "white coat" got me thinking of a backstory for Daisy. If you have a chance to watch the Rose Parade on New Year's Day, keep an eye out for the staff dressed all in white. You might see my friend whose behind-the-scene stories were a lot of fun!

I've had so much fun reconnecting with my "I Survived…" friends. Thank you for remembering and sharing stories with me and reminding me (or admitting you've forgotten too) of some of the details that have gone fuzzy. What a good time we had all those years ago!

Along the way, I hit some snags that were difficult to untangle. I have to thank Rachael and Paul for their advice on how to get the story moving again. Laughter through tears and stories that will have to make it into a future book. My sister, Kat, had never told me that she hoped her character wouldn't be limited to one book. I hope Linda knows what a gift it was to get to tell my sister about her cameo in this book. I will never forget those bedside conversations and laughing with my niece as I told her Kat's best lines.

Cath, thank you for helping me with clarity, catching the inconsistencies and giving such encouraging feedback. I'm glad I got to take you on a fictional pack trip since Albuquerque GCLS didn't happen this year. I was really looking forward to swapping stories in person!

Thanks to my wife for her unflagging support through the entire process a book takes, especially for the margin notes she leaves reading early drafts and nudging me to include the emotional content that does not come as easily as dialogue. Thanks, Ma for stepping in at the end to help with the "which word works better?" game.

Thank you to all of you who read my books and take the time to reach out and tell me that the characters touched you. I am truly lucky to be able to share these stories with you!

Dedication

For Louisa
After all these years,
the trail is still sweeter with you.

CHAPTER ONE

"Hot rats!" Jo Harding hissed, jumping on one foot and shaking the other that she had finally extracted from under Ladybird's devilish hoof. "You did that on purpose, you empty-headed jackass!"

"Step on her other foot for calling you that, Ladybird!" Gabe Owen's rich voice startled her all over again.

"Daggummit it, Gabe! I'm mad enough to swallow a horned toad backward! Keep running your mouth and I've got a special name for you too!"

"Keep tightening that cinch and you'll turn that poor mule into a peanut!"

"It's not that tight," Jo said as she loosened the girth.

"Not as tight as the jeans she's got on," the cowboy joked, tipping his head in the direction of the newbie leading a dirty white horse toward the upper hitching rail.

"Who?" Jo grabbed the next mule's pack saddle. She had no intention of following Gabe's line of vision. She'd already paid the price for watching the newcomer trying to catch a horse for the last fifteen minutes. Her irritation had grown with every hesitant step Tight Jeans had taken.

"Zorro, the newbie you've had your eye on all morning. Thinking about asking her out?"

"Thinking about chewing her out," Jo mumbled as she watched the woman loop the lead around and around the rail in front of the employee shed. Gabe's nickname was apt. Give her a black mask and cape to go with her flat-brimmed, unshaped black hat, and she could go trick-or-treating as Zorro.

"I wondered if she was your type."

"I wonder if she knows a daggum thing about horses."

"Looks like she needs help."

Jo refused to take the bait. She untied Ladybird and said, "I don't see anyone stopping you."

"Not true. My girlfriend's a sheriff. She's kept a close eye on me ever since she gave me that speeding ticket, and she's got informants everywhere. No way I could help out someone as hot as that without ending up in trouble."

"Not my job." Jo jutted her jaw in the direction of the lower pack dock where she had already sorted the guests' luggage and sleeping bags, her cook's kitchen boxes and camping gear like tables, chairs, shovel and ax. They were waiting to be loaded on mules and transported into the backcountry. "I'm one foot out of the yard. I don't have time to teach Zorro the difference between a horse's rump and its muzzle."

"You've got wagons of time." When she frowned at him, he added, "I'll help you out of the yard."

"Not my job," Jo shot over her shoulder as she led Ladybird and Dumbo over to the pack dock across the yard from the sheds and hitching rail where the dude horses were saddled each morning. The day-ride crew of Lodgepole Pine Pack Outfit led up to twenty tourists down to Rainbow Falls three times a day on the "bombproof" dude horses that could be trusted not to spook at unexpected things on the trail. Jo regarded the trip as the Disneyland of the backcountry, with families who wanted a quick thrill and a photo opportunity. Gabe had told her to be grateful for the revenue the two-hour-long rides brought in, but it was difficult since Leo was often forced to staff it with unskilled workers.

Gabe followed her to the shed with a raised wooden platform full of packing gear: boxes and the metal racks that attached them to the mule's pack saddle, huge leather panniers, ropes to tie down the loads and tarps to protect it all.

Away from the chaos at the Lodge, Jo was able to do her own thing. Out in the mountains, she always worked alone. In the yard, especially if she wanted to get an early start, she'd accept help but only from those who had proven their worth and skill. Gabe ranked at the top of that list. He was every inch a cowboy—and he had several above six feet—along with great upper-body strength from hauling hay bales his whole life. He wore his brown hair and beard short and usually put work before conversation.

"She's not hard to look at," he said, catching the straps of the heavy pannier Jo held in place.

"Being good-looking doesn't get the job done." Jo waited for him to lift the bag on his side onto the mule, with no expectation of his saying something about her ability to work and be pretty. Jo wore her dark brown hair as short as the men and though she lacked Gabe's bulk, she was nearly as tall. With her tight sports bras and her preference for working in silence, she was often mistaken for a man. Not that she minded. Jobs typically held by men held much more appeal for her and she was fine being "one of the guys." She checked the load and made necessary adjustments before she was ready to tie it off.

"But it makes the job more fun!" he said, uncharacteristically chatty. And distracted. She kept catching him glancing up at the day-ride crew.

For that she launched the end of the lash rope over the top of the mule without hollering the customary "Headache!" in warning.

"Hey!" Gabe barked when the long rope made contact.

"Sorry. Thought you were watching." Jo wasn't sorry. She had a job to do, and the sooner she got it done, the sooner she'd be in the saddle with only her five mules for company, the way she liked it. Takeisha, the cook, would take her time riding to camp with the guests, but once the equipment was loaded, Jo would travel faster, arriving at camp first to begin the setup. She expected Gabe to be as steady and hard-working as a mule, the highest compliment she could give anyone. Today he was acting as unfocused and as flighty as a hot-blooded horse.

"There are breaks in the day. You know, times that people stop working. Times when it's nice to sit next to someone easy on the eyes."

"When I stop, it's dark. Time to turn in."

"An even better time to have someone like that in your bedroll."

"It's not that easy." Jo nodded to the pile of gear she wanted put on Dumbo.

"I never said it was easy. But it's sure as hell not as hard as you make it."

"Come on. You're saying you'd hook up with someone from the day-ride crew?"

"Not anymore, but back in the day…"

"Back when you were helping on a trip, not lead packer."

"You're a snob. Those girls do a load of work every day."

"Not Zorro." Gabe's nickname suited her better than Tight Jeans. "I haven't seen her do a bit of work up there."

"See, you have been watching!" Gabe's smile made Jo regret her words. "So she has a lot to learn. You could be the one to teach her."

"And next summer, she'll be gone, and we'll have some new hoo haw who doesn't know…"

"…a 'daggum thing.' I heard you. And I know how much you hate flighty people."

"I don't have much use for people. Period."

Gabe slapped his palm on his chest as if to keep his heart in place. "That hurt."

Jo unclipped the packed mule and led it away from the dock to make room for the next two to be loaded up for their trip to Third Crossing. She tied Skeeter to Blaze and crossed paths with Takeisha on the way back to the dock. This was their second year as a team. Takeisha had been part of the day-ride crew for three years and itched to get into the backcountry. Since the pack station sent couples on travel trips and she was single, she had accepted the norm and stayed on day rides, stuck training greenhorns and seeing the same scenery day after day.

Jo had always been one to challenge the norm, and as Gabe liked to point out, she wasn't partnered, either. For Jo, dating meant permanence, and in her experience, animals were the only ones she could trust to stick by her side. Takeisha worked hard and didn't ask a bunch of questions, so Jo pitched the idea of being a team, not a couple, but a matched set of outsiders—her the only queer cowgirl, Takeisha the only black one.

She handed a brown bag to Jo. "Here's your lunch."

"Did you get good stock for us?"

"I snagged Mouse for a bell mare, and I made sure we don't take Bailey and Lumpy."

Jo took a bite of the apple she'd pulled from her lunch sack. "Sounds good."

"I'll stop the group for lunch right after that patch of granite, so you can pass us before the switchbacks."

"That'll work. Thanks for lunch."

While she and Gabe finished packing, she ate her apple and all the Starburst, except for the orange one which she gave to Blaze, and drank her juice box. The sandwich, she folded in half and shoved in her vest pocket to eat on the trail. She accepted Gabe's offer to string up her five mules while she grabbed her mount.

Mentally, she was already in the saddle, settling into the rocking gait of Tuxedo, the mule she'd be riding for the summer. But the sight ahead literally stopped her in her tracks. "Son of a biscuit eater," she mumbled under her breath.

Still tied to the hitching rail, Churchill leaned away from Zorro who held the bridle up as if she was trying to picture where to hang a painting on a wall. A wave of heat ran through Jo's body. She told herself it was the way the woman was holding the bridle all wrong, the bit up between the big white gelding's ears, the headstall at his muzzle, and the reins hung around her shoulders like a necklace.

Jo told herself that the heat had nothing to do with the jeans so tight they looked painted on. Nothing to do with eyes as blue as High Sierra skies that lifted to meet Jo's. She was at least a head shorter than Jo and wore a bright smile.

"The bit goes in his mouth," Jo said thrown off by all those straight white teeth.

"Bit?" The woman studied the tangle in her hands.

"First thing, you've got to untie your mount." Jo stepped forward to undo the mess of knotted rope at the rail. "How do you not know a decent slipknot?"

"I've never gotten a horse ready before," she admitted.

Jo took in her clean new coat and boots and immediately imagined a personal groom bringing a saddled horse to a mounting block. Girls like her spent the summer working on their tan. The deep tan on this one's skin and the golden highlights on her otherwise dark curls suggested she spent most of her time by the pool. They worried too much about keeping their nails clean to be bothered to tack up a horse for themselves. She took a deep breath, intent on counting to three to calm herself, but the smell of lavender cleared her mind completely. Who smelled like lavender in the midst of a dozen horses?

"I've only ridden once," the woman said, instantly reminding Jo of the trouble this woman was bound to be. "When I was ten, my aunt took me to Hansen Dam. It's in southern California. My horse went through a bush, and my shirt caught on a branch. The whole back ripped open!"

Too many words and too much stupidity. What was Leo thinking bringing in help that had zero riding experience? It was a nightmare, but not her nightmare. Across the yard, Gabe caught her eye and gave her a thumbs-up. Seeing her mules strung one after the other and starting to bunch up on each other, she decided not to link his gesture to the amount of time she'd talked to the newbie. She handed the lead to Zorro. "Hang tight. I've got to get my string out of here. I'll see if Gabe can give you a hand."

With that, she buckled into her chaps, slipped on her gloves and swung aboard Tuxedo. He danced underneath her, eager to get moving. She guided him across the yard and took Blaze's lead from Gabe.

"You two hit it off?"

Jo looped around Gabe, making sure each of her pack mules was in its place, the loads riding evenly. Satisfied, she said, "I don't know what she's doing on the employee side of the rail, and I'll bet she's long gone before I'm back from this trip. Good luck!"

With that, she pointed Tuxedo toward the wagon trail and gave him his head. "Cody!" she hollered. "Let's ride!" Her border collie darted out from underneath the loading dock and streaked out in front of her, tail wagging furiously. Jo lifted her hat both in farewell to Gabe and to release the stresses of the morning. Nothing but the mountains, the trail, and a set of mule ears in front of her, she finally relaxed.

CHAPTER TWO

Daisy Lucero shut her mouth before something could fly in. Blood pounded in her ears. She was embarrassed, there was that, but there was so much more. She'd convinced Leo to let her try working in the corrals and couldn't believe she'd seen *her* the first morning, the cowgirl who had been riding through her dreams since January. Temptation, the coffee shop where she'd worked, was on the Rose Parade route, so naturally she watched every year. She'd never seen anything like the Lodgepole Pine Pack Outfit's entry. More to the point, she'd never seen anyone like that cowgirl ride down Colorado Boulevard, one hand controlling her mule and the other guiding a whole string of them.

Of course, she hadn't known they were mules at the time. At home, she pulled up the Rose Parade on TV to hear the telecaster's brief description of the outfit. The camera operator must have seen what Daisy did because the picture zoomed in close on the cowgirl. It wasn't to capture another parade participant hamming for the people at home, only the somber cowgirl who didn't seem to acknowledge the camera or the enormous crowd. She was in her own world on that mule, like she'd been born in the saddle.

Never in her life had Daisy observed such sense of purpose, and she wanted it for herself. Six months and a five-and-a-half-hour drive north later, she was working at the Lodge. She had seen the cowgirl from the parade a few times in the café and the pull she had felt while watching the parade intensified.

She had hoped that working at the corral, she'd be able to share with the woman how she'd inspired this mountain adventure. Boy, had that gone wrong. She frowned at the tangle of leather in her hands certain that she had made a terrible first impression.

"You need some help with that?"

Daisy raised her eyes and matched the deep voice to a giant cowboy wearing a welcomed smile. "I really do, thanks. Heather is busy putting her riders on. The café is dead right now, so Leo said I could see about learning how to work the corrals."

The cowboy's shoulders relaxed and he let out a deep breath. "You work in the café?"

Daisy bunched up the tangle of leather in her left hand and held out her right. "I'm Daisy. I'm new this summer. Obviously. I have a lot of experience with coffee but none with horses, and I want to change that. I heard about how the pack station takes people into the mountains on horseback and I had to come."

"I'm Gabe. I do some of those trips. You know you can pay and go as a guest. Then we do all the work." He took the bridle from her hands.

"But I want to learn. I want to do this. I want to explore the trails and lead people through this national treasure."

"You sound like a commercial."

The look on his face made her bite back what she was about to say about the videos she had watched and how the mountains had called to her. She knew the mountains had something important for her. She didn't know what it was, only that she had to learn. "I did a little research." She hoped that sounded better.

Heather, the petite and spunky blond cowgirl leading the day ride, strode over, all business. "Are we ready?"

"I can do this," Daisy said. Everything about Heather and Gabe said they belonged at the pack station. Seeing their worn jeans and dusty boots, she willed herself not to inspect her feet to see if a layer of dust hid how new all her clothes were. Self-consciously, she wound her curly dark hair tight and looped it into a knot, wishing for a rubber band so she could get her tangled mess into a ponytail or keep it in a braid. Why hadn't that occurred to her?

Something passed between Gabe and Heather. He finally nodded and like lightning had the bridle on the horse and was directing her to put her left foot in the stirrup and swing aboard. Heather was a beat ahead of her and already directing her horse out in front of the small group of riders. Daisy tried to take in everything the cowgirl said about how to steer and stop.

Suddenly, Heather swung her mount around to a tiny trail. All the other horses, Daisy's included, fell in behind her. Daisy's heart raced. She clutched the horn in front of her on the saddle, trying to get used to the rhythm of her horse's step. Ahead, even though the trail seemed rough, Heather turned in her saddle and was talking to the guests behind her, a family of four who had driven over from the Modesto area and a boisterous couple from Arizona traveling with the woman's mother. She caught Daisy's eye and gave a thumbs-up. Shakily, Daisy returned the gesture.

The narrow horse trail met up with a wider pedestrian path, and Daisy sat taller as they passed hikers, partly out of the attention the animals received, and partly because she was afraid that they might inadvertently scare the horses and make hers move faster than she could handle. Her hips and knees had just started to complain about the way they were stretched around the horse when Heather stopped at a hitching rail. Daisy followed her direction to dismount.

"First stop: Rainbow Falls! The lookout is to the right, and there's a steep staircase to the left that goes down to the bottom. We leave for Lower Falls in fifteen minutes." To Daisy, she whispered, "Always tell them it's steep. They're a bitch coming back up, and slowpokes hold up the ride." In a matter of minutes, she had tied each horse to the metal bar.

"You're amazing," Daisy said.

"I've been down this trail so many times, I could do it in my sleep." The lilt in her voice said she didn't mind the repetition.

"Could you show me how to do that tie again? I didn't get it right up at the pack station, and the cowgirl who came to help me seemed mad about it."

Heather laughed. "That's Jo. If you're not doing things her way, pulling your weight, or getting work done fast enough, you're going to hear about it. The slipknot's simple. I'll show you on Peanut and you can do Rip's."

Daisy untied the little brown horse Heather pointed to and followed Heather's steps. She hesitated to say what she was thinking, but Heather seemed patient and understanding. "She kind of scares me."

"Oh, you're not alone. I was terrified I'd do something wrong whenever she was in from a trip, but I figured out that as long as I worked my tail off when she was around, she wouldn't give me a hard time."

"That sounds exhausting!"

"It is, but she spends most of the summer out in the backcountry, not in the yard yelling at us to get our heinies moving. Plus, as hard as she makes everyone else work, she works even harder. Takeisha told me the only time she sees her stop is when her butt's in the saddle. Dozer, on the other hand, will tell you a few beers will help get the job done. Watch out for him. He'll invite you to his cabin for some whiskey and hope you're interested in more. He used to be a lot worse before Kristine shot him."

Daisy's eyes grew wide. "Shot him!"

"Rubber bullet. He was fine."

"Does Kristine still work here?" Daisy wouldn't want to aggravate someone who would shoot a person, even if it was with a rubber bullet.

"Nah. She hasn't been back since that summer. You met Gabe, right?"

"Yes. He helped me with Churchill," Daisy said.

"Kristine's his sister. Get him to tell you about her and Gloria sometime. He has some good stories from that summer when they met. Sol's got some stories, too. He's the older-than-dirt cowboy with the red suspenders. He can get pretty crabby about things being done right, but don't let him scare you. He's really a sweetheart, and he knows absolutely everything about this place. He can teach you a lot, that is unless you decide you hate the corrals and run back to the café."

"No chance I'll be running away from the corrals," Daisy assured her, pretty sure that she could do the slipknot on her own now. "I used my coffee shop experience to convince Leo to let me work for him, but my real goal is to spend as much time in the mountains as I can."

Though Heather said she'd better teach Daisy more about caring for the horses and dealing with the guests, her expression betrayed her opinion that she wouldn't last out at the corrals.

In the daylight, she had been certain she would prove Heather wrong, despite the fact that when she got back to the little wooden box that was home for the summer her first thought was how fast she could pack what little she'd brought into her car and split. She had followed Heather's lead and stacked all her folded shirts and jeans on rough-board shelves, making the wall look like some kind of rustic clothing store. They shared one small dresser, two drawers each, where Daisy tucked away her toiletries and socks and underwear.

Later, lying in bed trying to fall asleep, she lost some of her certainty. Every muscle in her body hurt, and on top of that, she was freezing. She'd already piled her jacket on top of the blankets she'd brought, and she was still shivering. Her bladder doubted that it would allow her to go to sleep without another trip to the bathroom, but that would mean putting on boots and a coat to tromp over to a smaller box that held the toilets and shower.

Cowgirls had one sink and toilet; cowboys had another. Behind the two bathrooms was one shower. The space outside the shower had a wooden pallet to stand on, one small chair and three hooks on the wall. It had taken her a while to figure out how to arrange her clean and dirty clothes without anything getting wet. Not until Heather had expressed surprise when she headed for the shower in her boots did she realize how convenient a pair of flip-flops would be. If she couldn't find any at the store, she'd be heading back up to Mammoth soon. Her mind stayed busy on how else she was ill-prepared for the summer.

Then there were the noises. A critter skittered around. Heather had warned her that mice and sometimes squirrels usually visited at night to see if there was any food in the cabin. Daisy put her fingers in her ears but still heard a sound like someone being murdered. She froze, waiting to hear it again. Loud thumps, the thundering of hooves pounding in the corral nearby. She missed the thrum of traffic that typically lulled her to sleep. She missed being the person who answered questions about how to make the perfect Frappuccino. Would she be returning to that life at the end of the summer? *If she made it through the summer*, she heard Heather's voice in her head.

No. She would not allow her doubts to take over. Remembering the way Heather showed her how to pull the reins across her horse's neck to steer, she redirected her thoughts. Like she'd told Leo when she called him at his winter home in Bishop to find out what she needed to do to get a job, she needed a direction. She'd been wandering from major to major at the community college, barely passing her classes, with the vague hope that something would ignite a passion within her.

She heard amusement in his voice when he gave her the pack station's opening date, but the moment she had seen the majestic Minaret Peaks, the first breath of the crisp mountain air, she had known she was closer than she'd ever been to finding for herself the kind of intense focus she'd seen in Jo's gaze.

CHAPTER THREE

"I love that sound," Takeisha said.

Jo lowered herself into the camp chair next to her cook, stretched her long legs toward the fire and listened to the low ringing of the bell that hung around their bell mare's neck. "It'll sound even better in the morning when I find the stock. I always sleep better at Second Crossing when the distance makes running home less appealing to them."

"I'll sleep better if you and Cody sleep near the kitchen."

Cody lifted his head to meet Jo's hand. "Okay. The trail's close enough for us to sleep here, one ear tuned in on stock sneaking by and the other on bears trying to sneak into your kitchen."

The fire snapped and popped, tiny embers flashing briefly before they extinguished. Nightfall came earlier deep in the valley next to the roaring of the San Joaquin River. In their heavy coats, Jo and Takeisha sat close to the cook's fire, soaking in the warmth. When she and Takeisha turned in, Jo would extinguish this one as well as the one she had built for the guests. Tired from the long ride, both families had already abandoned the fire for their tents.

"How're you liking the new mule Gabe brought in?"

"Tuxedo?" Jo snorted. "Pretty is as pretty does."

"A handful?"

"Very much so. Granted he's young, but he has no sense. He made that clear when we drove the stock up from Bishop before the season started. I thought it would be a good chance for him to find a rhythm with the herd." She shook her head remembering how much she'd struggled with the fine-looking but flighty mule. "He jumps out of his skin at the littlest thing."

"You're turning heads on the trail, though. I've never seen such a handsome mule."

"He's sleek, that's for sure, but there's a reason you don't see thoroughbreds in the backcountry. I bet any mule you get from that cross is going to be hotheaded like its mama. This one sure didn't get any donkey smarts from his sire. His name fits him perfectly. A tux is hardly practical for the work that needs to be done."

Jo was enjoying the subtle symphony of the backcountry. For nine months of the year she made her living shoeing horses in Sonoma County, and she missed the sound the wind made rustling the tall trees out here. One of the things she liked best about Takeisha was how they could sit in companionable silence at the end of the day. No sooner had she finished the thought than Takeisha said, "You think the same thing about Daisy, don't you?"

"Daisy?" Mentally, Jo had been three-quarters of the way to bed.

"The newbie at the corral. I saw the way you were glaring at her when I was loading up our guests. You don't think she belongs here, do you?"

Jo sat up straight in her camp chair. "Zorro?"

"Tell me you did not call her that to her face."

"Why?"

"Because you sound like a racist asshole?"

"How is that racist?"

"Labeling a Latina with a Hollywood stereotype? Hmm. Let me see…"

"I wasn't labeling her," Jo said defensively. "It was her hat! And Gabe gave her that name."

"If you'd bothered to learn her name…"

"Waste of time. She'll be long gone when we get back from this trip. If I hadn't helped out, poor Churchill would have had a bit between his ears and a headstall in his mouth."

"You were glaring at her before that."

"I wasn't glaring!"

Takeisha's laugh popped like the fire in front of them. "Call it what you want, but your expression would have scared off most people."

"Probably wouldn't have hurt in this case. Leo's a daggum fool hiring someone who clearly doesn't know the first thing about horses."

"If you'd bothered talking to her, you'd know he hired her to work in the café." The humor in Takeisha's voice was absent now.

That made more sense to Jo. Cute young waitresses could lure hikers off the Pacific Coast Trail to splurge on burgers and milkshakes. "Then what's she doing out in the corrals in her Zorro hat?"

"She wants to learn all about our trips."

"Did you see the pansy-ass padded saddle she picked? Company saddle, I'm sure. One less Leo could be making money on this summer. I bet one trip down to Rainbow Falls gets her saddle sore enough to stay in the café for the rest of the summer."

"It sounds like you want to scare her off."

"There's no way she's prepared for how demanding this job is. She thinks the horse is doing all the hard work hauling her ass around the backcountry." Jo's job placed her in a catch-22. To do what she loved, she needed people who would pay for the privilege of her packing their duffels, tents, and sleeping bags onto mules, but then she had to suffer their company. The hardest part was listening to the complaints of guests who had a vision of effortlessly cruising through the magnificent backcountry.

They didn't think about the hours in the saddle or how they would feel after several nights sleeping on the ground. She'd even heard some pansy-assed morons complaining after she had packed their air mattresses and battery-powered pumps into the mountains. She couldn't decide what was worse, the whine of their machines or the whine of their unmet expectations.

That was why Jo did her best to avoid the guests for most of the day. She made sure to show up for meals in her hat and boots to give the guests the "authentic cowboy atmosphere" Leo often lectured them about. She would not have lasted a day in Takeisha's boots, stuck riding with the guests day after day. Takeisha had no escape. "If anything, she'd be angling for your job, wouldn't she? It could maybe make sense for someone in the café to do it. Course she'd have to cook the food before serving it."

"There's an idea! If I taught her how to do backcountry cooking, you might actually have a shot at doing these trips with someone you like."

"But I like you. You know that."

"I mean *like* like," Takeisha said. "The other teams get to keep each other warm in their bedrolls."

"Oh no you don't! I am perfectly happy out here with my mulies. And Cody keeps me plenty warm!" Hearing his name, Cody whined. "Sounds like someone thinks we should head that way. Probably worried about how much sleep he'll get if he's expected to keep the food safe."

Takeisha hmphed next to her. "Obviously you haven't shared your bedroll before. If you had, you'd be singing a different tune."

"I sing just fine on my own."

"C'mon. Don't you ever want to sing a duet?"

"I do not need to get laid."

"I'm not talking about sex. I'm saying that people are nice when you give them a chance."

Jo grunted. She did not understand the energy people invested in relationships that were bound to end. "Earl is nice, and you've never given him a chance."

"He comes out for a weekend trip. Daisy's here for months."

"Earl's into you."

"And Daisy's into you."

Jo cringed. "She's not into me."

"For someone who reads animals so well, you don't read people for shit."

"It doesn't matter whether Zorro's into me or not. No matchmaking."

"Daisy."

"Such a ridiculous name."

"Daisy, Daisy, Daisy…" Takeisha chanted.

Jo did her best to ignore her. "Bedtime, Cody." He accompanied Jo to brush her teeth after she'd collected a cup of water they had boiled. She didn't speak to Takeisha on her return and she crept into her bedroll, shoving tomorrow's clean shirt and socks to the bottom. She shucked out of her jeans, leaving them like an accordion for morning or in case she needed to pull them on quickly during the night. She unbuttoned her shirt and rolled that and her dirty socks into a ball she tucked into her duffel. It was cold enough that she'd sleep in her long underwear. Finished, she reached out and patted the canvas top to her sleeping roll. Cody circled and plopped down behind her knees.

Jo listened to the lull of the bell, the wind in the trees, the water rushing through the canyon…and Takeisha, still calling softly into the night, "Daisy, Daisy, Daisy."

CHAPTER FOUR

Now that she was on a ride other than the one that went down to Rainbow Falls, Daisy took in the expanse of the mountains. On the two-hour ride, all she saw were trunks of trees that lined the trail and a wide waterfall whose downpour kicked up mist that, at least for the eleven- and two-o'clock rides created a bright rainbow. Most of the guests admired the waterfall from the lookout near where they hitched the horses.

Since her first trip with Heather, she'd executed the slipknot at least two hundred times tying up horse after horse at the waterfall stop and when they returned to the pack station. Even so, she'd only convinced Leo to let her do one ride a day in between the lunch and dinner rushes. She didn't want to be stuck in the café all summer. She'd left the coffee shop in Pasadena to explore the mountains, not to wait tables.

Today Leo had agreed to send her on the half-day ride, which went to the Red Cones, two extinct volcanoes. Instead of following the trail down the mountain, Heather led the Japanese couple and their young daughter in the opposite direction.

Daisy rode drag. At first, the new scenery had captivated her. They rode through a lush meadow with bright purple flowers Heather identified as lupine. That's when Daisy started to feel cold. They began to climb switchbacks, and Daisy wished for a heavier coat than her denim jacket. Her toes went numb. She could barely hold the reins even though she kept switching, putting one hand and then the other into her pocket.

Finally, they rode out onto the face of the mountain, but Daisy barely appreciated the chance to survey the valley over the treetops. She soaked in the sunlight like a lizard, but instead of lounging on the warm trail to unfreeze her blood, too soon, they were back in the forest. Her teeth chattered. They rode through more forested area. Daisy shivered. She closed her eyes and imagined hundred-degree summers in Pasadena when she melted any time she got into her car.

Suddenly the horses in front stopped. Heather was saying something about the trail. Her mouth was moving, but Daisy's system had started to conserve energy, starting with her ears. Then, they seemed to be scaling the side of the mountain, and Daisy couldn't distinguish any sort of trail in front of them. The horses scrambled and lurched up an open expanse of soft red earth. Daisy took her free hand out of her pocket and held on to the saddle horn just like the guests. Heather stopped when they reached a sparse collection of trees. There, she instructed everyone to dismount, so they could walk to the top of the extinct volcano. Daisy did not want to. She was pretty sure her feet would shatter when they hit the ground.

She winced as she returned to earth and stiffly tied her horse to a tree. By the time she'd helped one guest from his horse, Heather already had two horses tied to trees. When they disappeared over the crest of the mountain, Daisy walked a few feet away from the horses and collapsed on the warm pumice-like surface.

"I forgot to warn you about how cold this ride is at the start of the season," Heather said, sitting down next to her. "Here, you can borrow one of my gloves for the ride back."

"I wasn't that cold."

"Yes, you were."

"How do you know?"

"You mean besides the fact that you look like a human solar panel lying on the ground like that?" Heather sat with her back resting against a log. She tossed the little chalky pebbles at Daisy.

"Gravity is super strong right here."

"Mmmm hmmm. But you weren't singing back there. You always sing on the rides."

"Oh. Guess I'm busted."

They sat in silence for a few minutes. Then Heather said, "Leo better get someone up here to get that tree out of the trail. It's too hard on the animals to go up the side like that. But I didn't want to turn around without the guests getting to see the view. You going up?"

"Still can't feel my feet."

"You need a better coat. As the season continues, the days will warm up, but if you end up on one of the overnighters, it's always cold at night."

"You really think I'll be doing those?"

"Why not? Isn't your goal to see a bunch of the backcountry? You'll see the same stuff over and over on these day rides. Five-night trips would get you out to Yosemite, six to Horse Heaven. Seven nights gets you out to the Silver Divide. Sol says that's the country to see."

"Why don't you do those trips?"

"And sleep on the ground? No way!"

"I don't know what I was thinking when I told you that's what I wanted to do this summer. I was swept away like a dreamy romance when I saw the riders leading those mules, the boxes all covered in roses for the parade."

Heather nudged her. "Break's over. We need to check cinches before we get everyone back on."

Daisy forced herself to her feet and trudged back over to where they'd tied the stock. She inserted her fingers between the cinch and the horse and tugged. It had too much give, so she tossed the left stirrup over the saddle and pulled the latigo leather to remove the slack. The leather connected the wide woven cord that extended around the horse's belly and the saddle itself. Once the loop was taut, she fed the excess leather around the ring on the saddle and tightened the knot that reminded her of a man's tie. She replaced the stirrup and moved to the next horse.

Checking the third dude horse, she sensed Heather's eyes on her. "What?" she asked, sure she had made a mistake.

"You learned how to saddle a week ago, and you're better at it than a whole lot of people I've worked with. You don't give yourself enough credit."

"I still have trouble getting the saddle on." Daisy cringed, remembering the first time she had tried following Heather's instructions about swinging the saddle up onto the square fluffy pads she had arranged on one of the horses. Instead of sailing onto the horse's back, she'd crashed it into the horse's side causing it to scramble. After that, Heather had shown her how to fold the right stirrup over the seat of the saddle and raise it to her chest and thrust it forward. Every other cowgirl swung the saddle with the stirrup free in an arc, so whenever she helped at the corral, she stood out like a sore thumb.

"They're heavy and awkward. Plus, in a few weeks, you'll have built up so much muscle, you'll toss them around like a sack of sugar."

"You're nice to say that. But there's still so much I don't know." Not for the first time, the way Jo's glare had pierced her when she took the bridle from Daisy's hands came back to her. Condescension mixed with anger in a big enough dose that there was no way she would share Heather's assessment.

"That you know that and will admit it puts you even higher in my esteem. You've got a good head on your shoulders which goes a long way around here."

While Daisy took pride in the knowledge she had acquired, it took a lot of effort to mask how very badly her body hurt that evening, especially after the longer time in the saddle. She could blame some of it on the cold, but she knew that her stride betrayed the stiffness in her knees and hips. The tourists never noticed, but the staff from the corrals enjoyed teasing her when she served them family-style at the long table, saying that she should accentuate her bowed-legged stride with a pair of jangly spurs. Not that she wore her jeans and boots to the café. She had her clean wardrobe of tank tops, chino shorts, and little white sneakers that she would never wear near the horses.

A plate piled high with pork chops in one hand and a bowl of mashed potatoes in the other, she pushed through the double doors and took a deep breath that normally gave her the equilibrium she needed to make it through the staff dinner. Five deep breaths could not have prepared her for the jolt when she looked up and found Jo's piercing eyes on her again.

Takeisha jumped up and jogged around the table, quickly taking the dishes from her to deposit on the table, so she could give her a hug. "Heather was just bragging about how much you've learned."

"I'm doing okay." Daisy warmed more from the cool assessment she could feel coming from Jo than Heather's praise. She tucked strands of hair that had slipped from her French braid behind her ear.

"We're out of juice," Jo said, extending the plastic pitcher to her.

The request felt like a smackdown, like Jo was establishing the hierarchy of the establishment. Daisy knew it came with the territory of joining a new team. What she couldn't understand was why her stomach tightened like she was about to fall. Why was she scared? She hadn't exchanged a dozen words with this woman, why should her opinion of her or her skills matter at all?

Jo was alpha in this setting, and her body language said she had been for a long time. For Daisy, that kind of confidence was both enticing and intimidating. When she reached for the pitcher, she could feel her own heartbeat at her wrists. Jo looked like she had come straight from the corral, the front of a plaid shirt covered with dirt. Her form-fitting shirt betrayed no feminine curves. Daisy flushed realizing that it might appear she was checking out Jo's chest. Her hand brushed Jo's as she released the pitcher. Her skin was heavily freckled from the sun, something Daisy associated with men who didn't worry about sunscreen and tan lines. Did her work make her more masculine, or did she work to present herself that way?

"We had to ride straight up the south cone because of a felled tree in the trail," Heather said, pulling Daisy away from her mental musings.

"What's this?" Leo joined the staff. He removed a battered straw hat, hung it on a pair of antlers on the wall and ran his hand through thin white hair. He hiked up loose-fitting jeans, and now that he was inside, carefully rolled up the sleeves of a dark denim shirt. He had owned and run the Lodge for more than thirty years and continued to be a part of the daily operation. From managing the business side of bookings to scooping up manure from the corrals, he was well-liked and respected by the staff.

Daisy excused herself to welcome and seat a family of tourists. She kept an ear toward the staff conversation, especially when Jo described the challenge of turning her string around when she had encountered the same tree from the other direction, adding an hour to her ride home.

"Forest service won't get to that for weeks, and there aren't any spot trips on the books tomorrow. Jo, you can take the two-man saw out there and clear it out."

"I'm a hard worker, Boss, but I can't work both sides of the saw."

So she does have some limits. Daisy smiled to herself. The way Heather had described her work ethic gave her the impression that Jo preferred to take on her job solo. She left the conversation to refill the juice pitcher and grab a water pitcher for the new table. Taking their orders and checking in on the other diners distracted her from the topic.

"Daisy!" Leo's voice caught her off guard. Once she delivered food to the staff table, she usually didn't return. They were responsible to bus their own dishes, so they didn't require her attention.

She hustled over, not about to give anyone on staff a chance to call her anything but a dedicated worker.

"You ever worked a two-man saw?"

"No sir?"

Leo met Jo's eyes. He worked something stuck around his eye-tooth with his tongue and took a drink of juice before he said, "You sure?"

Sure about what? Daisy glanced at Heather and Takeisha and found that they, too, were staring at Jo.

"Takeisha says she's a hard worker," Jo said.

Leo looked back at Daisy. She couldn't tell whether he was sorting out the schedule for tomorrow or assessing her potential on a two-man saw. He shrugged. "Suit yourself." He pushed back from the table, retrieved his hat and left.

Daisy stood rooted. What had just happened?

Jo stood and pulled a vest from the back of her chair and a tan cutter-style hat from another set of antlers behind the table. The hat molded to her head, dipping down dramatically in both the front and the back, and the vest brought Daisy's attention back to the lean frame she'd been studying earlier. "We'll leave right after breakfast. Have whatever horse you're riding saddled and ready to go."

Before Daisy could ask any kind of follow-up question, Jo picked up her plate and cup and disappeared through the double doors into the kitchen. Daisy turned to Takeisha and Heather who were hastily finishing their dinners.

"You'll be fine," Heather said. "You have a pair of gloves, right?"

Daisy held up her naked hands wondering what she'd agreed to by saying "No."

CHAPTER FIVE

"Two hotcakes, two sausages, two eggs—scrambled—and a piece of toast," Jo put in her standard order before grabbing and filling a bowl full of cornflakes to eat while she waited for her hot breakfast. She'd been up before dawn even though she only had to catch Tuxedo and Blaze before breakfast. The day-ride crew was beginning to emerge from their cabins when she had finished pouring grain in the trough for her animals and headed to the kitchen.

"Try to be nice today," Takeisha had said as she passed.

Instead of answering, Jo had looked toward the dude corral. Zorro was there haltering Churchill. This early in the season it didn't matter, but at some point, employees would have to give up the horses that guests could ride and take the spunkier animals. "She's still riding a dude horse?"

"I said be nice. Churchill is good and steady."

"There are plenty of other animals that need to learn the trails," Jo had replied. She turned her back on Takeisha's smirk choosing to let the topic go and get a jump on breakfast. The sooner she was in the saddle, the sooner she'd be back at the pack station. Ideally, they'd be home after lunch, which would give her time to shoe a few of the mules in her string.

The crew started to filter in as Jorge, the café cook, called her name. She retrieved her breakfast, pushing the eggs onto the toast which she folded in half and balanced on the edge of the plate. The rest she doused in maple syrup and dug in. Nobody said a thing to her, having learned that they'd probably get a warmer greeting from a bear woken from hibernation than from Jo at the breakfast table.

Jo sorted her own thoughts while the crew around her noisily discussed such matters as the number of riders signed up for the day rides and the destinations of spot trips. Spot trips weren't a bad deal. They required packing gear, and sometimes riders, to a set destination. None of the staff stayed with the party, and at a designated time, Leo would send someone back to retrieve the party. Many of the old-timers like Sol requested these, so they could sleep in their bunk at the pack station. Jo preferred the five- to seven-day travel trips in the backcountry, which allowed her to escape from these daily briefings. She tried her best to let the chaos wash over her.

She sat on the side of the table with chairs, never having cared for the way people crammed in on the bench-side of the table. Across from her, three or four bodies tipped to the side, Zorro dramatically leaning on Heather to extract herself from the bench.

"Sit down," Heather said through the laughter. "You're riding today. You don't have to fetch me coffee."

"You saddled my horse. It's the least I could do." Zorro disappeared into the kitchen.

Jo made eye contact with Heather and raised her eyebrows.

"What? Yesterday you told her to have her horse saddled. Does it matter whether she saddled it?" Heather asked.

"It matters whether she *can*," Jo said as Zorro returned with a pot full of coffee. She filled Heather's cup with a flourish and held the pot out to the others. She made eye contact when she circled around to Jo. "Coffee?"

Jo drained her cup and placed it on her plate. She slipped into her coat and settled her hat on her head before balancing her dirty dishes in one hand and pinching her toast and egg chaser in the other. "No time. I'm ready to hit the trail in ten."

Walking over to the workshop to find the necessary tools for the day, she finished her toast and eggs and tried to figure out why Zorro grated on her the way she did. It wasn't that she had leaped up to fetch coffee for the table, it was the *way* she had done it. For that matter, it was the way she had entered the café with Heather and Takeisha like a rowdy puppy stirring up a pack of dogs. Somebody had to snap at them to teach them order, she told herself.

Begrudgingly, she acknowledged Zorro when she crossed the yard from the café a few minutes later, three strips of bacon in one hand and two sack lunches in the other. "Do you need any help with the gear?" She smiled broadly.

"Almost finished here," Jo said. She took the lunches and lifted the tarp to stow them in the bag on the opposite side to the one holding an ax. "If you're ready, bridle up."

"Got it, Boss." Zorro's smile flashed again, and she strode with a purpose that surprised Jo up to the hitching rail where Churchill and Tuxedo waited.

Who smiled that much, especially before seven o'clock in the morning? Jo untethered her mule and watched as Zorro properly bridled her horse. A dude horse, Jo reminded herself. Let her try Rip with his tricky ear or Slick who refused to open for the bit unless you held some corn or oats in your hand. In contrast to her sunny smile, she was dressed all in black: black Zorro hat, black jeans that fit as tightly as those Gabe had ribbed Jo about last week and a black Sherpa-lined coat she must have borrowed from Takeisha that hid the rest of her figure.

Without speaking, Jo bridled Tuxedo. She pulled his lead rope through her belt and checked the cinch one more time. Glancing at Zorro, she was surprised to see her in the saddle. Score one for Takeisha who was convinced this hoo haw could make it through the summer. Jo swung aboard Tuxedo and pointed his jittery feet toward the wagon trail. "Cody! Let's ride!"

Jo had been wrong about the smiling. After a half hour of listening to Zorro singing behind her, she decided that was exceedingly more annoying than the smiling. Tuxedo seemed to be listening at first, his long slender ears swiveling back toward what at first had sounded to Jo like camp songs. Songs with numbers, songs that built on the same set of words verse after verse. She sang songs about Noah's ark that included ridiculous rhymes like twosies and kangaroosies. The woman was a child chasing after childish dreams. She probably thought Mary Poppins really could fit a hat rack in her carpetbag.

"Why a Zorro hat?" Jo called back after the song finally came to an end.

"It was all they had at Party City."

Despite the likelihood of Tuxedo spooking at something in the trail, Jo swung around in her saddle. She found a pair of amused eyes locked on her. When she snapped back around, she felt oddly exposed.

"I didn't realize you thought *that* poorly of me."

Jo shifted her weight in the saddle. Takeisha's "try to be nice" echoing in her mind. "I don't." The silence that followed told her she'd waited too long to deliver her response. *Shit*, Jo thought. *Now what do I say?* She wasn't used to thinking about someone's feelings. She wasn't used to thinking about anyone. She preferred to work with animals whose feelings were easy to read and respond to. Horses and mules didn't play games of innuendo or irony. They didn't manipulate. Animals had an uncomplicated language she understood. This gave her a decent out. "It's not your fault that you're a person," she called over her shoulder.

"What's that supposed to mean?" Zorro shot back.

"I read this book once. *There are No Problem Horses, Only Problem Riders.*" How was she supposed to explain that in her mind, even horses were a problem compared to mules?

"Thanks. That explains everything."

Jo couldn't miss the sarcasm that dripped from her comment. "It's hard to explain."

"Too bad we don't have time and nothing else to do."

A surprised smile blossomed on Jo's face, one she was glad Zorro couldn't see. "Riding is about communicating with your mount. It's our job to learn how to communicate what we want. The idea is that if the horse is misbehaving, it's because the rider hasn't offered clear instruction."

"So it's the person's fault if something goes wrong."

"The problem is that people don't take instruction well. They think they are smarter than the horse when it's the other way around."

"Horses are smarter than people?"

"Most." Jo accepted Gabe and Takeisha and a handful of other people as part of her herd. "And mules are way smarter than horses."

"That's why you ride a mule?"

"Exactly." Jo took in the expanse of the valley, glad Zorro understood.

CHAPTER SIX

Daisy waited for Jo to explain how a mule was smarter than a horse, but of course she didn't. And she didn't turn around to look at her, either. For more than an hour, Daisy's eyes were glued to the woman's hips and shoulders. Jo hooked a thumb into her pocket and went back to ignoring her. Daisy surmised that her singing had been bothering Jo and was tempted to sing some more to see if she could convince Jo to talk to her again. Normally, she considered herself a good conversationalist, finding topics that got customers to open up. That was the thing, though. Jo obviously had no interest in getting to know her. Every once in a while, she turned her head, usually in the direction of the black and white dog streaking through the forest, but mostly she stared straight ahead. Silent.

Hours of quiet contemplation were not what Daisy had had in mind when she called the Lodgepole Pine Pack Outfit. She had thought it would be more like camp—not craft activities, of course, but work that included the opportunity to talk and learn. She wasn't learning anything on this trail watching Jo's hips sway with her mule's stride.

And then she wasn't.

Daisy must've fallen into a trance watching Jo's ass in the saddle, and now Jo was swinging down, her eyes on Daisy.

"You okay back there? Y'got pretty quiet."

Daisy followed Jo's lead and dismounted, taking small steps to mask her stiffness. "Will we be here long enough that I should take off Churchill's bridle and loosen his girth?"

Jo's hands stilled on the knot she was tying, and Daisy tried hard not to color under her scrutiny. Why wasn't she answering? Daisy's eyes darted away from Jo's, and she realized Tuxedo's bridle already hung from the saddle horn.

Daisy hid her embarrassment by tending to Churchill. "Heather's been telling me about the all-day rides and what kinds of breaks the horses need along the trails. She said if I'm going to see more than the Red Cones and Rainbow Falls, I'm going to have to learn how to do an all-day ride. I'm not sure how I'd learn the trails, though. So far, I've been learning by following Heather, but we've barely even had any of the half-day rides, so I don't see when I'd be able to go out all day."

Jo methodically untied the rope that held the yellow tarp over the tiny load. Instead of removing the bag, she unbuckled one of the panniers and pulled out an ax.

"Sorry. I'm babbling."

"Stand closer to the tree, and you might be able to talk it off to the side."

Now Daisy's ears burned. She wished her hair were down, so she could hide the tips of her ears. Not that Jo noticed. She'd ducked under the mule's neck and gestured for Daisy to approach. She pointed to the end of a long saw that arched above the mule, a handle tucked into each bag. "Hold that end still until I take out my side. Then you can pass your side over. Careful, we don't want it to spring back and smack one of us."

Daisy did as instructed and waited for Jo to pull out more tools. Surely they were not going to clear the trail with just these two items.

Jo stared at her, disregarded her, and approached the log that cut across the trail at the level of their waists. About a foot away from the trail, Jo used a hatchet to clear branches from the trunk.

"I don't understand. Wouldn't this go faster with a chainsaw?"

"You think people hike all the way out here and want to hear a chainsaw?" Jo returned to her work without waiting for an answer. "They're forbidden in the backcountry."

Daisy knew she hadn't been expected to answer. She felt belittled. And worse, superfluous. Why had Jo asked her along when she had no idea how to help? As awkward as it made her feel, she vowed to remain silent until Jo talked to her.

Finally, she said, "Bring the two-man!"

Daisy grabbed a long saw with gigantic teeth and a wooden handle on each side. She extended one handle to Jo.

"Ever work a two-man saw before?"

"I grew up in Pasadena," Daisy said. Where would she ever have had a chance to use a saw like this in Pasadena?

"Didn't you go to the fair?"

"Fair?"

"There's the fair out in Pomona," Jo said. "Here's what you need to know. All the bite is in the pull. Don't try to push or you'll jam it. Ready?"

"How do you know about Pomona?"

"I grew up in So. Cal. Pull."

Daisy did, the saw blades bouncing along the cut Jo had made with the ax. Instantly, Jo pulled the blade back and almost out of Daisy's hands. She took a few quick steps to regain her balance and then realized that she'd have to step back to pull the blade again.

"Pull."

Daisy wanted to know more about where Jo had grown up and how her experience had included anything that prepared her for this, but the saw kept her attention completely. By the time she got the rhythm of the motion, her heart was pounding.

Her arms screamed at her from her fingertips to her shoulders.

Sweat began to roll down her back, but she wasn't about to take her hands from the saw. She breathed in through her nose, out through her mouth. Pull and let the blade be pulled. The work consumed her. Halfway through the first cut, Jo paused long enough to shrug out of her coat and get a drink of water. Daisy hadn't even caught her breath by the time Jo directed her back into position to "Keep the momentum."

One cut finished, Jo called lunch. Daisy sank to the ground, her lunch bag next to her. Food sounded good, but it would require using her arms, which hung limply at her sides.

Sitting next to her, Jo crunched through an apple.

"You must be a lumberjack during the winter," Daisy groaned. She rested her arm across her eyes.

"Nope."

Daisy waited for her to say more. When she didn't, she lifted her arm to peek at Jo. "You know, most people would say, 'No, I'm a barista, or whatever.'" She stared at Jo expectantly.

Jo finally regarded her. "What?"

"In a conversation, both people share things."

"You're the one having a conversation."

"Apparently," Daisy said grumpily.

"If you're not going to eat, we may as well start the second cut."

Daisy snatched her lunch sack without sitting up and fished out the sandwich. She took bites but chewed with her eyes closed. If Jo didn't want to talk, that was fine with her. It totally made sense to sit and enjoy the quiet with a virtual stranger. For Jo at least. For Daisy, it felt like a social experiment to see how long she could restrain herself from talking. The longer they sat in silence, the busier her brain became.

The sandwich gave her strength. Halfway through, she pushed herself up to sitting to find Jo's dog smiling at her. The dog had an uncanny ability to disappear until Jo was on the move. The moment Jo called for him, he was right behind her following with a tail-wagging adoration that Daisy understood. Jo had an inexplicable yet unforgettable magnetism. Long after the streets had been cleaned and the floats returned to warehouses to be fashioned into new floats next year, the cowgirl's image had remained in her mind. She had researched the job and daydreamed about spending her days on wilderness adventures instead of filling the same old coffee orders day in and day out.

She'd wanted to know what it would be like to follow a string of mules down a trail and see the things the cowgirl had seen. Experience what she'd experienced. And work with her? Hours of fantasizing had convinced to her quit her job and seek out the adventure. And, as it turned out, days of hard labor.

"How long have you had Cody?" The dog raised its head from its paws, but its owner's gaze stayed fixed somewhere in the meadow or the stream that turned back on itself, oddly snaking through it.

"Since he was a pup."

"Seriously?"

Jo's eyes finally came to her. "You're surprised?"

"No, I'm…" What was she? Angry was too strong for what she was feeling, but she was more than annoyed with Jo's terseness. "Why won't you answer anything outright? Are you a spy the rest of the year, and you're worried that if you divulge how long you've had your dog, your enemies will somehow track you down in the wilds of the California backcountry?"

Silence stretched between them. "Shit! You're a spy?"

"Yes, and I've been waiting for a crazy pants vigilante like you to team up with to eradicate evil up and down the coast of California."

Tell me where the bad guys are, and I'll grab my sword, Daisy grumped to herself, sore about the way Jo teased her about her choice of hat. It wasn't worth responding to Jo's barb. Daisy got the impression that doing so would not get the conversation moving. Instead, there would likely be absolute quiet for the rest of the day.

"I'm a farrier," Jo said. "And I've had Cody three years. Ready to get back to work?"

Daisy gathered her trash into the brown bag and followed Jo's lead, tucking it into the pannier hanging from the wooden saddle that looked like a skeleton with two X's pointing up. She wanted to know why the saddles they put on the mules were so different from the ones for the riders, but she knew better than to ask Jo. All the animals were napping in the warm sun, and Daisy wished she could shut her eyes and rest with them. Jo, however, was already working on picking the spot for the second cut. She got downright chatty as she explained that it was important to cut past the trail to allow the pack animals to pass through without getting caught.

"So you're a taxidermist?"

Jo turned a puzzled expression her way.

"You said you're a furrier."

"Feeeeeerrier," Jo corrected. "Not furrier."

"Oh. You captain boats?" Daisy asked once they were on opposite sides of the tree pulling the saw back and forth.

Jo pulled the saw blade and lifted her eyebrows.

"Isn't that what a ferrier does, ferry cars and people from one shore to another?"

A chuckle escaped from Jo before she shook her head and pulled again.

Daisy huffed as she pulled the blade back, frustrated by how much there was that she didn't know and certain the deficit affected what Jo thought of her. Why did she even bother trying to gain credibility with the aloof cowgirl? Did a ferry do something else that she wasn't aware of? It wasn't like she could Google it. She couldn't even get a signal at the pack station, let alone further into the backcountry.

After an awkward start to the cut, the women fell into the productive pattern of pull and release. A satisfying spray of sawdust accompanied the blade when Daisy pulled the saw to her shoulder. Ferry. Fairy. Fair. Jo had mentioned the Pomona Fair, maybe she meant fairee, like an employee of a fair?

"You work at fairs?"

Jo waited three pulls before she said, "Nope."

Daisy ruminated on more possibilities before she considered fairy tales. Though Jo's physique was the antithesis of the plump fairy godmother Daisy imagined, maybe she could make people's wishes come true.

"You're a modern-day fairy godmother who ferries people through spiritual and emotional duress?"

Now laughter erupted from Jo, and she doubled over, hands on her knees. She tried to contain it but guffawed again. "You're a hoot, you know that? Fairy godmother." For an instant, her grumpy and guarded expression disappeared. A wide grin transformed Jo, and even after the laughter subsided, she held Daisy in her gaze. From the few times she'd found herself in this position, she would have said Jo's eyes were blue, but now she could tell that they were flecked with yellow, creating something like a coral reef seascape.

With one more shake of her head, Jo said, "I'm a journeyman horseshoer. Now pull!"

Daisy pulled, but putting her muscles to work did not stop her mind from spinning. "What does that mean, journeyman? That's different than a regular horseshoer?"

Jo glared. "I did an apprenticeship. Now…can we work?"

Daisy complied, and soon she was breathing too hard to continue a conversation anyway. She kept her eyes focused on Jo's wiry forearms, fascinated with the ripple of her muscles each time she pulled the blade. Occasionally, she peeked back at Jo's distinctive eyes, always finding them trained on her. Her body tightened, not only the muscles she was working, but something deep in her core.

She wanted to tell Jo about watching her ride in the Rose Parade and how there was an intensity in her expression that had made Daisy want to see what she had seen. Now she was standing opposite the cowgirl, the wide sweep of the High Sierras her office, and she wanted to know more. Work that made her breathless made it possible to ignore the fact that Jo had no interest in talking to her. At Temptation, conversation always made her shift move swiftly. Even when they were busy, the team members chatted, building a rapport that she certainly didn't feel with Jo, despite the fact they had spent hours with each other.

Jo hadn't even asked what she had done jobwise before. In a normal conversation, the other person would reciprocate a question with a question. Enough time had passed that Daisy knew Jo did not feel the same. Daisy pulled the blade all the way to her side, releasing the spray of sawdust and the sharp smell of pine, and remembered how Jo had teased her about trying to talk the tree off to the side of the trail. She should have said that some conversation might help, a little "Spoon Full of Sugar" Mary Poppins' philosophy.

Mary Poppins, how old are you? she imagined Jo asking.

Twenty-six. You?

How old do you think I am?

Daisy studied Jo. Before Jo had laughed about the fairy godmother comment, Daisy would have guessed that she was ten years older than her, but the smile made her less certain. Minus the scowl, Jo had seemed much closer in age. Her expression, the one that had captured Daisy's attention during the parade, had come from experiences that had weathered her. She pictured Jo as a child on a ranch, going to bed hungry during lean years. Dropping out of school to help her family through but losing the ranch anyway.

Such hardship would age her, too.

"You need a break over there?"

Jo's voice startled Daisy out of her imaginings. "What?"

"You look like you're dragging over there."

The last thing Daisy wanted was to give Jo a reason to think she couldn't pull her weight. Although her muscles were screaming at her, she put her weight into the next pull. "Not me."

Jo nodded, and they continued to work, Daisy's mind spinning with unasked questions.

CHAPTER SEVEN

Jo rolled her shoulders a few times and shifted in the saddle. She'd overdone it a bit yesterday working the two-man saw with Zorro. If someone had asked, she would have had to admit that the woman could work. There were times she would have welcomed a break, but Zorro kept plugging along, and thank goodness she had finally caught a clue and stopped talking to Jo.

She glanced back at her five mules to make sure their loads were riding evenly. They were, and they looked smart. She took pride in that, especially remembering the awe in the voices of the eight guests when she passed them on their lunch break. Takeisha had caught her eye and mouthed something like, "You know you love it." Nothing wrong with taking pride in a job well done. Like the cuts she and Zorro had made. For the rest of the summer, on each ride through the now reopened trail, she would feel a swell of pride. It was nice to have those spots to balance out those that always brought an ache.

The ride up to Lake Minaret, which she was on now, had a switchback that had given her trouble the summer before. One of her mules had wrapped around a tree and pulled the whole daggum string down. Passing it, she remembered the shock of adrenaline, the fear she'd lose one of her mules and then the exhaustion of repacking them. She'd learned she couldn't give Blaze so long a lead rope and hadn't had a repeat disaster. Having learned, she could shake off the memory and let her mind return to the blessed silence of the backcountry.

The rhythmic beat of hooves beneath and behind her settled her in a way nothing else could. Some people complained about the long hours in the saddle. Never her. She could ride all day in the company of her animals with absolutely no need for human interaction. She almost looked behind her when she remembered Zorro singing on the way up to the Red Cones. She'd never met someone who made as much noise as Daisy. Such a ridiculous name, Daisy. It made her think of petticoats and proper behavior. Daisies were girlie-girls.

And clueless. Thinking that a farrier was someone who ferried people through spiritual duress. She snorted at the preposterous idea. Tuxedo spooked at the sound, and she stroked his neck in apology. "Can you imagine someone coming to me for spiritual advice?" Tuxedo swung his long ears back like he was waiting to hear more. "You missing Zorro and all those songs?" There were a few cowboys who busted out their guitars if there was a campfire, but she'd never heard one of them sing on the trail.

In the distance, she heard the call of the mountain chickadee, one extended high note followed by two lower chirps. It always sounded to her like they were asking for a cheeseburger. Zorro wouldn't hear any of that. The way she chattered would drown it out for sure. Even when words weren't leaving her mouth, Jo could practically see them battering the inside of her skull as they worked. Just thinking about it exhausted her. And why was she thinking about it instead of enjoying the quiet while she could? When the guests gathered to eat dinner around their campfire tonight, they would be asking the same questions Zorro had. Everyone was curious about what kind of a living a cowgirl could make. Luckily for her, Takeisha loved to talk and typically carried the majority of the conversation while Jo tended the fire.

After she had unloaded the mules, clustering Takeisha's kitchen boxes near the stand of trees she liked and tossing all the camp gear onto tarps for the guests, she led the horses away from the lake to set up her picket line, leaving the guests to find flat spots where they could pitch their tents. Lake Minaret was a favorite spot for base camps, with good day-hikes to occupy the guests, which typically gave Jo some shoeing time.

To create the picket, she headed off away from the camp, fashioned a lash rope as high as she could between two trees, pulling it taut, so it wouldn't sag when she tied her stock to it. She tied her mules well away from the base of the trees to prevent their hooves from damaging the roots and hiked back for the dude horses. Mouse's young rider still stood by her head, carefully stroking her forelock.

"Do you have experience with stock?" Jo asked as she untied two of the other animals.

The girl shook her head. She was pale, the only color on her face from a spray of freckles on her nose and cheeks. She was in the awkward preteen years, hunching in on herself to mask the height that almost pushed her past her older brother. Jo observed her guarded posture. It didn't surprise her that she'd gravitated to Mouse, a sweet mare who had earned her name for her mottled gray coloring.

"Well you're doing a good job there." Before she untied any of the other dude animals, she leaned over and poked Mouse's sagging lower lip. "They do that when they're nice and relaxed."

The girl's posture had begun to soften like Mouse's when a boy's voice startled her.

"Amelia! Dad said to get your butt over here to help with the tent."

Amelia swung around, looking for her brother, and Mouse jerked away from her. "I'm sorry!" she exclaimed.

"Not your fault." Jo stroked the mare's tense neck. Her ears were locked forward listening for the threat. Jo had heard it as well and hated to let the girl go. "If you want to brush her down on the picket line after you help your dad, it's right up this trail."

Shoulders tight, Amelia nodded and left the horses. Her posture stiffened as she approached her brother. Jo had seen the way the other guests had responded to the gregarious teen, his sly smile and stylishly cut hair that he kept sweeping out of his eyes. Hair that distracted them from the barely contained anger that pulsed through his body. Sure enough, as Amelia passed him, he stepped right into her path, hitting her with his shoulder. An old anger sparked hot in Jo's chest when Amelia silently shrunk away from him.

Jo quickly occupied hands that wanted to teach that boy a lesson. She untied the horses and led them up to the picket line, thankful again for the distance necessary to keep the smell of the stock away from the kitchen and give her the space she needed from the guests. Today it was difficult to walk away from Amelia, and when she didn't show up by the picket line, Jo worried. She unsaddled the stock as quickly as she could and headed over to the kitchen.

When she grabbed a handful of trail mix and the ax, Takeisha eyed her suspiciously. "What's wrong?"

"Nothing."

"Then why is your ass still in my kitchen instead of out digging us a privy or chopping firewood?"

"I can't walk away from your trail mix."

"Which is the same as always." Takeisha smirked but let it drop, returning to the wooden boxes for the food she needed for dinner.

Jo chomped a few more handfuls and poured herself a glass of juice, eyeing where Amelia's family had set up the tent. Once they had it erected, all four had disappeared inside. Jo's stomach had not relaxed, but she couldn't procrastinate any longer. She grabbed a shovel, tarp, and rope.

The campsite had a small, rocky clearing, and their guests usually tucked their tents within the canopy of the trees where the ground was spongier. Heading in the direction of the picket line, though keeping well out of sight of the trail, Jo passed the three tents to dig a latrine. When she returned for the boxes, the family was out of their tent, gathered around the snacks. Amelia stood off to one side eating from the handful of trail mix instead of snacking from the bowl as her brother and parents were.

Jo made eye contact with Amelia's brother as she walked up with the shovel in her hand. "I've almost got the privy set up. Do you have two empty boxes for me?"

"Gross," Amelia's brother inserted, scrunching up his face.

"It's a whole lot less gross than finding where someone has not quite buried their…" she didn't finish the sentence since everyone was eating.

Takeisha pointed under the table. "Trash bags and toilet paper are already inside."

"Thanks." Jo pulled out the two wooden boxes but hesitated. She wanted to pull Amelia away from the group, but it was far from appropriate to ask for help.

"I could carry one of the boxes," Amelia offered.

"You sure? I don't want to make you work on vacation," Jo said.

"I'd like to see how you put it together."

"I never say no to help!"

Takeisha coughed something that sounded a lot like *liar* into her hand as Jo passed.

At the hole she'd surrounded with a tarp for privacy, Jo instructed Amelia to place the box into a garbage bag. That would keep the boxes clean. They put one on either side of the hole and then placed the board with a toilet seat screwed onto it on top. "Voilà! Backcountry bathroom!"

"That was easy." Amelia sounded disappointed.

"The stock is a bit up the trail, and I haven't brushed anyone down. Want to lend a hand?"

The girl nodded.

They worked in silence, the way Jo liked. Amelia was no chatterbox like Zorro. Yet Jo worried about the kid. Couldn't her parents see how withdrawn she was? The longer she worked with the horses, the more relaxed she became.

"He's a hard one to get relaxed," Jo said when she saw Amelia eyeing Ninja's lip. "He tends to get into trouble, so he doesn't let his guard down."

"How can you tell?"

"See how the other horses put their necks down and have a leg cocked? They're relaxed. Ninja here is scanning the territory for threats. Feel how hard his muscles are underneath his skin? He's poised and ready to react. Ninja's kind of a tricky one. You have to watch him to make sure he's not mad, like when you tighten up the saddle, watch his ears. If he pins them back, he's likely to try to bite you."

"Then what do you do?"

"Stick out my elbow and pop him."

"Oh."

"It's not mean to set a boundary." She paused to make sure she had Amelia's attention. "Just because he's bigger doesn't mean he gets to push me around."

"Carl does that," she said so softly Jo would have missed it if she hadn't been watching. Amelia met her eyes. "My brother. He pushes me around."

"You tell your folks?"

"If I tell, he gets back at me when they're not watching."

"People suck. I don't get most of them."

Amelia blinked in surprise and then giggled.

"I'm serious. Why do you think I work with the animals? A horse is never going to try to get back at me for something I did. They have one job, to be a horse. They're much easier to understand than any person."

"I wish I had a horse," Amelia said wistfully. She ran the brush along Ninja's coat the way Jo had shown her.

"Doesn't hurt to tell your folks that. I was a little younger than you when I started to ride. There was a barn down the street from where I lived. I didn't like to be at home, so I pretty much lived there. At first I did all the chores the riders hated. I swept the barn, mucked out corrals. Took off winter blankets during the day when it was warm and put them back on in the evening. Eventually, I saved up enough to buy myself riding lessons."

"Your parents let you?"

The brush in Jo's hand stilled as she reflected on the years of using the barn to escape from her parents' screaming, trying to figure out what to tell this preteen. "They were busy and glad I had a place that kept me out of trouble."

"I wish I had a different place to be."

Before Jo had even thought it through, she said, "Your parents are hiking to the glacier tomorrow, right?"

"Yeah."

"Are you interested in that, or would you rather learn about shoeing a horse? Ninja here needs new sneakers, and it would sure be easier to get done with someone to distract him. Cody tries his best, but Ninja doesn't take him seriously."

Amelia leaned down to scratch Cody's ears. "He helps?"

"Like I said, not very well. I could sure use some backup."

Amelia's cautious hopefulness made Jo's heart hurt. "I don't think my parents would let me."

"Would you mind if I asked?"

Amelia handed the brush back to Jo. "You can try."

Four days later, Amelia was so much her shadow that Jo was happy to have her ride with the string instead of with the other riders and genuinely sad to see her go. Back at the Lodge, she told Amelia's parents they had a budding cowgirl on their hands and encouraged them to find a stable near their home. With a catch in her throat, she said goodbye to the youngster and tucked a slip of paper with her name and number on it into her hand. She doubted she'd ever hear from Amelia or her family again, but she hoped they would find a place that would help their daughter's confidence continue to grow.

After dinner and feeding the stock, Jo patted the log that made up one side of the mule corral. Cody jumped up and surveyed the stock with her. She heard the day-ride crew horsing around at the upper corral and had no desire to join them. While she had enjoyed Amelia's quiet company, the trip had exhausted her.

"You think you could have hidden her in with your mulies?" Takeisha said, joining her on the stump.

"Some kids would do fine raised by a herd of mules."

"Like you?"

"I wish. I was stuck with horses."

Takeisha grinned. "I figured. Taken in by a herd of wild mustangs."

They sat in silence and listened to thirty head of mules rustling through their feed. All those massive jaws grinding at the grass hay soothingly cleared her mind.

"That was a nice thing you did for Amelia."

Jo grunted. "There's a kid who deserves more nice than what she gets."

"And actually knew how to accept it."

Jo scowled at her and buried her hand in Cody's soft fur. "What's that supposed to mean?"

"First, you don't think people can be nice. And second, even if people are nice, you ignore it because it's too risky."

"How is it too risky?"

"I don't know. You tell me."

"Are you suggesting that you are nice, and I ignore it?"

"I'm used to you being an ass, so I ignore you. But Daisy's been nice to you."

"How's that?"

Takeisha slapped her arm. "That girl worked her tail off with that two-man saw instead of calling you out on your crazy. She waited a few beats and then said, "A bunch of us are headed up the hill to do laundry and get ice cream. Daisy's going. You in?"

Takeisha was testing her. Jo knew that. But she was tired. Amelia had reopened memories she thought she'd chased away for good. "I promised Cody an early night."

"Course you did." Takeisha surprised her with a quick squeeze around the shoulders before she hopped down from the log. "You're missing out!"

Jo sat by the corrals long after the rest of the crew had left. The tops of the trees disappeared into the darkness of night and the air grew chilly. Normally, she would have returned to the cabin to read until lights out, but Takeisha's words kept resurfacing. "Am I missing out?" she asked Cody. He raised his head and offered lickie air kisses. "You're just saying that because Takeisha sneaks you bacon at breakfast."

Takeisha was right about Daisy's hard work, but Jo was having trouble turning that into Daisy being nice. She was stubborn. Jo rolled her eyes remembering how hard she'd pressed for details about her life. What did it matter? When the season ended, if she made it that long, Daisy would go her own direction. Jo didn't get why she should invest the energy in getting to know her.

A tickle of interest flitted through her, suggesting a very nice payoff for engaging in Daisy's chatter. She rested her chin on her knee thinking about the way Daisy had held her bottom lip between her teeth as she worked to get the rhythm of the two-man saw. Wouldn't it be lovely to gently nip that full set of lips? Just as lovely as it would have been to explore the shapely bust that was so difficult to ignore as Daisy stood directly across from her. Working up a sweat...

She clapped her hands together, startling Cody to his feet. C'mon, then. I'll think myself right into trouble if I keep sitting here."

He happily jumped down and led the way to their cabin.

CHAPTER EIGHT

Daisy was so relieved that Jo was away on her trip the days following their sawing project. She'd barely slept that night because she was so sore. She turned on the thin mattress in her bed as gently and slowly as she could, like trying to dial in a distant station on an old radio. Just as she thought she had found relief from her aching shoulders, her muscles would roar like static. She kept telling herself to get up and find some ibuprofen, but once she had climbed into her bed, she didn't like to get out. The night grew cold quickly, and she knew her muscles would tighten on her if she left the warmth of the sleeping bag she'd bought from the store. There was also a nighttime critter that skittered around the cabin despite the fact that Daisy never kept any food there. Daisy was usually so tired she fell asleep before her nocturnal friend emerged.

"Someone was tossing and turning all night," Heather groused good-naturedly the next morning. "Thank goodness for earplugs."

Heather was always up before the sun to catch stock. Even when Daisy wasn't hurting from head to toe, she had trouble convincing her body to abandon her warm cocoon. She could barely move. She wasn't sure she could lift her toothbrush much less carry a tray of food, and she'd said as much to Heather.

"Good! We could use the help up here."

"I can't lift food, and you want me to lift saddles?" Daisy had asked incredulously.

"I'll lift, and you can tie the cinches. You'll see. It'll work."

"I'm broken. I can't work. I quit."

"You can't possibly be broken."

"Why not?"

"Because then Jo wins. I don't want Jo to win."

That had gotten Daisy's attention. "What are you talking about?"

"Takeisha said Jo doesn't think you'll last the season. But I put my money on you."

"Tell me you're joking."

"The money part, yes. But not about believing you'll make it."

Daisy had no words for the emotions that made her ears ring.

"Stock's waiting for breakfast!" Heather said cheerily, leaving Daisy dumbstruck. So that's why Jo had so inexplicably picked her to go cut the tree. Anger warmed her from her core and propelled her from her bed and into the morning ritual of catching, brushing, and saddling. While she worked, she kept Jo in her peripheral vision, waiting for her to see and acknowledge her. She wanted a chance to confront Jo, but completely immersed in the work of packing her string of mules, she didn't notice her once. And then, in a snap, she was gone, leaving Daisy to stew.

Over the course of the week, Jo's misgivings had fueled Daisy to lean fervently into the work. When Leo had driven in with fifty bags of the corn, oats, and barley mixed grain they gave the horses and mules each morning, she'd hopped right into line to carry them to the feed shed to lock it away from the bears. While the rest of the crew chatted among themselves, Daisy played an imaginary conversation with Jo on loop, listing all the attributes she brought to the job. *I am the first one to volunteer and the last one to quit. Three weeks ago, I could barely lift a saddle, and now I can get them up onto the top rack in the saddle shed. I ask when I don't know how to do something.* In her mind, Jo challenged every comment, belittling her personal assessment, and Daisy's arguments grew heated to the point of their shouting at each other.

When Jo had ridden back into the yard, Daisy's pulse quickened as if the two were scheduled for a duel and the countdown had begun. It was a ridiculous idea. Jo wouldn't even know that Daisy was aware of the wager. She told herself to pretend Jo was still in the backcountry. The way the summer had been going, she would probably be headed out again soon, so what did it matter what she thought? And why did she care anyway? The more she got to know Jo, the harder it was to remember what she'd been drawn to when she saw Jo riding down Colorado Boulevard. Essentially, she was the same, but what Daisy had read as purpose and dedication she now saw as disdain and condescension.

Daisy caught sight of Jo down at the mule corral with Dozer, another one of the packers. Up at the dude corral with the rest of the day-ride crew, she swung a hay hook into a bale and dragged it down the hill and into the trough jutting into the middle of the corral. Her heart pumped from the exertion, and she stood panting over the tightly strung bale, horses trying to rip mouthfuls from it. She placed the hay hook under one of the three nylon strands and started spinning. She spun and spun it until it popped. Then, the second. Then, the third. The bale opened, she yanked the twine out, looped and tied it, sticking it into her pocket so she could spread out the leaves of the bale for the stock.

She recalled Jo talking about how much she preferred mules to horses and understood that the corrals created a hierarchy—the lowly day-ride crew on the horses and the packers on the mules. Her internal dialogue kicked into gear again, arguing that they *needed the dude horses as much as the mules to do their prestigious trips into the backcountry. The day rides must pull in as much if not more money as the longer trips. We take more guests down to Rainbow Falls THREE times every day, and you're packing up a few animals and leading them to the next campground? That sounds a whole lot easier if you ask me.*

Still fuming, she grabbed another bale and kicked it toward the trough that ran along the edge of the corral. A hand on her shoulder startled her. "We're done," Heather said. "Pete's got the last bale."

"Oh."

"You okay?"

"Fine. I'll take the hay hooks in."

Heather handed hers over. "Great. You're coming into town with us tonight, right?"

Pete straightened and watched her as if he, too, were waiting for her answer.

"Sure."

"Good. We're heading out in five, okay?"

"Got it." As she walked by Pete, she extended the large metal hook that made her feel like a pirate. Pete rested the curve of his hook in hers.

"I've got room in my truck if you want to ride up with me," he said.

Pete had recently joined the staff, and while he clearly knew about horses and packing, he was newer to the Lodge than Daisy was which gave her a tiny bit of satisfaction. He was different from the other cowboys who wore their hair short and had more styles of beards and mustaches than she'd ever imagined. Pete, on the other hand, was clean-shaven and had waves of brown hair that nearly touched his shoulders. Sol, the grizzled old-timer, called Pete "The Hippie."

"Unless Jo goes, Heather has room, and I don't see Jo going."

He glanced toward the mule corral and then back to Daisy. She tried to interpret the tight-lipped smile he offered. "Let me know."

Daisy nodded and continued to the workshop to stow the hay hooks. Shutting the door behind her, she watched Takeisha jump down from the log where Jo and Cody were sitting.

"We knew she wasn't coming," she said when she reached Daisy.

Daisy fell in with Takeisha but couldn't help looking over her shoulder. Though she wasn't surprised, she wished she knew why Jo kept herself separate from the rest of the staff.

"Are you riding up with Pete?"

"I'd rather go up with you and Heather if that's okay."

Takeisha hmmed. "Pete'll be disappointed."

"Why?"

"A little bird told me he might be interested in you."

"Come on." Daisy scrunched up her nose. "He's been here all of three days. He can't possibly be interested."

"Not your type?"

Takeisha was studying her—Daisy could feel it. And she took too long to answer because she had lined up all the cowboys from the pack station in her mind to see if any of them matched her type. Jo was the closest. She was so startled to find Jo in the lineup of cowboys that her step faltered.

"It's okay if he isn't. And better for you to be blunt about it. It's kind of a thing for people to hook up for the summer around here."

Daisy blinked in surprise. "You're single. Why don't you drive up the hill with him?"

"The Hippie?" She pushed air through her lips. "I need someone sturdier than that. Hell, Jo's sturdier than he is!"

So she wasn't the only one who lumped Jo in with the guys. Would it make Jo mad to know that or was that exactly what she was aiming for with her short hair and... Daisy tried to pinpoint what it was that made Jo seem masculine. Everyone at the corrals wore jeans, button-down shirts and big belt buckles. She looked back at Jo again. It was something in the way she carried herself. The way that she walked.

Jo had pulled one leg up on the stump and was resting her chin on her knee. It was the most vulnerable she'd ever seen her. If she was honest, she'd rather spend the evening watching the mules with Jo than drive into town, but she knew better than to think Jo would talk to her, an occasional member of the lowly day-ride crew.

CHAPTER NINE

"Where's that god-damned Hippie with the rope I need?" Sol grumbled. He stood over a tarp that held fishing poles.

Jo led two of her mules through the packed yard. More than fifty head of horses and mules were tied to every inch of railing. All three of the wooden pack docks were laden with gear. Two were dedicated to the huge spot trip Leo had booked, a family reunion of twenty on their way up to Beck Lakes for four days. Many in their party had already left on foot. The nine who preferred riding to hiking milled around the saddle horses as the mountains of bags, food, and camping gear were sorted into one-hundred-and-fifty-pound loads for the mules.

Pete jogged by with the long rope slung over his shoulder. "All I could find are lash ropes," he said, arriving out of breath.

"Don't need lash ropes," Sol barked. The arthritic cowboy seemed to shrink over each winter. He returned more hunched, his posture and expression that of someone leaning into a bitter and powerful wind. He rearranged his chew with his tongue, spat off the side of the dock and took hold of the tie post as if he were going to step down.

"I got it, Sol. You stay put. You," Jo said to Pete, "take these two up to the upper dock. Clip Blaze to the post, but leave Skeeter tied to her."

He had the good sense to keep his mouth shut and follow her directions. Moments later, she emerged from the workshop and met Pete on the upper dock with the rope Sol had asked for. "You know how to manty the poles in a tarp?"

He looked at her blankly.

"Have Sol teach you how to turn the tarp and rope into a pack. It comes in handy with poles and if you have loose stuff you can't get into a pannier and end up needing to throw on top."

"Got it." He raised the rope toward her. "Thanks."

Sending Pete with information about what Sol wanted would smooth down the old man's feathers. Nobody thought Pete "looked Western enough," but Jo had kept a careful eye on him as he caught mules for his string. He had a quiet air about him and checked the adjustment of each sawbuck saddle as he worked. The only packing advice she'd had to give him so far was after he threw a double diamond hitch on a pack that would have gone down the trail with a single diamond just fine. She told him what she'd been told herself: unless you're riding through Yosemite where you'll have an audience, don't waste time working the rope to make the signature diamond shape on each side of the mule.

For Jo, the only thing worse than having to work her animals for a spot trip when they could have been resting was getting a late start. Leo helped her load and tie packs on her stock while Sol helped Pete. Amid the bustle, the eight thirty ride to Rainbow Falls gathered. Out of the corner of her eye, she watched Zorro working right alongside Heather, not waiting for any instructions about what horse to grab. She led the animals out to the yard, checked the cinches and helped several guests aboard. Even more surprising was seeing her ride out in front of the group to give instructions for the ride, still on the big white dude horse, Churchill, but clearly taking more responsibility by taking the ride solo.

"You have to admit she's improved a ton." Heather walked over to the dock where Jo was working.

Jo grabbed a tarp to toss over the top of the pack hoping to cover the fact that she'd been staring. "Leo lucked out there."

"What's your beef with her, anyway? I thought you liked hard workers, and she works freaking hard."

Jo frowned. "Isn't she supposed to be working in the café?"

"You say that like she doesn't deserve to be at the corrals," Heather snapped. "I bet you wouldn't last five minutes in the café, and she's so good out here that Leo hired someone else to waitress."

Heather's words punched her in the gut. Thankfully, the bustle of the yard whisked her away from the conversation, and Jo was able to let the tasks of the morning edge out the discomforting news. Heather was about to leave with the riders when a member of the hiking party returned. Jo gathered that one of them had sprained an ankle and wanted to ride to Beck Lakes after all.

Grateful she didn't have to deal with people, Jo strung up her five mules and helped Pete put his string in order. They bailed on the mess of Leo trying to find another horse and set out onto a blessedly calm trail. Riding through the grove of aspens, she accepted the applause of their leaves in the breeze. She smiled at the echo of hooves on the wooden bridge crossing the San Joaquin and even more so at the silence that followed. Maybe it was the five mules that separated them, or maybe Pete simply respected quiet on a trail because they hardly spoke for the three hours it took to reach where they had agreed to unload the mules.

Today, though, Heather's question returned and disrupted her preferred silence. What *was* her beef with Zorro? Her face flushed when she remembered how Gabe had caught her staring the first time she'd seen Daisy out at the corrals. He had said it was the tight jeans. She did wear her jeans tight, dramatically tighter than the rest of the crew. Jo had found it difficult to ignore the way they hugged every curve. She turned her head as if she'd been caught staring again, but there was no escaping the image that had wedged its way into her memory.

When Takeisha had asked about it in the backcountry, she'd denied her visceral reaction to being near Daisy, finding it easier to complain about how little she knew. But it was getting harder to argue that angle the more experienced Daisy became and the more she showed how willing she was to work hard. The singing was annoying as was the constant smile. And her questions! Jo had to cough to cover up the laughter that bubbled from her throat again when she recalled the guesses Daisy had made about what a farrier might be. She tried to picture herself as a spiritual guide. Daisy. And when had she stopped thinking of her as Zorro and allowed herself to think of the woman as joyful as the flower whose name she shared?

Arriving at the drop-off point allowed Jo to redirect her thoughts to business once again. She instructed Pete to throw down one of his tarps and unload the panniers and boxes onto it. He handily shouldered the heavy leather bags from his mules and tucked in re-coiled lash ropes and folded tarps into the empty bags for the return trip home.

By the time they had finished unloading, Heather had arrived with the ten riders. Jo was surprised to see Daisy—she pushed her mental conversation away—Zorro riding drag. She raised her eyebrows at Heather.

"What's she doing here?" Jo asked.

"Leo had to wait for the eight thirty ride to come back to get the sprained-ankle dude a horse."

"If Zorro wasn't still riding a flippin' dude horse, you could have left when you were supposed to."

Heather shrugged. "I don't mind, and Daisy was excited to see a new trail."

Before Jo could turn her frustration into words, Heather had bailed on the conversation and was teaching Zorro how to prepare the horses for a string.

"You guys are going to leave them out here all on their own?" Zorro asked.

"That's what a spot trip is," Pete said.

And this is why Leo should hire people who know how a pack outfit works, Jo thought.

"But what if something happens?" Zorro had at least started following Heather's lead, removing the bridles and flopping the stirrups over the seat of the saddle to tie them down, so they wouldn't catch on brush as they led the stock back to the pack station to unsaddle.

"Same thing that happens if a hiker gets hurt in the backcountry," Heather said. "Someone hikes in to get help. They have their wilderness permit, and Jo doesn't have to worry about trying to keep the stock from running home."

Jo snorted at this as she strung three of the horses together. "It's impossible to keep stock up here." She surveyed all the animals they had to get home. The horses were no fun to lead home strung together, but she couldn't take off with her mules and leave Heather and Zorro with a string of horses likely to get tangled at the turns on the way. "Pete, take two of the horses and put two of your mules on Heather's string." She tied two of her mules at the end of the horses she'd picked, leaving Zorro with a short string of her best-behaved mules.

"I get all mules?" Zorro asked.

Jo secured Dumbo's lead to Zorro's saddle with a quick half hitch. She didn't have to answer inane questions, did she?

"Because they're smarter?"

She listened to you on your ride to the Cones. Jo hated it when she heard Gabe's voice in her head. *And she retained it. That counts for something, doesn't it?* She mentally squelched his argument. *Still making more work for me.* Zorro seemed to be waiting for an answer, so she spit out a curt "Yes" and returned to mount Tuxedo. She was ready to be on the way home and annoyed to hear Pete explaining essentially what she'd already told Zorro.

When he finished explaining, instead of mounting, he said, "I'm going to water a tree before we head home." He flashed a wide grin as he wandered off.

Jo sagged in her saddle. Another delay.

"Two-and-a-half hours until we get back. Watering a tree sounds like a good idea," Heather agreed.

Jo could see in the way Daisy studied her that she was weighing whether to mount Churchill or empty her bladder. With an apologetic bow, she trotted into the woods.

Jo tipped her head back, trying to find peace in the tips of the Jeffrey pines that surrounded her. She inhaled their syrupy sweetness and waited for the others to return.

"Real cowboys don't pee." Heather egged Jo as she mounted. "How do you want the strings going back, Boss?"

"I'll lead. Then Zorro, Pete, and you on drag."

The others had returned. Heather waited for Zorro to mount Churchill before handing her the lead rope to her string of mules. She ate up more time explaining how to loop the lead rope around her saddle horn to prevent her from being jerked out of the saddle if the lead mule stopped unexpectedly. "And whatever you do, don't let the rope get under your horse's tail. He's a dude horse, but just about any horse is going to flip out if the rope gets under there."

Jo was pleased to see some trepidation on display as Daisy mounted and took the lead from Heather, but that evaporated when Heather added, "But Jo gave you her best mules, so I'm sure you'll be fine."

"Because this is Zorro's first time leading a string." She quickly reined Tuxedo toward the trail, hoping to put an end to the conversation.

"Don't worry. We won't spread any rumors about you being nice," Heather called after her.

Nudging Tuxedo into motion, Jo hoped to silence the conversation. It wasn't rumors of her being pleasant that worried her. She was frustrated with herself for giving Daisy any encouragement. She'd been briefly tempted to give her a string of squirrely horses to open her eyes to how little she knew, but Jo wasn't mean and she definitely wasn't one to put the stock in any kind of danger. Leo didn't seem to care.

Realizing that Leo's decision to send Daisy to lead a string had made work for her, Jo's mind finally settled. She started a mental list of all the ways Daisy increased the workload. She needed something to mute Takeisha's argument that Daisy would be good for her. Having her working the corrals instead of the café had made Daisy more difficult to ignore. There she was thinking of her as Daisy again. Zorro, Zorro, Zorro she repeated. She was out here pretending to be a cowgirl, and Leo's letting her was bound to have consequences.

Jo led them all to the trail where, with the number of animals in between each of them, she hoped to regain the silence of the trail. Unfortunately for her, all three must have been kindling as dry as Daisy, and all it took was those few sentences about her daggum mules to spark a wildfire of conversation that no amount of Jo's silence could extinguish.

CHAPTER TEN

When Heather handed her the lead rope for half of Jo's string, Daisy's heart pounded with worry. Her warning about keeping the rope out from under Churchill's tail scared her so much, she held the rope far away from her knee. This made her arm muscles scream in a matter of minutes, so she tentatively rested her left hand on her knee and glanced back frequently to check on the rope's position. And to receive a friendly smile from Pete who always managed to catch her eye.

"Is she the one who got people calling you Zorro?" Pete asked, pointing to Jo. After she confirmed his guess, he added, "You think if I wear your hat, they'll start calling me Zorro instead of The Hippie?"

"You know about that?" Daisy asked.

"Hard to miss when Sol is yelling it across the yard!"

His question reminded Daisy of Jo's similar one the day they rode out to clear the trail. In front of her, Jo rode as she had that day, back rigid in the saddle and not one hint of interest in talking. But when she looked behind her, she was met with three huge sets of swaying mule ears and Pete's easy grin. It didn't take more than that for her to launch into the story of visiting a store to buy western clothes.

"I don't know if the saleswoman could tell I didn't ride horses or if she didn't understand when I said I needed clothes for working at a pack station. She kept showing me things I'm guessing you'd see at a country music concert. The hats looked dirty and skanky and too small to give you any shade at all. When I said it was shade I was after, she brought me this one. I could tell by her expression that I was supposed to hate it, but I didn't. I loved it. It made me feel a little badass."

"You are badass," Pete said.

The way he said it made Daisy very aware of the fact that he was staring at her backside. For her, Jo's broad shoulders were on clear display and as tense as the last time she'd ridden behind her. She remembered the comment Jo had made about working with a vigilante, which brought a smile. "Man, if I had a sword, I could emblazon a tree when I do another spot trip."

"A big Z! You should do it! You don't need a sword. Your knife would work."

"I don't have a knife," Daisy said at the same time Heather asked why she needed a sword.

"Zorro is going to start marking off her successful trips by carving a Z onto trees," Pete explained.

"Z!" Heather yelled. "I'd give you a sword to wave at guests who ask too many questions. When you sweep it in a Z, it could make them zip it shut!"

In front of her, Jo's shoulders pinched together more tightly the more Heather and Pete talked about how the nickname suited her. Daisy grinned. Jo wasn't going to turn around, and she knew Pete and Daisy couldn't see her expression. When Jo called her Zorro, it made her feel degraded. Hearing Pete and Daisy call her Z made her sit up a little taller. It made her feel like she belonged.

Daisy knew Jo would prefer quiet, but she couldn't resist. "This group was awful, wasn't it? How old is my horse?"

"When is his birthday?" Heather volleyed.

"Are we going to cross that bridge?" Daisy shot back.

"Is the bridge very strong?"

"Who built the bridge?"

"Has anyone ever fallen off?"

Pete laughed harder at every question they recalled.

"When was the bridge built?" Daisy yelled.

"Do other animals use the bridge?"

"Do you ever ride through the water?"

"You know, I actually wanted to know the answer to that one," Heather said. "Ask Jo if there's a river crossing there."

Daisy turned in Jo's direction. "Jo did you hear that?"

She barely turned her head in acknowledgment. "What?"

"Can the horses go through the water instead of going over the bridge?"

"Why wouldn't you use the bridge?" Jo asked.

"The riders we took up to the lake asked if the horses ever go through the river."

Jo sat quietly for so long that Daisy thought she might have decided to simply not answer. That wouldn't surprise her in the least. She was used to Jo ignoring her and behaving like she was an impostor. Finally, Jo said, "I heard Sol talking about crossing downstream of where the bridge is. If the water is low enough."

"How do you know if the water's low enough?"

"I take the bridge."

Daisy passed this down the line, and her banter between the three riders continued. It didn't feel like any time had passed at all, and they were back at the bridge, a half hour from the pack station. As they clomped across, Daisy watched the San Joaquin roar beneath them. The banks of the river were steep and thickly lined with trees. Daisy couldn't picture a horse and rider making their way down to the river, much less a mule with a bulky set of leather bags.

When they returned to the pack station, everyone pitched in to help unsaddle the animals, and the evening progressed as usual. They sat by the corrals swapping stories about the rides of the day until the dinner bell rang. By that point, the stock was cool enough to put away, and they swung open the ten-foot wide gate that funneled the unhaltered horses right into the corral. All the halters were untied and hung by the gate, and the doors to the saddle shed were pulled closed. With the yard put to bed, they shared a family-style meal before the last chore of the day, feeding the horses.

"Who wants a ride?" Sol asked that evening.

"Oh! Did you finally get the four-wheeler up and running?" Heather cheered.

"Sure did. Bring your friend."

"Come on, Z!" Heather grabbed her by the hand and ran out of the café where Sol sat astride a four-wheeler that looked like it had been left in the middle of the mule corral and nearly kicked to pieces. She pointed to the rack behind Sol and explained how they would sit back to back facing out. "Hold on tight. He might be slow on foot, but he drives like a bat outta hell!"

Sol revved the engine and the machine jerked forward. He sped straight through the yard, passing the mule corral and the dude horses, circling the long way around. Daisy's teeth rattled together as the wheels bounced across the potholes. Heather squealed with delight while Daisy was mute with terror.

She leapt off when Sol finally slammed to a stop by a tower of hay. When he edged off and faced them, a whole lot of twinkle in his eye balanced his missing teeth. He removed his hat, revealing bristly sparse hair. He slapped the hat on his thigh to shake the dust free before jamming it back in place.

"You'll never get a job driving floats for the Rose Parade," Daisy said.

"Never said I wanted to," Sol cackled.

"You know people who drive the floats?" Heather asked.

"My dad does," Daisy replied.

"How many bales we need?" Sol asked.

"We'll get it," Takeisha said, handing out hay hooks she had grabbed from the workshop. She was slightly out of breath from walking up from the café. It wasn't far, but it was uphill, and the high altitude winded her. "You can rest."

"Like hell I can. Where's that pisshead hippie now?"

"He was grabbing something from the store and said he'd be right behind me."

The three women shrugged in unison and began counting the horses to calculate how many bales they needed. Daisy started pulling bales down a chute that allowed horses to eat from either side. As she scooped the hook underneath the twine, Pete jogged through the corral and ducked into the feeder.

"Hold up! Got you this!" He handed her a leather pouch.

He leaned closer as Daisy unsnapped the cover and pulled out a three-inch switchblade. "Oh, nice!"

"You like it okay?"

"It's perfect! I'll pay you back tomorrow."

He waved her off. "Don't worry about it. Anyone who works with stock needs to carry a knife."

"But I'll pay for it," she said as Heather pulled the next bale down the chute and watched as Daisy sliced through the twine before closing and pocketing the knife in its pouch.

"Sweet," she said, winking at Daisy.

Daisy was worried about accepting Pete's gift, and Heather's wink made her feel even more awkward. Was she indicating she liked Pete if she accepted a gift from him? She couldn't ask Heather with Pete standing right next to them in the feeder. "Thank you," she said.

He smiled and tweaked the brim of his hat. She'd definitely encouraged him. Her next thought was how relieved she was that Jo hadn't seen the exchange. This annoyed her. Why on earth would she care about Jo knowing?

CHAPTER ELEVEN

Jo might not have known about the knife, but she wasn't blind. The day after the spot trip, Jo noticed Pete and Zorro walking over to the café together and sitting next to each other. They talked so much, she was surprised they consumed any of their food. Though Pete was going in a separate direction than Zorro's half-day up to the Red Cones, he'd stuck around, bridling her horse and leading it out to her. Jo would have been an hour down the trail to Fish Creek if she'd been assigned his spot trip, but it was none of her business, and she was happy to pack up her mules and head out for a week in the backcountry.

A week should have been plenty of time to recalibrate. What Pete and Zorro did in their spare time was no business of hers. She kept herself busy on layover days when they weren't moving from one campsite to another. Typically, she took guests on day rides, but a few of her mules needed shoes, and layover days were a great time to get that done, so she occupied her hands and mind.

But none of this helped after the sun had set and she waited for the fire to die down before turning in. After the guests slipped away into their tents, and Takeisha put the kitchen to bed, balancing plates and pans on top of the food boxes to alert her if any bears came rummaging, Jo's thoughts would return to Daisy and the informal wager she and Takeisha had made about whether Daisy would last the summer.

She didn't like that Gabe and Takeisha had picked up on her staring. What they were trying to parlay into interest was more rubbernecked fascination that would cease to be an issue if Zorro left. Yet each time they were in the yard, there Daisy was again, poking at Jo's libido, and it became more difficult to flesh out her list of why it was best to ignore her.

Just the way she liked it, Jo and Takeisha were turning around after only one day back in the yard. Dozer pressed Leo for more days between trips, but the quick turnaround usually didn't bother Jo. This time, she found herself pushed because she wanted to modify the grill she'd made Takeisha.

She pulled her rig around. She'd chosen a standard truck and added a canopy with side doors. These gave her easy access to tools like nippers, rasps and hammers, iron to shape into custom shoes and some prefabs as well. Opening the back to the forge and anvil, she fired up the propane forge and selected a stick of iron to shape into an arm to hold a coffeepot by the cook's fire.

The first summer Takeisha had cooked, she'd complained about the way her grill tipped on the rocks around the fire pit. During the winter, Jo fashioned legs for a grill that she could remove for packing. Takeisha had been thrilled with the idea of being able to build a fire without having to balance her grill, but she was finding it difficult to fit all the pots and skillets on it. Jo had been brainstorming a feature that would create an arm that could free up cooking space.

Up the hill from her, the day-ride crew and some of the café staff had gathered in front of Sol's cabin. Someone had pulled out a pink plastic cow head and shoved it into a bale, and now Pete and Heather stood behind it messing with their ropes.

Cody whined and hid behind Jo's ankles. "Nobody's roping you, buddy," she said, bending to ruffle his ears.

"Not if they know what's good for them." Takeisha strode down to the shoeing shed.

Jo smiled, recalling the last cowboy who caught her dog and found himself eating dirt when she caught his foot in her own rope and tripped him.

"You're mean," Takeisha said, but she was smiling as well.

"Everyone thanked me for taking that asshole down a notch."

"That asshole needed it."

Something in Takeisha's voice made Jo look up. She waited, knowing Takeisha wasn't through. "But it's not your job to keep everyone in check."

Jo rolled her eyes. So this was about Daisy again. "I haven't said a critical thing about Zorro for weeks."

"You don't have to say anything. The way you act screams that you think she doesn't belong here."

"That's not true."

"Then pack this up and join us," Takeisha challenged.

"I've got to finish this hanger for the coffeepot."

Jo waited for Takeisha to go join the rest of the crew, but she didn't budge. Jo took the rod from the forge and worked the end over her anvil. When she had a nice curve on the end, she doused it in a bucket of water. "Think that'll keep the coffeepot from sliding off?"

"Absolutely. It's perfect. Now you have no excuses. You can head up there to give those hoo haws a roping lesson."

"I'm sure you remember fine."

"I still got it, girl, but sometimes people hang out just for fun."

Jo hmmmed noncommittedly.

"Promise you'll come up at least for a bit."

"Maybe. After I check the balance on this, make sure it's not going to tip your grill when we swing the coffeepot away from the grill."

"Excuses, excuses."

Jo took her time heading to the storeroom to find a coffeepot she could fill with water and hang from the new rod. When the volume at the roping activity jumped a few notches, she glanced toward the cabins.

Takeisha had hopped onto the bale everyone was trying to rope and was pretending it was a wild bull she was trying to ride, one hand gripping the bailing twine and the other swinging wildly above her. At the end of her ride, she dove off. Heather and the day-ride crew continued the faux bull riding, but Pete and Daisy stood away from the group facing her. Daisy held the rope, and Pete looked like he was explaining how to make the noose bigger.

Daisy frowned hard as she wrestled with the rope and finally shoved the tangled mess toward Pete. He held up his hands and stepped behind her, putting his right hand on hers to demonstrate the flipping motion she had to do to get the bend from the noose. Jo's body reacted, easily imagining the warmth Daisy would feel as Pete stepped closer to her and repositioned the rope in her hands. Close enough to feel the rise and fall of his chest as he explained how to position the honda, the circle where the rope fed through itself to create the noose.

She could easily imagine how it would feel to step closer to Daisy, to hold her wrist to explain the way she would rotate it above her head to become the fulcrum. The bend of her knee to position herself underneath Daisy's wind up would bring their bodies in contact and make it difficult to balance. She'd have to place her left hand on Daisy's hip to stay out of the way of the rope once Daisy got the hang of it.

The rope popped against the plastic cow's head, snapping Jo out of her daydream. She blinked to reorient herself and saw that Daisy was staring at her. Embarrassed, she turned back to her work even though she couldn't stop thinking about whether Daisy knew how to follow the coil of the rope how you would a garden hose. Over her shoulder she found that Daisy was still watching her. And Takeisha was too, wearing a huge grin.

There was no way she could join them now. She grabbed a few mule shoes from the shed and worked them like a puzzle.

Maybe she could connect the shoes and fashion a foot to give the arm more stability. Her mind shifted to the task, and she thanked her lucky stars that she spent the bulk of her time in the backcountry far away from Daisy and Pete.

CHAPTER TWELVE

Daisy was simulating Rainbow Falls, syrup flowing freely over the side of her tall stack of pancakes, when Leo walked in. Most mornings he had a cup of coffee in his hand and took his place at the head of the table. Today, he stood by the table scratching his head.

"What's up, Boss?" Heather asked.

Never big on words, he waved his hand and disappeared through the swinging doors.

With a shrug, Heather returned to her breakfast, so Daisy dug into her pancakes, and the familiar chatter of the morning resumed.

When Leo returned, he stood staring at the table. He hadn't poured himself coffee, and his hat remained on his head. Something was wrong. "I need a cook."

Daisy continued to eat. She was no cook. The others around her must have been thinking the same thing because, though the chatter ceased, the shoveling and chewing did not.

"For a travel trip?" Pete asked hopefully.

"No. Yes. Not a new one. I need to pull Takeisha in. Her father's had an accident."

Every fork at the table froze.

"Is he okay?" Heather asked.

"He's in critical condition. It's three plus hours to the Fish Creek camp. If I send someone right now, we might be able to catch her before she leaves for Second Crossing."

"Jo doesn't mess around," Heather said, her eyes on the clock. "She'll already have the saddle horses ready to go. Takeisha said she likes to clear the riders out, so she can pack her mules in peace."

"Don't you have a way to reach them to tell Takeisha to come in and Jo to wait?" Daisy asked.

Leo shook his head. "Too expensive. Only the rangers have satellite phones. I can try sending a message if there's a ranger down in the valley, but that doesn't solve that group needing a cook. And we need to catch them before they leave camp."

"Don't look at me," said Heather. "I do day rides. I don't sleep on the ground. I need my hot shower at the end of the day. I …"

Leo interrupted her. "I'm not sending you." As he scanned the table, every head turned away from him. He sighed heavily.

"Send Daisy," Heather said.

Leo did not look her way. "Daisy's not a cook."

"Leo, send Daisy," Heather repeated. "This is why she came to the Lodge."

"But I've never been to Fish Creek!" Daisy exclaimed.

"It's easy. You pass Rainbow Falls and ride a long time. Stay on the main trail, and you can't miss it," Heather said.

Leo considered Daisy, measuring her again as he had when Jo suggested her for the other side of the two-man saw.

"Send Daisy. She's worked in the café, and she can ride," Heather said.

"But I don't know how to cook!" Daisy said.

"You can make a cup of coffee. That's all that matters. As long as they have a good cup of coffee in their hand, you can feed them crap and they won't complain," Leo said.

All eyes were now on Daisy.

"Remember the Rose Parade? That's going to be you! You and your mule going through the backcountry!"

"You need to leave now," Leo said.

"I'll get Churchill saddled. You go pack."

"Pack?" Daisy's head was spinning.

"They're not due back for five more days. You need clothes, your toothbrush…" Heather was already clearing her unfinished breakfast. "C'mon. The longer you wait, the less likely it is you'll catch them! Pete! C'mon. You saddle a mule for her gear."

"Who?" He jumped up.

Heather looked to Leo.

"Matchbox is out there. He'll travel out."

Heather smacked Daisy's arm and snatched her plate. "Don't forget your sleeping bag!"

Daisy jogged to her cabin in a daze. She tossed clean clothes in a duffel and grabbed her toiletries. Travel trip! Five days more? Her heart pounded as she stood in the middle of her sparse cabin. What was she forgetting? Heather was at their door already, taking her bag from her and herding her toward the corral as she described what Daisy would pass on the trail.

"Meadow…small stream…switchback…cross the river…camp."

Pete took her bags and tossed them onto the waiting mule. Her head spun.

"You'll be fine. Just keep Churchill moving. You've got to travel fast if you're going to catch them. But slow down for the granite pass."

Daisy's eyes widened. "That doesn't sound good."

"Churchill will take you over it. But make sure your toes are loose in the stirrups and that you don't have the rope around the horn of your saddle. Dozer told me that if your mule starts to go over the edge, let it go."

"I can't do this! I can't ride three hours away to a place I've never been! What if I get lost? What if I don't get there before they leave? How will I know how to find them?"

"That's why you've got to go now," Heather said.

And then she was on her horse leading a mule into the dark of the pre-dawn forest.

She was going to throw up, her stomach was so tight.

An hour into the ride, the sun was high enough that she started to feel warm. Once she started to thaw out, she realized her shoulders were up at her ears. She tried to relax, rolling her neck. Maybe a song would help. Singing the songs that her parents had taught her when they'd driven up to Big Sur for what she'd always considered camping brought her some peace.

That vanished when she reached the granite. She was supposed to ride across a solid sheet of stone. As high as she could see on her left, the mountain was solid gray. And to her right, much too soon, the edge of the cliff dropped off. She stood in her stirrups and could see, down in the distance, the tiny blue ribbon of the San Joaquin River. A rough path about a foot wide had been blasted across the face about the length of a football field, and she weighed whether she should stay in the saddle or get off and walk across. The trouble was, she didn't know what she'd do with the mule.

She gulped and gave Churchill a tentative nudge with her heels. He stepped onto the granite, his metal shoes ringing on the hard stone. When Matchbox's hooves added to the clatter, she glanced back. He looked bored, his ears pointed to the sides like bent TV antennae. Daisy held the lead rope at her hip and kept her eyes trained on the chipped path, holding her breath until they were safely back on the soft and blessedly wide dirt trail.

After two hours of riding, she was surprised to find that she felt okay in the saddle. She smiled, remembering how at the beginning of the summer she could barely last the thirty minutes to Rainbow Falls without needing a break to stretch her legs. When she finally reached the switchbacks Heather had mentioned, she saw she'd congratulated herself too soon. Churchill pounded his way down the steep, snaking trail, every step rattling through her spine as they descended deep into the valley.

She reached the San Joaquin three hours in and tensed in the saddle, uncertain about her ability to spot Jo and Takeisha's camp. Then she remembered why she was riding to their camp in the first place, and her stomach dropped. Leo had shoved a folded piece of paper into her hand as she left the yard. She'd give that to Takeisha, but there would be questions that she couldn't answer. If she managed to find them.

Even with the roar of the turbulent river, Daisy heard a chorus of whinnying and braying and soon saw Jo striding toward the trail.

"Zorro? What are you doing here? And why do you have a mule with you?"

Daisy swung off Churchill. "Leo sent me. I need to talk to Takeisha."

Jo's face shifted from confusion to worry. "What's wrong?"

Should she tell Jo or insist that she talk to Takeisha? "It's her dad."

"Dead or hurt?"

"Hurt." Daisy pulled the note from her pocket and handed it to Jo.

Jo snapped the paper from her hand. "Wait here."

Daisy stood in the middle of the trail holding Churchill and Matchbox trying to decide whether to follow Jo. It felt good to be on her own feet, so she tied the two animals to trees off the trail. Twenty feet beyond, three of Jo's mules stood with tidy packs already in place. Two neat piles of gear waited to be loaded. Beyond the broken down camp, riders were gathered by their mounts. They trained confused expressions on her.

Takeisha was hurrying to her horse. Her worried eyes paused on Daisy.

"I'm sorry," Daisy said, feeling responsible for the fear in her eyes.

"Thank you for getting down here. I told Jo where my menu is. My kitchen…"

"Don't worry about it. You need to get back," Daisy said.

"Tonight is pork chops. Jo won't know where the seasoning is…The cooler with the tape on it is for the meals in Horse

Heaven. If you open it too soon, the ice melts too fast and won't keep the meat…" She put her hand to her forehead as if trying to still her thoughts to search for essential information.

"We'll be okay. Go!" Daisy urged.

"Thank you!" In a flash, she accepted her horse and a hug from Jo. A flicker of envy fluttered in Daisy's belly when the two women embraced. Jo's warmth surprised Daisy. All summer, she'd seemed nothing but cold and aloof. For a moment, she thought perhaps Jo was more personable in the backcountry, but that idea quickly skittered away with Takeisha. At the trail, she burst forward disappearing quickly and leaving Daisy alone with Jo and a bunch of strangers she was supposed to feed for the rest of the trip.

Mirroring the breakfast table less than four hours before, all eyes were again on Daisy, but she sensed Jo's most keenly. Hands on her hips, she stared at Daisy for several moments. A long sigh escaped her lips, and she shook her head.

"C'mon. Takeisha was about to head out with the guests. Let's get you out of here."

"I don't know where I'm going."

"Stay on the trail and to the left any time you come to a fork. I'll pass you before you have to worry about finding our camp at Grassy."

Daisy's mouth was dry. She nodded.

"You can load up the guests, can't you?"

"Sure."

"I'm going to fix this pack you've got on Matchbox. Who tied this for you?"

"Pete."

"Box hitch wasn't tight enough. See how it's rubbing his shoulder raw?"

She hadn't been with Jo for five minutes, and already Daisy felt as if she couldn't do anything right. She dreaded the next five days. "I'm going to find a tree to water first."

As she walked away, she heard Jo swear under her breath, "Oh, geez."

CHAPTER THIRTEEN

When Jo finally got Daisy and the eight guests pointed toward Grassy, she was at least a half-hour later than she wanted to be on a travel day. And knowing that she would have to slow her pace to let Daisy follow her instead of leaving Takeisha in her dust in order to start getting camp set up before they arrived soured her mood even more. Running late always put Jo on edge. And Takeisha was always there to say it didn't matter. *It's supposed to be relaxing*, she'd argue. How was she supposed to relax with Daisy in the backcountry?

Worried you won't be able to resist her? she heard exactly what Takeisha would say.

"Well, poop on a stick and fry it up hot!" Jo growled. Cody joined her with a yap that made her laugh. "So you're with Takeisha?"

He wagged his tail.

"Some friend you are. You should be thinking about whether she knows how to cook on a campfire."

Soon enough, her mules were packed, strung together and moving at a good clip behind her on the trail. Too soon, they caught the slow riders. Though she passed them and tried to set a good pace, asking Zorro to remind them to encourage their horses with hearty kicks, they fell behind to the point of Jo needing to wait for them. Tuxedo fidgeted. The mules in her string kicked at each other. It took so long to climb the switchbacks up to their lakeside camp that she felt like she was carving the trail.

Her back was killing her by the time they rolled into camp five hours later. If she was hurting, she knew the guests would be even worse off, not to mention Zorro with the hours she'd ridden to catch them. She knew everyone would feel better once they had snacks, something Takeisha knew and always dealt with while Jo set up her picket line. Even if Zorro knew what she was doing, which Jo thought was unlikely, she would have no idea where Takeisha had packed anything, and Jo would be no help to her.

"I took the bridles off all the horses and left them tied to trees. What's next?" Zorro asked.

Jo looked up from coiling a lash rope to see the newbie standing there, hatless, her face covered in dust. The guests were gathering to collect their sleeping bags, tents, and duffels having scoped out flat areas to settle for their two-day stay at the lake. "The kitchen needs to be set up. Takeisha usually puts it over here away from the guests' fire pit. I'd get the tables set up first and pile things on top as you try to find a snack. Here's Takeisha's menu."

She peered at the menu and then back to Jo. After more than eight hours in the saddle, she looked every bit a barista who'd been put through a wringer, but she pushed back her shoulders and walked over to the tables Jo had leaned against a tree.

Usually, Jo would take the time to set up her picket line and unsaddle the stock before she stopped for snacks and a cool drink, but she had a feeling…Zorro? Without her hat, the nickname didn't feel right, yet Jo still couldn't bring herself to call a grown woman Daisy. She remembered Heather and Pete joking about her drawing a Z on trees after successful spot trips and heard the "z" sound of Daisy's name. She worried that Z wouldn't know how to make the water safe for drinking. Even more exhausted, she returned to the kitchen. "Z, you know how to treat the water, so nobody gets sick?"

Daisy stared at her. "Huh?"

"Once you have water, you'll need to kill the bacteria before you make juice."

"What did you call me?"

"Z?" Jo tested once more.

Daisy said nothing.

"Is that okay?"

"Fine. Whatever. What's the deal with water?"

"Takeisha has iodine that she puts in before the flavor packet." She scanned the boxes and bags. Takeisha would probably keep them in the juice container, but would she put that in a box or a bag? The water bucket, she knew, was too big for the boxes. She rooted around in the bags and held out the soot-blackened bucket. "Here, fill this from the stream while I find what we need."

When Z came back sloshing water from the heavy bucket, Jo had nearly everything in the boxes and bags on the tables, including what she needed to make juice.

"That's the iodine?" Z asked as Jo added a few drops to the pitcher.

"Yep—kills any bad stuff. The punch flavor covers it up pretty well. Should keep us from getting the runs."

Daisy seemed appropriately overwhelmed by the unpacked and unassembled kitchen. She held up a box of crackers and said, "All I have to do is dig out cheese and salami from the coolers, right?"

"And then make dinner."

"I don't see the grill and fuel."

"Grill's here." Jo pointed to the grill she'd assembled while she waited for Z.

"But where's the fuel?"

Jo bent down and picked up a stick which she extended to Daisy. "There's some bigger stuff over by the guest's fire pit. Use that until I get your kitchen pile restocked. First, I've got to get the stock situated, but you've got enough to get a decent fire going."

"Fire? Isn't there a butane stove?"

"Nope. Just the grill."

"But how do you control the heat?"

"Big fire—real hot. Little fire—not so hot."

"That's helpful," Z said wryly.

"You know how to get a fire going, or do you want me to help?"

"I can make a fire."

"Good. I'll be back with more wood in fifteen, twenty."

Jo felt a little bad leaving Z on her own with the mess she'd made. She honestly had no idea how Takeisha did her job, how she kept things organized and prepared the whole meal on one grill. Even if Jo had been interested in learning trade secrets, with all her own chores she'd had no time to hang around the kitchen. She strung the picket line, one line for the horses, another for the mules, saddles slung over a nearby log. She returned to the kitchen dragging several long branches and was grateful to see that Z had the snacks out, and several guests were eating and chatting by a small fire. Jo quickly broke apart the branches she'd brought and added them to the fire.

They had eight on this trip, three siblings and their spouses. Two of the families had children. Jo crossed her fingers that they would keep the trend of catching up with each other instead of asking her and Daisy a lot of questions about their jobs.

Though Daisy was talking with the guests, her smile was only at half the normal wattage. She held a jar of jam in one hand and a bag of marshmallows in the other and was scanning the table like she was playing some kind of game where she was supposed to match the items in her hands to their mates in the mess.

"Why don't you have the boxes stacked to make shelves like Takeisha did yesterday?" Monica asked. The amount of padding she wore on her frame had brought to mind jolly grandmas, but she had proved this wrong with the amount of criticism she'd already slung Takeisha's way. She continued needling Z. "Have you done this before?"

Z turned panicked eyes to Jo.

"Sure she has," Jo answered. "Z's one of our best cooks. She just doesn't get out here very much because she's so handy around the pack station."

The daggers Z shot her hit like a bucket of ice water. Jo didn't understand. She'd been trying to help Z out by throwing Monica off her hunt.

"How long have you worked for this outfit?" Monica asked.

"About seven weeks." She glared at Jo again and said, "Before that, I'd never really ridden a horse."

Jo couldn't understand why Z was throwing herself to the wolves. She ate a few peanut-butter cracker sandwiches and gathered the supplies to build the privy, glad for the excuse to leave the kitchen area.

Z's fierce glare continued throughout the evening, so Jo gave her generous clearance. She built up the guests' fire and was forced to sit with them instead of enjoying the quiet of the kitchen. Sadly, this gave her a courtside view of how poorly the dinner went. The guests cut their pork chops into tiny pieces, partially to excavate bites that were not charred but also to masticate what was essentially jerky. They also used their knives for the near-raw potatoes. Z hadn't ruined the corn, and there was plenty of salad that, with a healthy squeeze of ranch dressing, served to round out dinner well enough.

She dumped the scraps of her dinner into the fire and went to release the stock for the night, and when she returned, she found that the guests had cleared out for the night. Jo sat poking at the burning logs of the guest fire while Z did dishes by lamplight. She missed Takeisha and selfishly wished that Z had not caught them to deliver the message. The awkward silence lengthened as fog crept in over the lake.

The long day in the saddle and the lull of the cowbell around the bell mare's neck almost put Jo to sleep by the fire. She hadn't noticed the clang of dishes had ceased until Z was standing over her. Caught completely off guard, her eyes locked on Daisy's chest, the fabric of her shirt stretched tight across her bosom. She stood quickly and the camp chair fell back. Cody growled.

"Happy now?" Z's voice carried the same timbre as Cody's growl.

"About what?" Jo saw now that Daisy had started a braid at the base of her neck. She pulled it around to finish taming her curls.

"That epic failure? You've been waiting all summer for me to make a fool of myself. This must have been a great day for you."

"I haven't…"

Daisy held up her hand. "It doesn't matter. I just want to know where I sleep. I can't keep my eyes open another minute."

"Takeisha usually sleeps between the table and the boxes to scare away bears. Once you turn in, I need to make sure your fire's out."

"Bears."

It was a statement, not a question, so Jo wasn't quite sure what to say. "My bedroll is over by the picket line."

"Can't you tie the food up in trees? Isn't that what you're supposed to do out here?"

"We bring too much to haul into a tree. That's why the cook sleeps near the kitchen. To scare them off when they come."

"When," Daisy said. Again, it wasn't a question. "And you sleep with the stock."

"I sleep close to the trail to listen for the stock to make sure they don't take off for home."

"How would they leave?"

"If they're not hungry enough or barn sour, some of them'll hightail it when I turn them out."

"You turn them out? As in you let them go?"

"To graze. How did you think we feed them?"

"How do you find them if you turn them all loose?"

"We have one mare. All the mules think she's their mama, and all the geldings think she's their girlfriend. I stick a bell on her, and that helps me find her. I find her, I find all the stock. Usually."

"And Takeisha keeps bears from getting into the food."

"Usually," Jo said.

"Usually!" Daisy's voice conveyed clear concern. "What does that mean, usually?"

"Every once in a while, a real sneaky bastard will get in and steal the cold cuts or get into the snacks. That's mostly on the other side of the valley, though. Over here, usually a stern holler will scare them off."

"Holler at them."

"Sometimes you have to chase 'em. Knock some pots together. That works."

Daisy crossed her arms over her chest. Each suggestion made her look more uneasy.

"I can leave Cody with you to help with the bears," Jo offered.

Cody's tail wagged hesitantly under Z's glare. "Sure."

They stood staring at each other, awkward silence stretching out between them. "I'll put the fires out while you get situated. If you're not in bed, he's likely to follow me."

"Fine." She grabbed some things from her duffel and walked off toward the privy.

"See that right there, Cody?" He turned to face her. "That's why I prefer your company."

CHAPTER FOURTEEN

Daisy had thought she'd never hurt like she did the morning after her first day in the saddle. Sawing had proven that wrong, and now waking up after a night of trying to stay on top of her thin sleeping mat, Daisy's hurt-o-meter again rose above the previous register. She opened her eyes when she heard Cody jump up. This time, he only whined, a change from the crazed barking that had woken her several times in the night. How was a cook supposed to get any sleep at all guarding the kitchen from bears each night?

The sky had the barest hint of light when Daisy cracked her eyes open. "Go back to sleep!" she groaned.

He lay back down but whined again. Then Daisy heard the bell. She sat up and used the sound to locate Jo. She sat astride the bell mare, and like magic, all the other animals were following along as if they were stuck to her exactly how Jo had described.

"Go."

Cody leapt from the saddle-blanket bed Jo had set up for him the night before. Daisy lay back down. Could she hit snooze in the backcountry? Or did she have to get to work immediately? The morning was so cold, and her bed so warm. She decided she could rest her eyes for just…one…more…

A strong *whoosh!* woke her again. She sat bolt upright to see a flash of flames leaping from the cooking fire.

"Sorry to startle you," Jo said. She looked like she always did at the Lodge in her jeans, boots, coat, and hat. Her ruggedness matched the backcountry perfectly. "I thought I'd get the fire started for you."

Obviously, Daisy thought. "Be up in a minute."

Daisy swore inwardly. Not only had she missed her opportunity to get up and give Jo a reason to think that she might actually belong in the backcountry, now she was stuck trying to change from her pajamas into her clothes with Jo standing right next to her. She stuck her arms out into the frigid morning air and pulled her duffel bag toward her and rummaged around for clean clothes.

"I put my clean clothes at the bottom of my bedroll at night. That way, I can pull them up to my body to warm up a bit before I have to change."

Kind of her to share that after the fact, Daisy fumed.

"I'll get the guest fire going. And then, unless you need me, I'll go brush down the stock."

"I'll manage," Daisy croaked. She waited for Jo to leave, so she could get dressed. "Was there something else?" she snapped.

"Sorry. I…Your shirt…Mickey Mouse?"

Daisy clutched her clothes to her chest and sank into the bag cursing Jo for the tears that sprang to her eyes. It seemed like everything she did made her slip further down the slope of Jo's disdain. Just as her clothes had warmed enough to change, she heard the *whoosh* of the second fire coming to life. Finally, Jo's footfall faded as she walked over to the where she'd tied the horses and mules.

As quickly as she could, Daisy contorted herself out of her pajamas and into her clothes, praying that none of the guests exited their tents before she escaped her cocoon fully clothed. She envied them their tents which Heather had told her the cooks and packers never used. She'd thought, foolishly she now realized, that there would be some kind of privacy in the kitchen.

Leaving her sleeping bag wadded under the table, she tried to direct her brain away from the cold to the task of making breakfast. Coffee. Heather had said that as long as she could make a good cup of coffee, everything would be okay. She found a kettle to get the water warming over Jo's nice big fire while she searched for a French press. But Jo had unpacked all the kitchen boxes yesterday, and Daisy didn't remember seeing one when she reorganized the food and dishes. She smelled the kettle. It had definitely held coffee. She did not want to ask Jo for help. She measured what seemed like a good amount of grounds into the kettle and then looked for the bucket Jo had given her the night before.

It sat on other side the table, full.

Kind, she conceded. *But it doesn't make up for her mocking me.*

She poured water on the grounds and put it on the fire. Takeisha's menu was pancakes, scrambled eggs, and sausage. At the café, Jorge always had his bacon and sausage cooked by the time they came in to place their orders, so she started there. After she'd plunked the near-frozen sausages into the iron skillet, she peeked at the coffee, which was boiling furiously. It smelled good, so she lifted it off the grill and was about to hang it from the hook attached to one corner.

"Wait till you have some pots on the grill to use that," Jo said, striding to the kitchen. "Glad you have coffee ready."

Daisy didn't particularly feel like talking to Jo, so she simply nodded. Jo poured herself a cup. She kept an eye on Jo as she mixed pancake batter waiting for Jo's assessment of the coffee. Jo carried her cup over to the guest fire and messed around adding logs before she finally took a sip. Coffee spewed into the fire, and Jo quickly turned her back to Daisy. Daisy's heart fell when she watched Jo splash the rest of the cup into the coals. It looked like she was wiping her tongue before she finally turned around and returned to the kitchen fire.

Without a word, she rinsed her cup and filled it with cold water. She returned to the coffeepot, raised the lid, and poured the cold water in with a swirling motion.

Daisy was furiously turning the sausages, trying to keep them from burning and sticking to the skillet. She wished Jo would leave again before she had to figure out how to get an even heat to cook the pancakes without burning them. Instead, Jo poured another cup of coffee and stayed by the fire. "A cup of cold water after it boils settles the grounds."

Daisy would have gladly taken instruction or advice from Jo. She obviously didn't know what she was doing, yet Jo had effectively muted her with the comment about being *one of the best cooks*. She pushed the pan with the unattractive but hopefully fully cooked sausage to the corner and pulled the pan with heated oil to the center. The first pancake she flipped was three shades darker than she would have liked and instantly started to push up in the middle.

"That's going to be gooey in the middle," Monica said, looking over her shoulder.

Daisy pushed the coals underneath the grill apart, hoping to disperse the heat, and steeled herself for another torturous meal.

* * *

Already exhausted, Daisy sat down and gnawed on a barely warm, overcooked sausage having tossed most of her scorched eggs and gooey pancake middle into the fire after a few bites. Everyone was quiet again, and she knew it was because nobody had the courage to complain. Jo added her plate to the wash bin and left with the big bucket. She returned with water, filled a large pot on the grill and stoked the fire.

"For the dishes," she said.

"I know how to wash dishes," Daisy barked. "I thought maybe I could eat some breakfast before I got back to work." She would have liked some of the cantaloupe she'd frozen her fingers cutting, but the guests had demolished it. She'd find a snack once Jo took the guests on their day ride. If Jo would ever leave.

"I'm going to saddle up the horses and take the guests out to see an old mining cabin."

"Fine," Daisy croaked. The smoke from the fire made her throat burn.

"We're…going to need…lunches."

Daisy's whole body sagged. She hadn't even cleaned up breakfast, and she needed to make lunch? How did Takeisha get everything done? Not by sitting on her ass. "I'll get right on it, Boss!"

"And…" Jo looked really uncomfortable.

"What?"

"Takeisha usually uses the Dutch oven on layover days. I didn't know if you knew how to work it."

"I don't even know what a Dutch oven is." Daisy felt like crying. How could Leo have sent her into this mess? Why had she agreed? She wanted to leave so badly, yet she had no idea how she would even find her way back to the pack station. "Did you have some advice you wanted to share?" Daisy's voice was tight.

"Look, I'm sorry I don't know very much about how Takeisha does all this."

"Well, it would be nice of you to share what you do know before I try instead of after I make mistakes."

"I'm trying to help you, but you're not making this easy."

Daisy could tell that Jo was trying to keep her voice down. Though she wanted to scream, she did her best to keep her voice level. "*I'm* not making this easy? *You're* the one who told the guests that I'm a great cook."

"I didn't think it was a good idea to tell them that you don't know what you're doing. They pay a lot for these trips, and it's not right for Leo to send someone who doesn't know a da…"

Daisy had heard enough. "Don't you have horses to saddle?"

"Yes, I do. I'll bring you the shovel when I come back for the lunches."

"Shovel."

"For putting coals on top of the Dutch oven. That's how it works, I think. All I know is Takeisha needs the shovel when she does roast or ham in the oven."

"Perfect." Daisy pasted on a smile thinking it was a good thing she didn't have the shovel in her hands at that moment when she wasn't sure she could resist the urge to smack Jo with it.

CHAPTER FIFTEEN

"What did I do wrong now?" Z snapped the next morning after breakfast.

When she got up to catch the stock Jo had been surprised to find her awake, dressed and making sandwiches. She had to admit that Z was trying hard. Last night's ham had been burnt like she'd snatched it from the gates of hell, but she'd actually managed to make the zucchini taste all right. But then, her mom had always said hunger was the best sauce, and she'd had to put something in her stomach.

After dinner, as delicately as possible, she'd reminded Z that they had a long ride ahead of them to Horse Heaven in the morning, and the earlier they got started, the more time she'd have to get her next camp put together. That hadn't meant she expected Z to get up before dawn. The circles under her eyes suggested that she hadn't slept at all.

"Nothing."

"Then why are you moving stuff around?"

Jo kept her head down. "It's what packers do. I have to make sure the base load is weighted evenly on both sides, so it doesn't tip over." She'd had to do it early on for Takeisha, too, not to the extent that she was having to rearrange Z's boxes, but adjustments that would help the balance.

"Thanks for telling me that before I packed everything up."

Jo stood and stretched her back searching for something to say that would defuse Z's sarcasm. She took a deep breath but didn't get to utter a word. When she glanced at Z, a chortle escaped her. She tried unsuccessfully to cover it with a cough.

"Now you're laughing at me?"

"No, not laughing. You got a bit of soot on…well, on your face."

Z growled. "I cannot stay clean out here!" She balled her fists at her sides and blew like a volcano. "I can't sleep. I can't cook. I can't put stuff in boxes. And I can't stand your smug attitude!"

Jo looked around for their guests and was relieved to find that they were all still inside their tents. "I'm not smug. I'm just doing my job."

"Like you're the only one who can do it. I want to learn how to do this, and you refuse to show me. It's shitty. I can't wait for this trip to be over, so I can get the hell away from you!"

Z's words stung even though Jo had also been counting the days. "I would have given you some tips, but you were already packing things up while we were eating breakfast. You seem hell-bent on figuring this all out on your own, so…" She threw up her hands at a loss for words. "So more power to you."

"I *have* to figure things out on my own! You're good for grabbing water for me and bringing firewood, but beyond that, you avoid the kitchen like a typical male chauvinist!"

"I am *not* a male chauvinist."

"No? This whole setup is a chauvinist's dream. Here I've spent all this time admiring you for pushing gender norms, but you're not. All you're doing is playing the man doing all the important work while you wait for your woman to make food for all the guests. It's ridiculous."

Jo didn't know how to respond to that, and even if she did, the guests camping closest to the fire pit stepped out and headed toward them. Jo hung her head. They paid a lot to get away for a peaceful experience in the backcountry, not to hear her and Z bicker. She rubbed her face failing to see how they could resolve Z's frustration before breaking camp, and they needed to get a move on. "I'm starting to put together our loads, so if you've got your bags set, bring them on over," Jo said, shelving the discussion.

"Tell me what I can do to help with the boxes. I know that having me out here is slowing you down, so why won't you let me help with this?"

"That takes time. I can work faster alone."

"Then I'm taking the guests. That's what you told me to do the first day."

"You don't know the way." Jo didn't feel comfortable sending Z across the Silver Divide on her own. There was the suspension bridge and tricky stock fences to navigate.

"I found the Fish Creek camp. The trail to Horse Heaven must be marked, and you said you always pass Takeisha at lunchtime. So let's get crackin!" She projected the words with an upbeat tone toward the guests, but Jo could feel the unexpressed anger radiating from her as she strode away leaving Jo to grit her teeth.

They hadn't spoken since. Though the guests cheered when Jo passed them with the mules all loaded, Z had maintained her stony silence. The long ride to Horse Heaven felt even longer with her mind spinning on Z's accusation.

It wasn't like Jo was sitting on her ass by the campfire waiting to be served dinner. She had a heck of a lot of chores she had to get done, and it made sense for the packer to get all those done while the cook worked on dinner. Man or woman. So all the cooks were women. Leo let Jo pack, so if a guy wanted to do the cooking, she couldn't see him shooting that down.

She'd spent her whole childhood listening to what her mom wanted and could never find in a man. As Jo grew older, she filled in what gaps she could, learning how to fix things, mowing the lawn. Like the breakdown of jobs at the Lodge, it just made more sense. She wasn't afraid of the kitchen. She could make her own meals. She didn't see why she should help Z do her job to prove she wasn't a chauvinist. The way she and Takeisha ran camp had never been a problem, so in Jo's mind it was Daisy's problem and one she didn't have any interest in fixing.

Why had she mowed the lawn instead of making dinner for her mother after her father had left? She tried to picture working in the yard with her mom before making dinner with her, sharing duties the way it seemed like Z would have it. But the lawn was a problem her mom never tackled. She handled dinner. Jo clenched her teeth remembering how hard her mom worked to please each new boyfriend with her cooking. Some boyfriends ate only steak. Others were chronically late, but her mom would never think to serve before they arrived. Taking on duties like mowing the lawn helped Jo avoid how frustrated she became with her mother.

Once they reached the meadow, Z continued to push at Jo. When Jo approached the kitchen to gather what she needed for the privy, Daisy curtsied and extended a cup of juice.

"I hope it's to your liking," she said with syrupy sweetness.

"Would you rather dig the privy and have me make dinner?"

"As tempting as it sounds to get my hands on your manly tools, I have plans to kick this dinner's ass tonight."

Jo walked away from the kitchen baffled by the change in Z's demeanor. It unsettled her, and rightly so. After a much-improved chicken dinner, Jo was trying to think of how to play the evening when Z disappeared with the bucket. She hauled water back to the kitchen fire and poured it into the large pot as Jo had been doing the last few days.

"You don't need a hand?" Jo asked carefully.

"Nope! I fetched you water, so you can do the dishes. I feel gross. I've got to get clean, and I'm not going to wash up in the dark. I need some daylight to let my hair dry before bed."

"But dessert!"

"Luckily for you, I already mixed up the cheesecake. It's in the cooler. All you have to do is cut it and serve it."

Jo stood, words once again failing her.

"And if you're worried about bears, I suggest you move your sleeping bag to the kitchen. I'm not dealing with them all night again."

She grabbed a bag of toiletries, tossed a towel over her shoulder and stalked off through the grassy meadow toward the stream.

Jo didn't know how much the guests were likely to have overheard from the larger fire. Takeisha usually saved herself some washing by serving dessert on small paper plates, but Jo didn't see them on either of the camp tables. Where would Z have packed them? She rifled through the large leather bags, trying to picture the things she had rearranged that morning to even out the loads. After all the work she'd done, she was exhausted, yet Z expected her to pick up the kitchen work? She knew this was about Z thinking their roles were outdated and chauvinistic, but had she thought it all through? Was she willing to get up before dawn to go hiking after the horses?

After Jo plated the cheesecake, Z hadn't returned. She eyed her slice and then the pile of dirty dishes. With a sigh, she rolled up her sleeves and poured warm water into the wash bin.

CHAPTER SIXTEEN

Daisy discovered one of the reasons the meadow they camped in for the last two days of the trip was called Horse Heaven. Their stock, having eaten well all night, wandered back to the picket line where she had finally gotten to rest. She haltered the mare and left the bell in place while she gave all the animals small bites of grain from the bag she'd had under her head while she was sleeping as Jo instructed.

She heard Jo's voice in her head: *If you're lucky, the stock will come to you.* She smiled. *If you're lucky, you'll figure out the Dutch oven before you burn everything to a crisp.* Today's menu included biscuits and gravy as well as pot roast, and Daisy had decided she was never again going to attempt to cook with that evil pot.

Once she had secured the stock to the picket lines, she marched down to the kitchen to start the morning fire. On her approach, Cody poked his head from the large canvas square Jo had wrestled down to the kitchen area after she'd finished the dishes. Jo didn't stir, Daisy wondered how much sleep she'd gotten chasing a persistent bear away from the food. Each time she'd heard Jo shouting, Daisy had smiled with deep satisfaction and turned away from the kitchen, wriggling down deeper in the warm sleeping bag. Stacked on top of several saddle pads, it was almost comfortable. That, combined with not having to jump up for the bears, had given her a decent night's sleep.

She found the lighter fluid that Jo, true to her nature, hadn't mentioned the first day. Daisy started with a triangle of sticks balanced above tinder. As she worked, she noticed movement next to Cody and wasn't surprised when Jo emerged from bed, dressed.

"I can do that." She pulled on her boots and stood. "The packer…"

"I'm not stupid," Daisy said. "I have the roles all figured out, and I know that today the guests go on a day ride. That I can do. Since I don't know how to cook biscuits on a campfire, and I know nobody wants me to try my hand at cooking a roast in the Dutch oven, you can have a go. After I get your water, I'll be brushing down the stock."

Jo attempted to tame her short hair with her fingers before settling a ball cap in place. "But I don't know how to make biscuits!"

"I'm sure you can figure it out. You've made bacon gravy before, right?" she called over her shoulder like Jo had done the first day Daisy had been in the backcountry.

Feeling more at ease among the horses, Daisy took her time brushing them down. She knew she'd have time to saddle them after breakfast while Jo made lunch, so she was in no rush. With every stroke of brush, she became more relaxed and the thrum of self-doubt that had been blaring critically for days finally quieted. From the small grove where the stock dozed at the wide meadow before her, Daisy watched the sun rise. It took the chill off the crisp mountain air and promised another beautiful day. Birds chirped, the horses swished their tails. Away from the popping fire and clatter of dishes, this was all she heard.

Daisy took in the vastness of it all, the snowcapped mountains in the distance unobscured by shops or smog as the San Gabriel mountains were across Colorado Boulevard back at Temptation. She'd been following a string of mules identical to the one she'd seen back in January, and now she was seeing for herself what she had only ever imagined. No image she had clicked on as she researched pack outfits could have prepared her for the majesty of the backcountry that was hers to explore by horseback today. Deeply satisfied, she strode back over to camp and poured herself a cup of coffee. Jo looked as harried as she'd felt the past two mornings, but she poured in sugar and milk and joined the guests who were awake around the guest fire she had started that morning.

"We were surprised to see Jo in the kitchen this morning," Monica said, her wavy brown hair pulled off her face with a visor. She, too, had a cup of coffee, and her son sipped cocoa with one hand and poked sticks into the fire with their other.

Loudly enough for Jo to hear, Daisy said, "She's been wanting to work on her Dutch oven baking, and today is the perfect day for that."

"It's so interesting how differently you two work together than the team last year. Sam and I came on our own and we convinced his brothers to join us this year. I can't imagine last year's cowboy cooking us breakfast, can you?" Monica said.

Her husband, Sam, looked uncomfortable and kept his eyes on the fire. "No," he finally answered.

"What was his name? It was something so interesting."

"Dozer," Sam said.

"That's right, Dozer! He was like a cowboy right out of the movies. I'll be honest with you, I was worried about the Lodge sending us into the middle of nowhere with two women, but you've both done such an amazing job."

"I wouldn't say amazing," Daisy said, remembering Jo's criticism about the food and how much the guests paid for their vacation.

"Don't be hard on yourself," Monica said. "You're worried about your friend. That would throw anyone off their game."

"That's very generous of you. I'm sorry she wasn't able to cook your whole trip."

"Still worth it to have real food, not freeze dried, and to not have to carry any of it. This has been great, hasn't it?" Sam asked the others.

"I want to run my horse today! Can I run my horse?" Timothy asked. He and the other boys had adapted to mountain life with ease. Instead of wearing sweatshirts, they sat close to the fire, and it didn't look like they'd brushed their hair since the beginning of the trip.

Daisy didn't need a coat or the fire. Her whole body flashed hot. She had no idea how to answer Timothy's question. What if they were allowed to run the horses? She'd never gone faster than a walk all summer. She'd probably fly right off. Even though she had plenty of coffee, she held up her cup and said, "Time for a refill."

Jo stood like she was about to have a gunfight with the Dutch, two oven mitts serving as her pistols.

"How's it going, Cookie?" Daisy asked.

"How do I know? There's no window! But I think it's too early to take the lid off."

"Exactly! Now do you get why…" Thinking about the ride, she knew she couldn't afford to continue picking the fight about equity that she'd started. "Timothy was talking about whether he could run his horse."

"Hmmm." Jo stuck the thick handle of a wooden spoon through the loop on the lid of the oven and nudged it aside. They both peered inside. Uneven lumps had pushed together in the pan, but they were a pretty golden color. A surge of jealousy ran through Daisy.

"Looks like they're done," Daisy said begrudgingly.

"Hot dog!" Jo wore a look of pure jubilation. "I just hope they're not gummy in the middle." She carefully removed the lid and lifted a pie tin out of the oven. When she pried one biscuit away from the bunch, her jubilance faded like a dark cloud covering the sun. The bottom was burned black.

"It happens in an instant," Daisy said. The first three times I checked the ham, it was fine. Then the next time…well…you ate it. You know how badly it burned. We'll cut off the bottom. They'll be fine."

"But now there won't be enough."

"I'll start another batch. Or you can, and I'll give the gravy a try. I've watched my mom make gravy at Thanksgiving."

"What happened to you not cooking today?"

Daisy dug around for the container of flour. "I don't know what to tell Timothy."

"That sounds like a pickle."

Jo didn't sound concerned, and it was maddening that she refused to say whether they were even allowed to run the horses.

"The horses ran when you turned them loose last night, so I'm guessing it's safe."

"You're the packer today. It's your call."

Daisy added flour to the bacon grease in the pan and heated it on the grill. She didn't meet Jo's eyes when she said, "I've never run a horse. I don't know what to tell him or what to do if something goes wrong."

"Sounds like someone changed her mind about cooking a roast."

Daisy had been looking forward to taking the day ride and getting out of the kitchen, but even more she hated to admit that she couldn't do Jo's job. She searched for a bright side. "I guess there's a chance I'll redeem myself from that ham disaster. Otherwise, there's no way Leo's sending me into the backcountry again."

She wasn't sure, but when she looked up, she thought she caught Jo smiling.

CHAPTER SEVENTEEN

Jo had never been as happy to roll into the Lodge as she was the next day. Z had allowed her to pack up the camp without question. The packs were light, especially with the extra mule Z had added to her string, and the ride home had been blessedly quiet since she was able to give Z easy instructions to find the Red Cones, and from there she'd be able to get the guests back to the pack station on her own.

She tossed her lead rope to Gabe. "Boy, am I happy to see you!"

"How was your trip?"

Jo dismounted. "It's a miracle I survived."

"Don't tell the boss that."

"I know. Tell me Takeisha's back."

Gabe turned and led her stock down to the pack dock closest to the store and café. Jo tied Tuxedo, aware that Z had now joined her and was on her way to help the guests from their horses.

"No, no, no, no, no! My shoeing buddies come for our annual trip tomorrow. Takeisha is cooking that trip! Please don't tell me she's not back."

He clipped Dumbo to the post and started to untie Ladybird.

"Say something!" Jo loosened the half hitch on the first load, waiting for Gabe to speak. When she'd removed the tarp and the top load of chairs, Gabe was back to help remove one of the boxes. They met on the dock, thunking down their boxes. "Gabe!"

"You said not to tell you, so I'm not."

"Rats! She has to be here! She came in days ago! At least tell me Leo found a replacement. Tracy?"

"Isn't it *hot* rats?"

Gabe's teasing only fueled her frustration. "Gabe!"

He raised his hands to calm her ire. "Nope."

"*Hot* rats! Cleland?"

"Nope, she's busy being mayor of Mammoth."

"Fried farts on toast!" Jo barked. Her list of possible cooks was as empty as the corral on an overbooked morning.

"Got any more guesses? This is fun!" Gabe said. She angled a glare that only made him laugh as he led Dumbo over to the tie rail where she'd give all her stock grain before putting them away for the night.

Jo stomped away and returned with Blaze and Skeeter. Once she'd secured Blaze to one post, she moved Skeeter to the other. She and Gabe worked quickly, dismantling the loads and carrying the bags and boxes to the dock. As they were finishing up, the guests clustered around making piles of their duffels, sleeping bags, and tents. Z was there with them as well, but instead of going to fetch a truck to move her kitchen boxes off the dock, she walked to Skeeter's head.

"Matchbox was my mule. I'll take this one down and bring him…" She took Skeeter's lead rope, unsnapped the line that held her to the post, and started to lead her away from the dock and from Blaze.

"Do not move that mule!" Jo lunged for Skeeter's lead rope.

It was too late. Not seeing Blaze in front of her, Skeeter lunged away from Daisy, easily pulling free and galloping away.

"Shit! You can't lead Skeeter without Blaze," Jo hollered. "Gabe, take Cody around the dude horse corral. Let's see if we can drive her toward the mule corral."

"What can I do?" Z asked.

"Stay out of the daggum way!" Jo barked. She was already running, but she hadn't missed Z standing there looking like she'd been socked in the stomach. Ready to explode with frustration, Jo continued to chase the mule, hoping that their long travel day would make her easy to catch.

When the dust had finally settled and all Jo's mules were lined up at the rail and unsaddled, Gabe turned his level gaze on Jo. "What?" she said.

He looked pointedly at Jo and then up to the dock where Z was talking to their guests. She could tell he was disappointed in her. She was tired of having to be so careful. She wanted to do her job and be done with it and stop having to teach Z and watch what she said. Gabe's expression told her that she was going to have to try to make it right. Without any lecturing at all, he helped her turn out the stock.

Z remained on the dock even after the guests left. Turning to her, Jo said, "You'll want to track down a truck to put the boxes in. That's how Takeisha always takes them to the storeroom to restock them for the next trip."

"Leave the heavy lifting to the guys. Understood. Wouldn't want to mess up my nails anyway." She turned on her heel and left.

Jo didn't have to see Gabe to know that he was smiling. Z's comment meant she'd have to tell Gabe everything, including Z's ridiculous accusations about her being a male chauvinist. All through dinner, she could feel the question coming. After they'd eaten and fed the mule corral, she wasn't surprised when he walked up to her cabin with two camp chairs in one hand and two beers in the other.

"Still hiding from the humans," he commented after they'd settled in. Her cabin sat furthest from the corrals and the store and few ever approached. Said humans were gathered several cabins down practicing with the rope again.

"Still waiting for you to say Leo's found someone to cook my trip."

"What's wrong with the one you've got?"

"I do a good job. Nobody's ever complained before. Then this one shows up…" She bounced her chin in Z's direction. "And suddenly I'm a chauvinistic asshole."

Gabe threw back his head and whooped. "I like her more and more."

"You don't know a thing about her, and you're taking her side?"

"Here's what I know. First time I saw her, she didn't know what side of a bridle was up. Two months later, she's leading in a bunch of guests and offering to help unload the mules. I don't get why you're not asking her out for a date."

"She thinks I'm a chauvinistic asshole."

"So you *do* think she's hot."

"Quit matchmaking, Gabe. I've heard the stories about Kristine, and the parts about the rabid bear are a heck of a lot more interesting than the stuff about how she fell for the bear expert."

"Some people like the hooking up part." He was still watching Z and Pete.

They were doing their flirty dance masked as him teaching her how to throw the rope. Seeing her have so much fun irked Jo. "What right does she have to march in here and say there's a problem with a cook doing a cook's job and a packer doing a packer's job." Gabe sat patiently listening as she ranted about all the things that had gone wrong on the trip and how on top of it all, Z had found fault with their delineated jobs. "I'd like to see her tell The Hippie that it's his turn to cook breakfast."

"I never had any problem cooking my lady breakfast," Gabe said with a sly smile.

"That's different. You're in a relationship. That's not about the job, it's about showing you care."

"Exactly!" He raised his beer in salute. "You're not as clueless as I thought. This is good."

"I tell you you're wrong and I'm the one you think is clueless?"

"A little. But not as much as I thought."

Jo frowned and drank her beer trying to figure her friend out. "I'm talking about a woman I work with, and you're talking about your girlfriend. That's not the same. I don't care about Z."

"Who?"

"Daisy."

"Don't you call her Zorro?"

"We all did a spot trip a few weeks ago, and she talked about putting a Zorro 'Z' at every successful trip she helped with."

Gabe nodded.

"It doesn't mean I like her."

"Okay."

"What's the rest?"

"What?" he asked innocently.

"Of the stuff in your brain. I can feel you thinking."

He kept her waiting for a while, both of them watching the toss of the rope, the re-coil, the next toss. "You haven't shown any of them how to throw a rope?"

Now he'd baffled her. "Not about roping. About Daisy…Z."

"You keep watchin' 'em, so I thought maybe you were creating a lesson for them. You're figuring out what they're doing wrong, not enjoying the view?"

"You're the one watching them!"

"Me? No! I'm keeping an eye on my girlfriend, so I know when she's had enough of all that racket."

"You didn't say you brought your girlfriend."

"You didn't ask. You had a lot of complaining to do about that girl you don't like."

"I'm trying to wrap my brain around doing another trip with her in the backcountry."

"Her cowboy friend over there is thinking the same thing."

"Daggummit, Gabe! Will you shut up about it?"

"Maybe if you get up off your ass and catch that *daggum* pink cow before it stampedes the place."

Jo plunked down her beer bottle and strode over to the gathering. Daisy was winding up before her throw, the loop much too small to catch anything. The way she snapped it after she threw, it cracked at the plastic cow head like a whip. "Mind if I have a go?"

Daisy finished pulling in the slack and held the rope out to Jo. Jo grasped it, but Daisy didn't let go. "That depends."

"On?"

"Whether you say roping is part of the packer's job."

With Gabe behind her and Daisy standing her ground, Jo had to find an answer. She knew that Z was waiting for her to accept that the separate jobs for packer and cook were sexist and if she didn't, the next trip was going to be torture. Luckily, roping was not a necessary skill for either. "It's not part of the job."

Daisy made no move to hand over the rope.

"Gabe's worried the cow is going to get away. Let me show you how to catch it. Please?"

Reluctantly, Daisy let go and walked out of the space Jo would need to wind up for her throw. She situated the extra rope in her left hand and fed out enough to make a loop as big as two bales of hay. "First you need a bigger loop. Then get the end of the rope out halfway." She began her windup. "Most important, you've got to throw over your shoulder and point at your target." She followed her own instruction, and the loop fell neatly over the pink head. She pulled as it did and tightened the loop right around the horns.

While the group clapped, she loosened the rope and re-coiled it. Gabe stood there smirking, so she handed the rope to him. "Happy now?"

"Maybe. If you understand that you have to throw the rope if you ever hope to catch something." He handed the rope to Pete and kept a level gaze on Jo.

Jo was confused. What was he talking about? "I know. I caught the cow for you."

"Clueless," she heard him whisper under his breath. "Come meet who I caught."

"You make no sense, you know that?"

"Not now, but you'll figure it out. I hope."

She followed to meet his woman, leaving the immobile pink-headed hay cow for Pete and Daisy to deal with.

"Look! I convinced Jo to socialize a bit," Gabe said. "Jo, this is my girlfriend, Brenna. Brenna, this is Jo. She doesn't like people either."

"I hear you give tickets," Jo said. "Is there a citation for public annoyance?"

Jo liked the way Brenna looked at Gabe. She matched Gabe in height and physique, but where he had an air of joviality, she was all seriousness. "He bothering you?"

"Write me up later," Gabe said with a twinkle in his eye.

Brenna didn't look amused, if anything she looked confused. She was staring at the horses in the corral. "Is that Houdini?"

Gabe laughed. "Nope, different white horse."

Jo didn't understand why that would make Brenna relax, but it did. Gabe explained, "Our friend Madison has this horse, Houdini, that doesn't exactly stay in one place."

"I owe that horse a ticket," Brenna said.

Gabe shook his head at Brenna. "Madison runs a small resort in Quincy called Hot Rocks. It's worth checking out if you're ever out our way."

The pause made Jo aware that she'd lost track of the conversation. As they'd talked about their friend's horse, her eyes had drifted back to Churchill's rider and her persistent attempts to catch the plastic cow head. When she looked back, Gabe was smiling.

"I'd tell you how Houdini helped Madison hook up with Lacey, but I know you're not into that sort of thing."

Jo turned, so Daisy was out of her range of sight. She wouldn't give Gabe any reason to think she was interested in any kind of backcountry romance.

CHAPTER EIGHTEEN

Daisy luxuriated in her twin bed. What she had considered cramped in comparison to the queen she slept in at home now felt like a five-star hotel after her days on the flimsy camping mat. The windows of the cabin she shared with Heather showed the barest hint of light, and Heather had yet to stir. She listened for movement out at the corrals and missed the sound of the bell that had woken her the last four mornings.

She'd hear that bell again tomorrow night when Jo turned out their stock at Second Crossing. Four more days in the wilderness she'd left her city job for. Four more days of being put in her place by Jo. A scale tipped in her head as she weighed the prospects trying to determine whether she could feel happy about the trip.

She'd been so relieved when she rode in and Pete and Heather met her at the corral. They chatted easily about what had happened while she'd been away, Heather full of day-ride disasters like the large man whose saddle tipped sideways, him holding on the whole way over and around until he was underneath Lurch. Pete complained about picking up a spot trip to Sharktooth Camp where at least three loads worth of gear greeted him and Leo had only sent him with two mules. She would have loved to add her own stories, but she wasn't about to say anything with the guests lingering by the pack dock and Jo working with her stock.

Later when they'd gathered for roping practice, she'd finally been able to describe her cooking debacles. To her surprise, stories of other cooks' failures tumbled out: the one who served raw sausage versus one who took a "burn-and-turn" approach. Another foisted the lunch-time sandwich making onto the guests, and worst in everyone's book was the one who prepared food without washing her hands. Instead of criticizing, everyone around her applauded the way she had stepped in for Takeisha and congratulated her on the progress she'd made. They assured her the most important thing was that she tried her best and shared their confidence that it would go more smoothly on her next trip.

A shiver of anxiety mixed with anticipation tickled through Daisy's belly. Tomorrow morning she'd be in the café making sandwiches for all of Jo's friends before they left, and then she'd be cooking dinner over a fire again. When Leo had told her Takeisha wasn't back, he'd assured her the next trip would be much easier because it didn't require packing up the kitchen to move every other day. Instead, Jo would keep the stock at Second Crossing where the grazing was good and would do day rides to various fishing spots with her friends. She was happy to have Takeisha's menu from the Horse Heaven trip but wished she could talk to her to find out whether she'd prepare the same meals if she was cooking for a base camp.

Jo wasn't happy about it. She'd made that clear sitting in front of her cabin, her expression shooting daggers. Even before Jo had marched over and taken the rope out of her hands, Daisy had felt Jo's eyes on her. She and Pete kept laughing at each other as the rope fell short of its target. Cute, fun, uncomplicated Pete whom she hadn't thought about for an instant while she'd been in the backcountry.

Then Jo had stormed up, her stride communicating her position at the top of the herd. Once Daisy had relinquished the rope, she couldn't help admiring Jo's form as she snapped her loop around the bull's horns on the first try. She walked away without a backward glance but managed to maintain Daisy's attention. Pete's breath whispered against her neck when he leaned in asking whether Jo was hard to work with, but that wasn't what tightened Daisy's core. Even when she'd seen Jo from a distance riding in the parade, something about her pulled at Daisy. Too bad her personality threw water on the kindling of desire.

Thinking about Jo made it even harder for Daisy to motivate enough to get out of bed. It was too easy to imagine what it would feel like to be in Jo's arms instead of Pete's. Hearing Heather yawn and stretch, Daisy was forced to shove the idea aside.

"You awake?" Heather asked.

"Knowing I'll be sleeping on the ground tonight is making it hard to get out of bed."

"I bet." In typical Heather fashion, she went from eyes open to out of bed and fully dressed in less than a minute. She ran a brush through her hair and said, "No hurry for you, right? All you have to do is get your kitchen packed?" She pulled on a coat, ready to go catch up a dozen horses before she walked to breakfast.

"All I have to do. You're joking, right? I don't even know where to start."

"That's what's really keeping you in bed." Heather punched her feet into her boots and quickly laced them.

"I know," Daisy groaned. Heather hadn't been with her in the storage room down behind the café. The walls were lined with shelf after shelf of camping gear, all of it battered and smelling of smoke. After Jo had told her to drive the kitchen boxes over to the café and ask Jorge for help, he'd popped in for all of five minutes to suggest that she unpack the leftovers from the trip. He explained that unused meats and dairy were to be put in the kitchen refrigerator for him to repurpose in employee meals.

Backcountry cooks were to restock with fresh dairy. Daisy knew she had to lay it all out on the massive wooden counter in the middle of the room to figure out what she needed to restock, but even the thought was daunting.

Today, she was supposed to gather as much as she could for what she needed from the store itself. If there were groceries she couldn't find in there, she would have to go into Mammoth to shop. Regardless, Daisy planned on going to town to find a Wi-Fi signal and see what tips she could find on YouTube for cooking with a Dutch oven on a campfire. All of it overwhelmed her.

"Can't I come help you at the corral where I know the drill?" she groaned.

"Avoiding it isn't going to make it any easier. See you at breakfast!" With her omnipresent smile, she settled her hat on her head and slipped out of the cabin.

Daisy listened to Heather's boots crunch against the rocky soil. She couldn't stay in bed all day. The kitchen was not going to pack itself. She pushed back her covers and swung her legs over the edge of the bed, anxiety tumbling in her belly like shoes in a dryer. Why was she so nervous?

Well after lunch, Daisy returned to the pack station with a few bags of groceries and pages of notes she'd taken while she'd been in Mammoth. She'd been tempted to call someone while she had a constant signal. Her old high school friends who had gone off to university might chuckle at the image of her scribbling notes about cowboy cooking, but since she had not followed them on their four-year track, they'd lost touch.

Her coworkers at Temptation wouldn't understand. The beauty of that job was in the immediacy. Nobody would appreciate trying to anticipate everything she would need for four days knowing that if she forgot something, there was no running to the market or to her cabin to retrieve it.

It saddened her to realize how tenuous her friendships were. She could call her parents, but she knew they would counter with a Rose Parade example that would make her complaint sound trivial. The mountain of food and supplies she had amassed over the course of the day impressed her enough that she took out her phone to take a picture, even though she had nobody to show it to or a way to post it on social media. Still, it was evidence she would share at the end of this crazy summer when the season ended.

For a split second, she entertained the idea of learning more about cooking. Time had flown by as she clicked video after video of craggy old cowboys sharing tricks for trail cooking. But no way was that a career. She knew that her future wasn't in a coffee shop and while she loved the work she was learning to do at the Lodge, she couldn't imagine what she would do during the winter.

No time to think about that when she had hundreds of pounds of stuff to put into loads that wouldn't make Jo blow her lid. She kicked herself for unpacking without taking note of Takeisha's system. She put loaves of bread in the wash bins. That she remembered. The big pots and pans she tucked in the two leather bags which filled much too quickly—Jo had said they were the only panniers she got. Everything else had to fit in the smaller wooden boxes and coolers. Would it be better to cluster the food with her boxes like grocery-store aisles or by days?

The sound of approaching footsteps pushed her into action. She didn't want Jo to find her idle. Heavy things on the bottom seemed like a good idea, so she grabbed cans and started lining a box. She paused when the footsteps stopped right next to but out of sight of the doorway and waited a moment before resuming her work.

A little rap on the doorframe made her stop again. "Yeah?" she asked. Jo stepped into the doorway, and the myriad of feelings that always chased each other when Daisy saw Jo scampered about again, defensiveness running into excitement and in turn bumping intimidation.

"I called Takeisha," Jo said.

"Oh." Daisy slumped. She tried to sound indifferent. "Is she going to make it back?"

"No. Her mom needs her to watch her brothers and sisters while her dad is in the hospital. At least he's out of danger now."

Daisy wasn't quite sure what to do with that information, not sure why Jo would come down to tell her something that didn't change the trip at all.

"I asked her what her strategy was when she put the kitchen together."

"You did?"

Jo lifted a shoulder. "She's done it enough. I figured she had to have a method."

"I was going to try alphabetizing. Is there a better way?" It was too dark in the room for Daisy to say for sure, but she thought she might have seen a hint of a smile.

"Tetris."

"The video game?"

Jo approached the table. "That one. Where are the pots and pans? She said it's important to fill every nook and cranny."

"Like the bread in the wash bins."

"Exactly. She said once you approach all the stuff on the table as bricks you can move, you'll be set."

Daisy removed the pots from the leather bags and scanned the table. What would fit inside? She grabbed a bag of apples and fed them to the coffeepot.

"Nice!" Jo exclaimed. "Now they won't get banged around and bruise."

They worked like this for several minutes, trying to best each other, grumbling at awkward things like the silverware tray and lanterns. Jo occasionally paused to pick up each of the boxes, checking the weight to see that they paired with another of equal weight. She didn't lecture, and Daisy found herself relaxing and enjoying herself.

"What are you usually doing when Takeisha is packing the kitchen?"

"Depends. I have stuff to gather on the dock, the chairs and tables and such. Sometimes I fix things in the workshop."

"Anything that keeps you away from people?"

"Pretty much," Jo said simply.

Daisy hadn't expected her to say that but was not surprised when Jo didn't elaborate. Even after spending almost a whole week with Jo out in the backcountry, she couldn't say she knew her any better. Did Gabe? They'd sat in front of Jo's cabin for a long while the night before, but after Jo had met Gabe's girlfriend, she quickly escaped from the group. When she wasn't working, Jo seemed to spend more time with the mules than the humans.

"You know that you're a person, right? That you belong in the people herd?"

"I prefer my mule herd, thanks," Jo said.

"What do you have against people?"

"They're selfish."

"Okay." Daisy reflected on that for a moment. "But mules aren't exactly unselfish. They want their hay, their grain."

Jo hmmmed noncommittedly.

"People smell better," Daisy countered.

"That's a matter of opinion," Jo said. "People judge."

"Horses probably do too. They just can't talk," Daisy said.

"They communicate if you pay attention."

The conversation felt very much like roping practice. She threw out an idea. Missed. Spent time coiling another topic to pitch at Jo only to clearly miss her mark again. She tossed out her next reply. "Still, sometimes you want to talk to someone who will talk back."

"People talk too dang much."

"Ouch." She mentally coiled her rope to prepare for her next throw. "Especially me. I'm a talker. A lot of people find that appealing, if you were wondering. I have some great stories."

She'd expected Jo to take the bait, but Jo did not. The noose had missed the target again. Daisy had once held her coworkers riveted with a story of a body discovered in the trunk of one of the Rose Parade cars. And there was the time her mother had thrown up out of the window of their car on the freeway with disastrous results. People loved that story. Jo wasn't interested. She hadn't even looked up from the box she was filling.

"Horses, mules, dogs…they're all better listeners," Jo said, her focus on the work.

Daisy was no closer to understanding Jo's distant nature. She paused on that. She'd been hoping Jo would share something that would explain her behavior, but maybe that was who she was. It certainly wasn't Daisy's nature. She could appreciate that Jo seemed to thrive on the community she built with her animal friends, but they couldn't possibly satisfy all your needs. "That may be so, but I bet they're terrible kissers."

Jo's head snapped up. Just as quickly, she returned to her work, but her expression divulged exactly what Daisy had suspected. Jo's attention could be caught. All she had to do was learn to throw the noose correctly. She coiled for her next throw.

CHAPTER NINETEEN

Daisy stood by her fire, savoring for a moment how well the day had gone. Her hackles had started to raise when Jo approached her at the saddle shed to explain how all her colleagues were expert horsemen who didn't need any instructions on riding.

Jo had met them at a farrier convention when she first started shoeing. It was hard for Daisy to picture Jo being social at such an event, but it made sense when Jo explained that she'd been sucked in after she divulged she was from California. A dozen Californian farriers had established their own group for networking and welcomed her into the fold without much choice.

Daisy's grumpiness because of Jo dissipated quickly when she met the gregarious group. She quickly saw how hard it would be for anyone, even someone as prickly as Jo, to decline membership to their group.

They charmed Daisy from the get-go. When she'd handed out lunches, Ethan, with eyebrows as bushy as his mustache, had said with absolute seriousness, "Daisy's cooking our meals. Do everything you can to keep her happy."

After that, she'd enjoyed the easiest day of her summer. She had already caught and saddled the five horses she wanted to take on the trip, but instead of having to deal with the guests individually as she had every day of the previous travel trip, Jo's friends worked out which mounts they wanted. Two wanted to pack and ride with Jo. The other three were already ready to go when Daisy rode back on Churchill.

Daisy had enjoyed listening to the easy conversation between the men who rode behind her as well as answering the typical questions about where she was from and what had brought her to the Lodge. They had almost finished their lunch when Jo and the others passed with two neat strings of packed mules. Those with Daisy ribbed the others about how long it took them to do the work and warned that they would not get a good review if camp wasn't ready when they arrived.

Having learned from setting up Takeisha's kitchen, she was pleased with her camp and had an easy dinner to prepare. Jo's friends worked on the snacks she'd set out and juice to chase away the dust of the trail but were discussing how much better their beers were going to be after they'd been sitting in a stream of snow runoff for a few hours.

Before she got to work on dinner, Daisy wanted her camp sneakers and her ball cap. From the pile of gear Jo and her friends had heaped on a tarp, she extracted her bag which had once been bright yellow but now was covered with oil from the leather panniers and dirt. She pushed aside the other bags in search of her purple sleeping bag. Her sleeping mat was there, but not her bag.

Jo returned from the picket lines and was talking to Earl about fishing in the morning. He had merrily cracked up when he'd read the nametag on his horse's saddle. His friends had quickly decided that it would be appropriate to call him Baldy for the weekend, giving Daisy a chance to observe that it would be easier for her to call any guest of the summer by their mount's name.

"But then you'd have to trust them to remember what their horse was called," Jo had added with her typical pessimism.

"And people are stupid," Daisy had muttered.

Jo's friends chuckled. Their ease around Jo's fractious attitude helped Daisy relax her guard. She handed Earl the fishing poles she had found while looking for her sleeping bag.

"Always a step ahead of us," Earl said. Daisy liked the resonance of his bass voice.

"Jo taught me that anticipating what guests need is an important part of making the backcountry experience a vacation."

"I like this one," Earl said. "Shame that Takeisha couldn't be here but seems like you found us a suitable replacement!"

"Were you finally going to ask her out this year?" Jo asked.

Earl's smile revealed straight white teeth. "I only come on this stupid trip of yours to fish. You know that."

Even though Daisy could tell Jo was taking a much more relaxed approach to this trip, she didn't for a second think that she would be forgiven if dinner was late. She needed to keep moving. "Has anyone set up their tent yet?" she asked. "Looks like someone grabbed my sleeping bag by mistake."

"We've all been busy destroying your bean dip," Earl said. "Anybody grab their gear yet?" he hollered.

The others joined them, all confirming that they had been busy eating. Daisy's stomach started to free-fall. They'd ridden five hours that day. What would happen if her bag hadn't ridden with them? "I don't have my sleeping bag," Daisy said.

Jo frowned but sounded unphased when she said, "That's impossible. There are seven of us. Five guests and us two. The two bedrolls rode on top, and three sleeping bags in one pannier and two in the other. I added the fishing poles on that side to even it out."

"But I don't see it."

"Okay! Time to set up tents!" Dave announced. He was the most softly spoken of the group and had thinning blond hair. "It'll probably turn up once we clear out our junk."

"What happens if it doesn't?" Earl crossed his arms instead of jumping to pull his gear out as the others were.

"It'll show up," Jo said. She dismissed Daisy with a *trust me* look.

Without a tent to worry about, she returned to her cooking duties. As the fire burned to coals, she boiled water for coffee and the rice pilaf. That could rest in the Dutch oven while she grilled the chicken and prepared zucchini with butter and garlic salt.

Later, Kevin ran his hand over his beard after he polished off a healthy second serving. "I guess we'll keep you! That was delicious!"

One of the quiet ones, either Dave or Terry returned from the stream with a bucket clinking with beer bottles. "Have a beer with us, Daisy!"

Daisy should have been elated that the first meal was going so well and happy to join them to eat. Without the pressure of moving camp and all the videos she had watched, she should have been feeling confident.

"Terry's right!" Earl boomed. "Sit! You deserve a beer!"

As Terry passed beers around to his buddies, Daisy tried to catch Jo's eye to see whether she should join them or not. She had seemed so certain the bag would appear that Daisy had managed to put the problem out of her mind while cooking. Now she only had to serve the cherry pie Jorge had given her for the first dessert, but all she could think about was the slight shake of the head Jo had given her when Daisy had served her dinner.

There was no way anyone was riding all that way back to find her bag, especially not with dusk upon them.

"Jo told us about your sleeping bag," Terry said. "That's the shits."

Many mumbled similar sentiments. The quiet extended as they sipped their beers.

"You could share with me," Kevin said.

Ethan coughed on beer that must have gone down the wrong way. "As if the two of you would fit in a bag!"

"We could unzip it. I could keep you warm all night." He lifted his beer and his eyebrows.

"Dude, you have a wife," Terry said.

Kevin flipped him off. "That counts you out too. Dave doesn't have a girlfriend, and he's got a bedroll."

Dave threw his hands in the air. "You guys are disgusting. Daisy doesn't want to share a bedroll with some dude she just met." Silence stretched as the fire crackled. "Do you?"

Daisy was getting worried. How was she supposed to respond to that?

"Buzz off, Dave," Jo finally said. "She'll bunk with me." A very different silence settled on them. Even Jo looked uncomfortable and quickly added, "If you want."

Daisy sipped her beer again. It was the best beer she'd ever tasted in her life. Terry was right. The mountain stream did get it perfectly cold. "I figured I could pile up the horse pads like I did on my last trip. I have Heather's nice coat. I'll stay by the fire. It'll be fine, right?"

Another silence.

"Those saddle pads stink to high heaven," Jo said. "But it's your choice."

Daisy didn't know what to say, so she drank her beer. It made her feel better. She waggled the bottle. "Do you have another one of these?"

Boisterous laughter filled the canyon. "I have allllllll you need to make that arrangement look good, little lady," Terry drawled. He jumped up from his chair and headed to the stream.

CHAPTER TWENTY

They stayed up for hours, partly because they hadn't seen each other for ages—Earl, Ethan, and Dave since the summer before and longer for the others who came less frequently because of their families. They drank and started dredging up stories. This wasn't new. Stories and campfires were a backcountry staple, but the fact that Jo would be sharing a bedroll with Daisy changed the tone of things. Takeisha never stayed with the group for more than a single beer before calling it a night. It occurred to Jo that maybe Daisy would do the same if not for the fact that she didn't look prepared to leave the campfire without Jo.

"Does Daisy know about the mule you got stuck in a tree your first summer here?" Dave asked. Even though only a few of the guys had seen the accident firsthand, the story was a good one and had passed among the group.

"How do you get a mule stuck in a tree?" Daisy asked. She leaned closer to the campfire instead of getting up to look for her coat.

"My first summer here, I had crap choice for mules," Jo said. "My string was made up of a bunch of cranky old-timers. Pesky was the worst. He'd kick the shit out of anything that was behind him."

"Trouble was," Dave jumped in, "he was the smallest damn mule. Jo was all set to impress us. Like today, she cruised by with all our stuff loaded onto the mules, tipping her hat and saying she'd see us at Second Crossing. Then we come moseying along the trail and see this little mule, his hooves what? A foot off the ground?"

"At least," Jo said. Surrounded by colleagues who had become friends, she relaxed into the story, temporarily distracted from the fact that she'd soon be sharing her bedroll with Daisy. "We were cruising right along when the mules stopped up short. I had that leggy giant, Orion, in the lead, and he nearly pulled me out of the saddle. I dallied up my lead rope on the horn of the saddle and spurred my horse. Nothing."

"When we rode up, she was standing there looking at him scratching her head."

"Somebody didn't cut out a fallen tree wide enough?" Daisy guessed. "We had to cut a section of a fallen tree out earlier in the season. You said it was to allow for small mules to pass through."

She looked at Daisy, arms wrapped around her knees, face rosy from the fire, the hair that had fallen loose from her French braid floating ethereally with a gentle breeze. There was no denying that she was much more than hot. Gabe himself had pointed out how Daisy had relaxed, and Jo could now see that Daisy's demeanor had as much to do with her friends' clamoring to share a sleeping bag with her as her physical beauty did. Daisy was a good person, jumping willingly into anything that was asked of her, and she had remembered what Jo had told her weeks and weeks ago which made her even more appealing.

Jo gulped. Sharing her bed with the cook whose bag got lost was one thing. Sharing her bed with someone she was attracted to was a different thing altogether.

Jo shook off this realization quickly, hoping her friends had not noticed her falter. "Worse. In that case, you could take the string around the tree or, worst-case scenario, unpack and repack the load on either side. This trail had trees on either side rooted close to the trail but leaning out, so they made a huge V shape. The tall mules walked through the larger space no problem, and then here came Pesky at the end. He could see that the boxes he carried weren't going to fit, so at the last minute, he jumped."

"And that's how we found him, wedged in that V. Took all of us to get into the cinches and get him out of the saddle without someone getting kicked in the head," Dave added excitedly.

"I'm so glad you kept the promise to bury that story on the trail," Jo said wryly. Embarrassed, she glanced at Daisy who wore a huge smile that shot a rush of sparks through her. She caught a glimpse of what Gabe and Takeisha had meant when they said how nice it was to share a bedroll with someone like Daisy to keep her warm. She needed a distraction from the way her thoughts were going, and one appeared immediately. "I swore I'd never tell about the time we had to rope Terry off his horse, and that story has never left the group."

Earl whooped and, as Jo had hoped he would, ran with the story about their drunken friend galloping off toward the Devil's Postpile where the Lodge was forbidden to take any stock. Jo relaxed as Earl relished every detail of Terry's attempts to cut away from the group which finally resulted in Jo having to chase him down and rope him off his horse.

The story diverted from her, she had the opportunity to watch Daisy as she took in the details Earl was sharing. He was a good storyteller, and his rich voice made it even better, especially since he had a new audience. Daisy's smile widened as the story built, and Jo wondered if she would have stayed with the group if she'd had her own sleeping bag to escape to, like Takeisha did. Did Takeisha leave her with her friends for Jo's sake or her own?

Friendly laughter once again reverberated around their campfire pulling her from her thoughts. "You had to rope anyone lately?" Earl asked when the laughter ebbed.

"Naw."

"She could, though," Daisy piped up. "We've been trying to learn how to rope all summer. One of the day-ride crew has a plastic cow head he puts on a hay bale. I haven't figured out how to get my loop right, but last night Jo walked up and snagged it in one throw."

Daisy's sparkling blue eyes met Jo's. No. Not sparkling. They merely reflected the dancing flames. Still, she held Jo's attention until Kevin spoke.

"That sounds about right. All work all the time. The only reason she agrees to this trip of ours is because it's her job."

The familiar jab aligned with Gabe's words. His goading about the roping had been to make her show off in front of Daisy. Had Daisy noticed and read it as a play for her attention? Cody roused himself from Jo's bedroll and edged under Jo's outstretched hand. "Okay. This one is dragging me off to bed. He knows the bears will likely have us up all night. Everyone got what they need?"

Her friends groaned as they stood and moved away from the warmth of the fire. Flashlights bobbed into the woods where tents awaited them.

Daisy and Jo stood side by side by the fire, studiously not looking at each other. "You can get ready first. I've got to let the fire die down a bit before I go to bed, anyway."

"Scared of me?"

Electricity ran through Jo's body. The way Daisy's confidence had grown since their last trip was making it more difficult for her to ignore how beautiful she was. That was scary. "Should I be?"

"I don't bite." Daisy playfully butted Jo's shoulder with her own.

All that did was pull Jo's focus to Daisy's full lips, lips that she could easily picture finding in the night, lips that would feel like heaven on her skin, lips that now ticked up at the edges. Jo met Daisy's eyes.

"How many beers did you have?" Daisy asked.

Not enough to stop her mind from spinning on how she was going to be able to sleep squeezed in next to Daisy in her bedroll. She couldn't think about that, about how the easiest way to share the pad that wasn't quite twin-sized with another person was to spoon in the same direction, and then where were their hands supposed to go? "Enough that I'm going to have to pee all night. I'll probably stay by the fire for a while. You go ahead."

Instead of blossoming, Daisy's smile faded. "I should make a bed out of saddle pads and my coat. It's what real cowboys in the Wild West did, right?"

"The guys would never forgive me. You'd sleep like crap and then ruin breakfast. Remember what Ethan said about keeping the cook happy."

"Well the cook is tired and ready for bed, and if you're staying by the fire, there's no way I'm crawling in your bed and falling asleep wondering how long you're going to be out here. So if you want to keep me happy, brush your teeth. That's what I'm doing." Without waiting for a reply, she marched over to her bag and pulled out her toiletries.

Cody whined and Jo reached down to pat him. "Okay. Here we go. It's not like she can see into my head, right?"

CHAPTER TWENTY-ONE

Daisy wished her heart would quiet down. She had seen how wide Jo's bedroll was and worried that when they crawled in next to each other, Jo was going to be able to feel the way her pulse raced through her whole body. At first, she'd been relieved that after Jo had said they would bunk together, not one of her friends said anything about two women sharing a bed. But then she had felt Jo's eyes on her. What had that meant? Jo talked like she didn't care much for people—man or woman—but when her gaze had lingered on her lips, Daisy had to wonder if that was just talk.

Daisy unzipped her coat hoping to temper the heat coursing through her when Jo had responded to her lighthearted comment about not biting. Jo had seemed to study her mouth, flooding Daisy with ideas of the various parts of Jo's body she would very much like to nip and tug with her teeth.

Enough of that. She ran a cold washcloth over her burning cheeks. At least in the dark Jo would not be able to see her blush. She'd disappeared with her own toothbrush and had returned to the fire, poking the logs away from each other, her toothbrush hanging from her lips like a pipe. Crouched down to avoid the smoke, she lingered as the flames died away. Daisy knew Jo was stalling.

Jo's bedroll was tucked into the trees a few feet away from the kitchen. Daisy made some last adjustments to the tarps covering the food, gathered clothes for tomorrow and stood next to the bedroll. As she had hoped, Jo finally lay down the stick she had been using to poke the coals and joined her. She knelt and folded back the protective canvas of her bedroll.

Inside was what looked like a twin bed made up with real sheets and blankets, even a full-sized pillow.

"You want to put your clothes and boots down at the bottom to keep them clean and dry."

"You have a bed in there!" Daisy sat on the opposite edge to remove her shoes. "Oh my god. There's a mattress in here? You sleep on a mattress?" She pressed her hands into the thick foam and then flopped her whole body down. The soft bed felt like heaven to her tired body.

"What did you think I had in here?"

"A sleeping bag?"

Jo snorted, making Daisy feel a little more comfortable. "Sleeping bags are for hikers and posers."

"You're calling your friends posers?"

"They are my guests."

"So I'm a poser." Now Daisy warmed for a different reason. Jo continued to regard her as a temporary disturbance despite all her hard work, including pulling off what she'd considered a pretty damn good dinner. She set her change of clothes and sleep shirt on the canvas that extended out beyond the little bed. The soft bed that was calling her name. "You know what? Don't answer that. I'm too tired to care."

With her back to Jo, she shucked off her sweatshirt. Again grateful for the dark, she unbuttoned her blouse, all too aware of Jo's proximity. Keeping her bra on, she quickly pulled her Mickey Mouse sleep shirt over her head, removing the bra through the armhole like she had in eighth-grade sleepovers. The cool night air made the hairs on her arms stand at attention. To preserve her body heat, she wiggled out of her jeans and immediately into Jo's bed. Quickly, she rolled the jeans and wrapped them in her sweatshirt to tuck under her head, leaving the pillow for Jo. She shut her eyes to give Jo privacy but could sense her movements as she changed. Into what? Did she have shorts or pants that she slept in or did she sleep in a shirt as well? Daisy felt exposed in her shirt, her bare legs appreciating Jo's soft flannel sheets. The heavy blankets were already capturing and returning Daisy's heat, as was the foam mattress underneath her.

Daisy couldn't help but sigh with utter contentment. It felt so good to be lying down on a bed as soft as the day had been long. Jo froze next to her and Daisy realized how it might have sounded like relief to have Jo settling down next to her. It was so easy to imagine herself rolling into Jo and being held by her, savoring her warmth. Instead, she held her breath until Jo somehow found the space to settle in without coming in contact with Daisy.

"Do you have enough room?" Daisy whispered.

"Wagons."

"What?" Daisy rotated onto her back and tipped her head toward Jo's.

"I've got wagons of room."

There was no escaping the sarcasm in her voice. There was also no escaping Jo's scent, a bold spiciness that matched her personality. The two of them together warmed the bed quickly and instead of feeling sleepy, every breath made Daisy feel more and more awake. She barely knew the woman next to her, and what she did know usually ticked her off, yet she wanted to turn and bury her face in Jo's neck to breathe in her scent directly. Working with Jo, she wouldn't dare touch her, yet next to her in bed, she longed to turn over and let her hands wander. So inappropriate! she scolded herself.

"I'm sorry," she said, both for her thoughts and for the situation.

"Not your fault." Surprisingly, Jo sounded sleepy. She yawned and turned her body the same direction as Daisy. Every nerve in Daisy's body waited for some kind of contact, but Jo was careful not to touch her. "We'll have to turn at the same time, so we don't end up face-to-face when one side gets tired."

So practical. All work, she remembered Kevin saying. Would it even occur to Jo that there was something beyond the job? She remembered Heather saying that all Jo did was work. Did she do that as a defense mechanism or was she truly uninterested? She certainly seemed unmoved by the close quarters they shared. Jo's breath fell softly on her neck, and it was all she could do to hug her edge of the foam mattress and keep herself from leaning into Jo.

A real bed, her hips and shoulders said. In the middle of the forest. A gentle wind rustled the tips of the evergreens above her and carried the sound of the bell mare broadcasting her movements in the meadow. If not for how uncomfortable Jo clearly seemed about Daisy sharing her bed, Daisy might have felt like she was right where she belonged.

* * *

Daisy couldn't say what woke her the next morning. It wasn't the bear that, with Cody's help, they had taken turns chasing from the kitchen. It wasn't the sound of the bell mare anywhere near camp. And it wasn't Jo who breathed deeply next to her. Daisy's arm gently rose and fell with each of Jo's breaths. Her eyes flew open. Her arm was draped over Jo's hip! What was it doing there! A zing of pleasure rushed through Daisy's body, but she quickly pinched it off. She had to move before Jo woke up. What would she say if she realized that Daisy was holding her? What would her friends say if they were to wake up and find them spooned from shoulder to ankle?

Desire pulsed through Daisy urging her to pull Jo's hips closer. She must be dreaming. Just because Jo had looked at her from across the fire didn't mean that she would welcome Daisy's touch.

She had to move.

But Jo's body felt so good next to hers.

She had to turn. Stealthily. First, she took the weight off. No movement. She would sigh with relief, but she couldn't breathe, not until she extracted herself. Slowly, she rotated onto her back, pulling her arm to her own body. Safe, she kept scooching until she faced the other direction, away from Jo. Not three breaths later, she heard the jingle of Cody's tags followed by a quiet but deep yawn. Jo rose up on her elbow, and Daisy forced herself to take deep breaths praying that she had managed to cover her mistake.

Letting in very little cold air, Jo slowly extracted herself from the bag. Daisy heard her pull on her jeans and boots. Then she was gone, Cody trotting after her. With the mattress to herself, Daisy rolled into the middle and stretched. She pulled her clothes into an embrace for a few minutes warming them before forcing herself into the cold morning. The last thing she wanted was for Jo to catch her in bed when she returned from gathering the stock.

By the time Jo got back, Daisy had been hard at work in the kitchen long enough that she had a cup of coffee in Earl's hands and was concentrating hard on getting her homestyle potatoes browned to perfection.

"Try it yet?" Jo asked Earl. Jo didn't even look in Daisy's direction. Her gaze was locked on the fire.

Had she noticed Daisy's arm draped over her waist? Was that why she was being weird and distant? *Ridiculous*, Daisy scolded herself. *This is how she always is.*

Earl raised the liquid that was as dark as he was to his lips. "Oh, man! Nothin' in the world like cowboy coffee!" His booming voice matched his large frame.

From inside a nearby tent, Daisy heard one of the others holler, "Did I hear someone say 'coffee'?"

"Better come quick before Jo polishes off the pot!" Earl bellowed. "That'll get up the stragglers! You girls get any sleep?"

Daisy glanced at Jo who was intent on pouring her cup of coffee. Without answering the question, she brought the blue enamel cup to her lips. Steam swirled around Jo's face as she inhaled deeply. One of them should answer Earl's question, but

Daisy could not form any words, completely transfixed on Jo's lips as she took a tentative sip.

Her eyes met Daisy's. She knew. Something in that look probed at Daisy, wordlessly asking whether Daisy had nestled behind her on purpose. "Honest to gosh, that is good coffee. You been studying?"

More than your mouth? Daisy's face warmed at the direction of her gaze and thoughts. "YouTube is an amazing thing. Cowboy coffee is more than settling the grounds. It's boiling out the acidity." Earl's unanswered question expanded in her mind. Had Jo intended to change the subject? If that was the goal, she wasn't successful, not with her other four friends now stumbling toward the fire and the coffeepot like zombies.

"Sounded like you had a visitor last night," Kevin said, rubbing his hands above the flames of the guest fire.

"Stubborn thing," Jo said. "I chased it off twice."

"I only had to get up once," Daisy said, recalling how she had been stuck with all the bear chasing on their last trip until she had made Jo sleep by the kitchen instead of by the stock. Now they had shared the burden as well as her bedroll. The list of reasons she did not miss her own sleeping bag grew longer, even without the memory of her arm nestled over Jo's hip, pulling her dangerously close.

"How much longer till breakfast?"

Jo's words snapped Daisy back to attention. "Right now! Come 'n eat!" She mimicked the cowboy cook whose videos she'd studied. She grabbed a nice flat rock and tucked it between the grill and the pan, raising one side where she scooched the cooked potatoes. On the lower side of the skillet, she poured a bit of bacon grease into the empty space. "Earl, grab a plate and tell me how you like your eggs."

Earl jumped to attention. "Fried."

Daisy cracked two eggs into the spitting grease and sprinkled salt and pepper on them. While the eggs cooked, she scooped potatoes and bacon onto his plate. "Tell me when," she said, "and whoever's next, tell me how you want your eggs."

"Make mine sunny-side up!" Terry said. "Man, eggs to order? You're spoiling us!"

When she peeked up to serve Earl's eggs, she found Jo's eyes on her. She couldn't read the expression she had never seen before, but when the bacon grease popped and sizzled in the skillet, it was very easy to imagine how her skin would react to Jo's touch.

CHAPTER TWENTY-TWO

"Good breakfast." Jo cleared her dishes hoping her friends would follow suit. She needed to get away from the campfire where she had to keep telling herself not to look at Daisy. To look at her was to remember waking up pressed close to her. Her body flushed. She had to stop thinking about it, especially accompanied by Takeisha's comment about how nice it was to share a bed at the end of a long day. "I'm getting ready."

"Can't we wait until the sun warms things up a bit?" Earl asked as usual.

"We're in the valley, man. It'll be hours until it warms up here. It's warmer up at the lake," Jo argued.

Daisy laughed. "You sound like my dad. He's a Rose Parade volunteer, so he stands out on the street with the floats the whole night before. He wears four layers of clothes and drinks coffee from a truck that makes the rounds to all the cold volunteers, and he still freezes."

"How cold does it get?" Terry asked.

"Thirty-five was the lowest, I think. That year he rode one of the scooters and came home wanting to put his face in the microwave to thaw." The guys beamed. Caught in her spell, they stayed right where they were, plates balanced on their knees. By then, Daisy had joined them at the campfire with her own breakfast making it even harder for Jo to ignore her. Unlike the last trip where Daisy had buzzed with nervous energy, she now appeared to be fully in her element. That all but ruined Jo's argument about Daisy being a liability in the backcountry.

And then there was the memory of waking up with Daisy's arm at her waist adding warmth to the bed, the rise and fall of her chest against Jo's back adding a comfort she wasn't sure she'd ever felt before.

"What happens if he's got to piss?" Dave asked.

Jo jerked back to the conversation.

"Oh, they've got another truck that pulls a portable potty. It's covered in Christmas lights," Daisy said.

"That'd spruce up our privy, don't you think, Jo?" Dave asked.

"I'll get right to that after our ride," Jo said, attempting to motivate them. Kindergarten teachers probably had better luck coaxing children away from the playground.

But Daisy was already sharing a story about the driver of the potty-on-wheels getting distracted and driving off with a volunteer inside.

Jo rolled her eyes and went to brush her teeth, but she had to admit that it was hard to walk away from such an animated storyteller. It was clear she enjoyed the attention. The more the group listened, the brighter Daisy shone, making it impossible ignore how beautiful she was. When she returned, Daisy was telling a story about a fire drill on a float that almost took out the rose queen and her court.

"I'm saddling the stock," Jo announced to the group. To Daisy, she said, "We'll be gone till three or four, so we'll need bag lunches."

"Boss says it's time to get a move on," Daisy drawled.

A week ago, she would have bristled at the label, but she heard humor in Daisy's voice. She met and held Jo's eyes. She knew. She knew that Jo knew she'd been holding her before she'd turned this morning. How was she ever going to get through this day?

"What do you know about Daisy?" Dave asked after maneuvering his horse onto the trail right behind Jo.

"Basically nothing. This is her first summer, and I hardly saw her at all until Takeisha had to go home for a family emergency."

"She have a boyfriend?"

"Don't think so. But there's a packer who's interested in her."

"But she's not with him?" Dave asked hopefully.

"Get her number, man," Earl shouted from behind him. "Pasadena is probably, what? A half hour from Chatsworth?"

She heard someone further down the line comment but couldn't follow the conversation.

"Jo! Terry says she's gay. You would know if she's gay, wouldn't you?" Dave squeaked.

"She didn't do the secret handshake when we met," Jo said. And on that first day, it hadn't mattered to Jo whether she was gay or straight. She was a nuisance, nothing more. Did it matter now?

"Jo doesn't think she's gay," Dave shouted down the line. "Wait, you slept in the same bed. How can you not know?"

"We work together, Dave. I come out here to work, not to look for girlfriends. Unlike you and Earl. He said he was going to ask Takeisha out this year. Ask him if he wants her number. Santa Cruz and Santa Barbara are both on the coast."

Dave passed the comment down the line, as she knew he would. The day trip was supposed to be an escape from Daisy, not a debriefing, and she was sure Earl would bite on the fact that his town was more than four hours away from Takeisha's. That gave her time to chew on why Terry would say Daisy was gay. And if she was, why hadn't she said anything to Jo? Because Daisy didn't like her. Because Jo had given her such a hard time at the beginning of the summer. How was she supposed to know the city barista would turn out to be her cook?

This propelled her back to that first day and how she pawned her off on Gabe when she'd needed help bridling her horse. She had nothing else to do on the trail, so she allowed herself to imagine an alternate summer. In this version, it was her, not Pete, who stood behind Daisy to offer lessons, first on bridling and later on roping. She would have angled to spend every minute of her time between trips with Daisy.

By the time she took over the trip for Takeisha, they would have been sharing a secret smile to be able to spend their every day together. And each night. Would they have dared to share Jo's bedroll on purpose? A shudder ran through Jo when she imagined being welcomed into Daisy's arms, molding her body to Daisy's wonderful curves.

If she was gay.

Is that what she was asking in the looks that she had given across the fire this morning? Did she want it to happen again? Did she want more?

At the lake, she was bad company, lost in such questions. She wished she had strangers with her that she could ignore, people who were solely focused on their escape with no interest in Jo beyond getting their stuff where they wanted. With her friends, she obviously couldn't sit by the stock lost in daydreams, while they went off fishing.

Even though she was trying her best to pay attention to the conversation, she had slept so poorly with the bear visitor that it became harder and harder to keep her eyes open as the sun rose higher in the sky.

A pebble tossed in her direction snapped her awake.

"We should take Jo back to camp, so she can get a proper nap," Dave said.

"Dave's missing Daisy. Worried about whether she's having trouble keeping camp safe from the bears?"

"Don't be an idiot, Kevin. Bears don't come out during the day." After a few beats, he turned to Jo. "Do they?"

"She's probably chasing off scary chipmunks and squirrels," Jo said. "If you're ready to head back, say the word. It's your vacation."

She listened to the others rib Dave, and Terry said again that his desire was misplaced. "Weren't you listening when she told that last story about the year the Rose Parade got rained out? She and her *girlfriend* got drenched."

"That could mean a friend who is a girl," Dave said. "Straight women call their friends girlfriends all the time, don't they?"

Nobody answered, and Jo realized they were waiting for her to answer. "Don't ask me! Most of my friends are here. Do you see any straight women?"

They all looked at her. "Nope."

She had to laugh along with them.

* * *

She waited for one of them to bring it up when they got back to camp, but by some unstated agreement, now they were all mute on the subject. When they rode in, Daisy already had snacks and juice set out, which her friends were happy to spike with something Terry had tucked away in his duffel.

Like a well-oiled team, she took care of the stock and came back down to camp to find Daisy well into her dinner prep to which she had agreeably added the fresh rainbow trout the guys had caught and cleaned at the lake.

Self-conscious about sharing her bed again, Jo excused herself for a quick bath in the cold river. Cody followed her down to the water where she stripped quickly, plunged in her whole body. As quickly as possible, she washed with biodegradable soap, rinsed and jumped back onto the granite slab to absorb its heat while she waited to dry enough to slip into clean clothes.

She couldn't stop thinking about Daisy, about whether or not she dated women or men. How had she not asked before now? Because she hadn't ever asked a single personal thing about her. She looked like she was in her twenties. Was she still in school and working at the coffee shop to pay her way? What did she study? These were the type of questions Daisy had asked back when she'd been Zorro. Jo chuckled remembering her joke about getting her hat at Party City. The way she'd been treating Daisy filled her with shame now. And regret. She didn't deserve the way Jo had treated her. Her looking like the girls who had turned their backs on Jo didn't mean Daisy would behave that way.

Life was so much easier when she'd been a tomboy. Nobody questioned her clothes or the activities she enjoyed. She galloped around the barn with a whole herd of tomboys like her, girls who filled their days mucking stalls and grooming ponies every spare minute they had.

Until puberty. And boys. Makeup. Cute clothes. One by one they had deserted her. The horses didn't. They were there for her no matter what. In the middle of the night when her mom argued with her latest boyfriend and it turned nasty, it was easy to slip out of her window, jog to the barn and curl up in the corner of a box stall. Nobody missed her.

If it was her choice, it didn't sting.

But it left her as she was now. Alone.

During dinner, her friends easily pulled Daisy out of the kitchen and into their conversation. Such small talk usually seemed pointless to Jo. Why learn about people's hometowns, careers, and interests when everyone went their separate ways after the trip? None of her friends, except if Dave got brave enough to ask for Daisy's number, would ever talk to her again after this short trip, yet they happily asked about her family. Mom and Dad? Still married. Siblings? None. Interests? Hiking in the mountains and roller blading on the coast. School? On hold until she figured out what she wanted to do with her life.

"The only thing I've ruled out for sure is dentistry."

"But you take such good care of your teeth. I don't see anyone else flossing out here," Kevin said.

"Good hygiene never goes on vacation," Daisy said seriously. "Both of my parents are dentists. Their passion is teeth. I've always wanted that kind of singular focus." Her eyes unexpectedly found Jo's. "I saw it in you when you rode in the parade. You looked like you were born to ride."

"Just about," Jo admitted. "There was a barn down the street from my house. I was a barn rat before I even hit double digits." She thought about how much Daisy had learned in the few weeks she'd been working at the Lodge. She'd been so conceited about Daisy's lack of knowledge instead of impressed with her desire to seek out a new skill.

"I know it sounds ridiculous, but I've always loved being outdoors, and I thought spending the summer in the backcountry might help me find my own direction."

Unexpected words galloped into Jo's thoughts like wild mustangs. "It's time to turn out the stock. Did you still want me to walk you through it?"

Daisy looked bewildered, and the quiet that fell over the group told her that her friends would be discussing her motives the second she left the fire.

"I've got dessert to serve," Daisy said.

Variations of "I'm stuffed, maybe later" went around the campfire.

"It'll be quick. But you don't have to learn how to turn out the stock if you don't want to. It's not your job," Jo said.

"No, I'm game," Daisy answered.

"Good." Jo grabbed her feed sack with a bit of grain and the cowbell and motioned Daisy to follow her through a narrow patch of forest to the picket lines. Cody trotted beside her, and the animals nickered at their approach, all primed for the evening routine. She first attached the bell to Mouse, their one mare and gave her a few bites of grain.

"The mules wear the leather halters out in the pasture, so you can unclip the lead rope. But take the halters all the way off the horses."

"Because horses are stupid," Daisy said.

Jo caught and held Daisy's gaze. The conversation about belonging to the human herd ran through her head, and she heard how ridiculous she sounded when she said that horse company was better than human company but not as good as a mule. She'd asked Daisy to learn about turning out the stock because she very much wanted her company. "Because their halters are nylon. If they get caught up, they'll strangle themselves. Mules can break the leather ones if they happen to get into a bind." She smiled realizing she'd circled around to Daisy's point.

"Which they rarely do."

"Exactly." Jo couldn't hide her smile, and Daisy returned it. "Leave Churchill haltered, so you can ride him."

"But he's not saddled."

"It's not that hard to ride bareback, and we're not going that far." Jo was already turning the stock loose, and Cody trotted around the perimeter.

Daisy headed for the horses and removed a few halters. She looked worried, not excited as Jo had anticipated. "You don't have to help out. The way the last trip ended up, I thought you wanted to learn more about this side of the job."

That made Daisy look even more wary.

"What?"

"Nice is not your normal which makes me worry that you're planning on ditching me deep in the backcountry where nobody will ever find my body."

"I was trying to apologize for not taking you seriously when you started here, and you take it as a death threat?" With all the animals loose and milling around, Jo untied Mouse and gestured to Churchill. "Either hop aboard or take off his halter. We don't need the stock roaming into the kitchen."

"I didn't mean to piss you off. I just hate being in yet another situation where I don't know what to do." Daisy gestured to Churchill. "How am I supposed to get on without stirrups?"

Jo couldn't blame Daisy for thinking that she was trying to point out her ignorance. She had a lot to make up for. One step at a time. She looped Mouse's lead through her belt and held out her hands. "I'll give you a leg up."

"I'm supposed to put my foot in your hands?"

"Most people are fine with a knee. C'mon!"

Perfect eyebrows pushed together in deep concentration as Daisy took hold of Churchill's mane and put her knee in Jo's hands. "Why weren't you like this at the beginning of the summer?"

Anyone else would be hopping aboard, but Daisy simply stood there close enough that Jo could have leaned forward to kiss her. Whoa there! Jo reined in thoughts and tried to redirect them to Daisy's question. Why had she been so mean? "Girls like you don't stick around."

Daisy put her foot down. "What's that supposed to mean?"

"The barn rats I ran with when I was a kid… When they started to look like you…" She couldn't say the words.

"How do I look?"

Was she flirting? Jo couldn't tell. "When they outgrew being a tomboy, they outgrew the barn. They disappeared."

"You stayed behind."

"With the other misfits," Jo said. She held out her hands again. "We'd better get going. We don't want the stock wandering. Count of three, hop. I'll give you a little lift."

Daisy did as instructed and shifted uncomfortably on Churchill's back. "How far are we going?"

"Not far. But it's boggy, so I ride to keep my feet dry." She grabbed hold of Mouse's mane and leapt aboard.

"How did you do that?" Daisy exclaimed.

"Lots of practice." She didn't add that she had a lot of time after all her friends found boys more interesting than the barn.

Jo gave Mouse a nudge and led the animals out toward the meadow like the Pied Piper. They rode in silence deep into the meadow where the grazing was best, and Jo demonstrated how Daisy should put her tummy to Churchill's back before dropping to the ground. She slung Mouse's halter on her shoulder. "There's a shortcut this way that I use to collect them in the morning if Mouse doesn't come in on her own."

She'd taken several steps when she realized Daisy wasn't following her. She turned back and thought she saw Daisy swipe quickly at both cheeks. Was she crying? Jo wasn't sure what she should do. Horses and mules didn't show emotion like this. Before she could think through her options, Daisy turned.

"Sorry." Her smile was timid. "It's just so beautiful. Sometimes it overwhelms me."

Jo walked back to stand next to Daisy. The sun was disappearing behind the Sierra Nevada range softening the light. It softened the trees that lined the edge of the meadow, softened her own edges and softened the space between her and Daisy. It wouldn't be long before they were plunged into utter darkness, but she didn't want to interrupt the moment. The impulse to put her arm around Daisy surprised her. She put her hands deep in her pockets, chalking her feelings up to the scenery. This kind of seclusion and quiet begged to be acknowledged with an intimate action—a hug or a kiss.

She tried to chase that idea out of her thoughts, but like a sassy pony, it circled back around again, and she knew they had to talk about how they had woken up together. She built a mental corral to trap the words she needed to say.

"When I invited you to share my bedroll, I thought you were into Pete. But then, this morning…" She wasn't any good at this and wished Daisy would take over. Ugh. Now that she needed her thoughts to be words, they had abandoned her.

Daisy turned to face her. It was nearly dark now, and Jo could barely read her eyes, but she was pretty certain Daisy was laughing at her. She took a step toward the trail, but Daisy rested her hand on Jo's arm. "Pete's not the type I'm typically attracted to."

Her whisper made every nerve in Jo's body stand at attention.

She took a step closer and leaned toward Jo. To whisper who she was attracted to? To kiss her? Voices and flashlights in the woods prevented her from finding out.

"Jo! Daisy!"

"Here!" Jo called. "We're on our way back. Don't come through the…"

"Aw fuck it all to hell. My boot's stuck!" someone yelled.

"Think we should help them out or take the shortcut and avoid the muck?" Jo asked.

"I say they deserve it for thinking that women need rescuing instead of a moment alone."

Jo was so tempted to ask what Daisy would have done with a few more moments, but she couldn't leave her friend stranded. She reached for Daisy's hand to lead her back to camp. She couldn't remember the last time she'd held someone's hand and feeling Daisy's palm pressed against hers brought unexpected regret. Soon enough she would have to let go, knowing if she didn't, she would have some major explaining to do to her friends. But for now, she held firm and led the way back to camp.

CHAPTER TWENTY-THREE

Daisy wasn't surprised when Jo had stayed up with her friends long after she'd turned in early. For a long while, she wished for supersonic hearing, curious about whether Jo was talking about her. Would Jo tell them what had kept them so long in the meadow? Would she berate them for interrupting Daisy's attempt to kiss her?

She'd been about to make it clear to Jo that she was attracted to her and had been from the moment she'd seen her in the parade. She'd been telling people that it was Jo's look of satisfaction that drew her into the backcountry when it was Jo herself. Had their first day gone differently, would she have been able to confess that? No use pondering it. Jo was never going to take a greenhorn seriously. The real question was whether she would take Daisy seriously now that she had worked her tail off. She imagined finishing what she had wanted to start in the meadow, sure that had they kissed it would have been very, very hard to stop there.

Despite the plan to stay awake, Daisy had succumbed to sleep before Jo joined her. Warmth from Cody curled at her back combined with the drone of the campfire conversation lulled her into slumber.

* * *

Having been rising before dawn for nearly two months, Daisy sensed the day approaching. As she came into an awareness of her body, she became cognizant of the arm around her waist, the knees and hips nestled perfectly behind hers. She blinked awake trying to ascertain if she was still dreaming. The barest hint of day lightened the patch of sky above them, and Jo was most certainly spooned behind her. When would Jo notice? What would she do? What happened next wasn't up to Daisy. Unlike the previous morning, there was no way to extract herself without Jo noticing.

Daisy had certainly noticed. She tried to quell the heat growing inside her as she remembered Jo's eyes on her lips. She had to have been thinking about kissing Daisy. People didn't stare at your lips unless they were thinking about what a kiss would feel like, did they? The way their bodies fit together now, it wasn't hard for Daisy to imagine what Jo's lips would feel like on hers. Daisy shut her eyes again, memorizing the sense of being close enough to feel the rise and fall of Jo's belly against her back.

In the distance, the bell around Mouse's neck clonked. Was she heading to the picket line? Jo had said that the more days they camped, the earlier the stock would come in, well grazed and looking for their grain. She lifted her head to assess how close they were and immediately felt Jo tense behind her as she woke. Daisy smiled. Certain that her movement had woken her, she thought it was amusing that Jo would attempt to slip away.

Daisy grasped Jo's hand, and Jo sucked in a breath of surprise. With her hand on top, Daisy directed Jo's hand to her hip, up to the dip of her waist using her hands to ask the question she had been poised to ask with her lips the night before. Daisy's heart kicked up a notch as Jo allowed her to guide her hand to the soft of her belly and back to her hip. Every inch of her begged to be under the attention of Jo's hand. Daisy pressed herself deeper into the warmth of Jo's body remembering how she had wanted to pull Jo to her the morning before.

"What are you doing?" Jo whispered.

Still holding Jo's hand, Daisy rotated toward Jo. "I never got to tell you who I'm attracted to."

"We can't..." Jo scooted back an inch but this gave Daisy more room to maneuver herself all the way around, so she was now facing Jo and able to snake her own arm around Jo's back. It was barely light enough to see Jo, but Daisy could feel the rapid rise and fall of her chest. Her gaze fell again to Daisy's mouth, the signal Daisy had been waiting for.

She closed the distance between them, nestling her lips on Jo's before the moment passed. Jo's lips and nose were cold against Daisy's face, and for a split second, Daisy worried that she had misread everything. Her worry evaporated when Jo's lips parted. Daisy took advantage, exploring the lips that had held her attention all summer. Lips that had been quick to frown their disappointment and slow to crack a smile were now supple against Daisy's.

Daisy ran her arm down Jo's side and over her rear to pull Jo's leg over her own. In the same movement, she nestled her thigh in between Jo's.

Jo's free hand swept up her body, making Daisy shiver with pleasure.

"Cold?" Jo whispered.

"Cold?" Daisy repeated, pushing every inch of herself that she could against Jo. "You're kidding, right? You are so incredibly hot." She took Jo's lips again. They were softer now, and Daisy traced them with the tip of her tongue, asking for more.

When Jo threaded her hand through Daisy's hair, Daisy felt all the gates Jo had kept secure swing open. Jo was at once playful and demanding with her tongue, and Daisy met her every step of the way. She felt like the horses finally turned free in the meadow, galloping, nipping, weaving against each other, and she was breathing as heavily as she would at a full run. Her blood rushed like the hooves of a hundred horses on the trail.

"The stock..." Jo gasped.

She pulled away, and Daisy tried her best to hold on, not ready for the ride to be over.

"Goldie..." Jo wiggled away and struggled into very cold jeans whispering, "Shit, shit, shit..."

"Goldie?" Over the pounding of her heart, Daisy realized the sound of hooves was not in her imagination. In the morning light, she could make out actual hooves and muzzles snuffing at the boxes in her kitchen.

Jo was pulling Goldie by the halter on her huge head. Jo's jeans were bunched above hastily pulled boots, her sleep shirt hung below her unbuttoned coat, and her short hair poked up every which way. Daisy couldn't resist. She dug her phone out of her boot to take a picture. Cody yipped, chastising Daisy's warped priorities and spurring her into motion. She pulled on her own cold jeans and threw on a sweatshirt, her head spinning with the memory of Jo's mouth on hers.

* * *

For the most part, Daisy didn't miss having cell reception. She didn't feel the pull of social media to share pictures of the breakfast she served (pancakes, cooked to the perfect golden brown by thinning the batter so they cooked more quickly over the coals) or the stock lazing on the picket line. She didn't crave updates on the lives of her friends in the city. Even when she found reception at the pack station, she didn't use it because she couldn't imagine trying to explain everything to her friends back home.

But this morning, sitting alone in camp, guarding the kitchen from rodents, she wanted someone to talk to. She'd run down her already low battery revisiting the picture of Jo she'd taken this morning. Today she wished she could call the Lodge to catch Heather between her rides and tell her what had happened. Daisy tapped her useless phone against her thigh and shut her eyes, running again through the luscious predawn kiss that the stock had so rudely interrupted.

Once the stock was secured on the picket line, Daisy had tried to revisit the wordless discussion of attraction, but now vertical and surrounded by her animals, Jo was infuriatingly all business again. Nothing in her posture said that Daisy could touch her, let alone kiss her. She'd put up such a wall that Daisy looked around expecting to see one of her shoeing buddies up and about. For all she could tell, the early dawn was theirs alone, but Daisy had been reading Jo all summer and knew she would not be open to discussing what had happened until they were alone in the dark again.

Daisy rolled up the sleeves of a blue gingham shirt. Either the day was finally warming up, or perhaps thinking of being alone with Jo in her bedroll was enough to raise her body temperature. She examined her arms, admiring the definition she was acquiring on her forearms and biceps. Even the one summer she had tried to do a hundred sit-ups a day, her body had never been as toned as Jo's. When her breasts started developing, her body seemed to round everywhere—hips, belly, ass. Her friends would be impressed, but they would also tease her about developing a farmer tan. She licked her finger and rubbed a spot on her arm. How much was sun and how much was dirt? In all her years, she'd never been this filthy.

She was going to seduce Jo tonight. Even if Jo avoided going to bed at the same time, there was no way Daisy was letting Jo go to sleep without resuming their kissing. And from the way her body had reacted this morning, she did not see them being able to stop at a kiss. She trailed her fingertips along her own arm, deliciously imagining the feel of Jo's hands on her body.

Her very dirty body.

She had to have a bath before bed.

Yesterday Jo had slipped off to the river to bathe, but Daisy would be too embarrassed to go down there and have a bath when everyone was back. She had to go now. She wouldn't have

to be gone long. Grab some clean clothes and her natural soap…
Jo had left Cody with her, suggesting he could help guard camp,
but Daisy suspected that Jo didn't want her to be lonesome
while the group was gone for the day. "Cody, you could watch
camp on your own while I go to the river, right?"

He lifted his head and cocked it to the side.

"I wouldn't be gone long. You could chase off any rodents
who try to sneak in?"

He cocked his head the other direction before resting his
head on his paws as if to say such a request bored him.

Daisy hurried to pull the things she needed from her duffel.
"I'll be super quick. Promise." She crossed the trail as Jo had
done the day before and picked her way down to the river. She
followed a tiny path that led to a slab of granite next to a pool
of deep, slow-moving water. Perfect for a dip. She looked over
her shoulder to make sure she wasn't within view of the trail.
Satisfied with the privacy, she shucked off her clothes and leapt
in the river.

Cold! Cold! Cold! her brain screamed. She pulled herself
onto the warmth of the rock and soaped herself while she
shivered. Before she could chicken out, she jumped back in
again, this time dunking her hair as well. She scrubbed her
hands over her face, behind her ears. Her skin was numb enough
that it started to feel good to be in the river and be completely
clean. She ran her hands through her hair. She hadn't brought
shampoo, but it would at least remove the dust.

When she could barely feel her extremities, she sprawled
on the rock grateful for the warmth from the sun above and the
stone below. She lay there melted like a perfect grilled cheese.
She shut her eyes and considered variations of grilled cheese she
could pull off on a layover day. Add some fresh basil or tomato.
Avocado would turn to mush in her boxes.

She smiled to herself. When had she ever daydreamed about
ways to improve the job she was doing? Never. *Take that*, she
wanted to say remembering how Heather had told her how Jo
didn't think she'd last the season. Perhaps she hadn't wanted
her to last the season because of the attraction she'd felt. Her

smile broadened thinking about the possibility that Jo had been trying to avoid feelings she had. If that was true, it couldn't take much to convince Jo to explore Daisy's bare skin. Her body hummed with the sweet anticipation of pulling Jo's naked body to her own.

From where they had left off this morning, Jo would ease Daisy onto her back, slowly inching the fabric up to expose more of her body. Following the lead of her imagined self, she turned to her back to help Jo free her of the shirt. She'd be naked as she was here. A gentle breeze blew across her chest bringing her nipples to attention. Too bad it wasn't Jo's breath… she opened her eyes…

Jo!

She pushed up from the rock, blinking from the glare and then shrieked, "What the hell! How long have you been standing there?"

Jo threw up her hands and said something that Daisy couldn't discern over the roar of the water. Thankfully, Jo spun on her heel and marched back toward camp. Daisy grabbed her small towel and made quick use of it before tugging on her clothes. Raking her fingers through her hair, she jogged after Jo, red as much from her embarrassment as from the hot sun.

When she reached the trail, she was relieved to see that Jo was alone in the kitchen. She walked slowly, trying to assess whether she was angry. Jo met her eyes. Yes, she was angry. This wasn't what Daisy wanted at all. "I didn't expect you all back for another few hours," she attempted.

"What were you doing away from camp!"

"It was quiet. I took a quick bath."

Jo's glare brought her already low eyebrows down another notch. "Be grateful we came back early, so I was here when Dozer came through."

"What was Dozer doing here?" An uncomfortable heat swept through Daisy.

Jo pointed toward the kitchen, which, Daisy observed, looked the same as she'd left it. Leaning against the cooler was a familiar purple shape. "My sleeping bag!"

"He found it coming down the switchbacks and figured it was one of ours. They moved to Third Crossing today."

"They came through with all their stock? I didn't hear a thing!" Daisy said.

"Obviously. You didn't hear me calling for you, either."

"I'm sorry." The apology had no effect on Jo's visage. Daisy tried humor. "You could have asked Cody. I told him where I'd be, and he promised to keep camp safe."

"You had one job and you couldn't manage it."

Jo's words stung. The camp was fine. Daisy didn't see why Jo was making such a big deal out of her popping down to the river to get clean. Jo had done so herself. She wasn't even looking at Daisy now. Just like that, all the fantasizing about what might happen on their last night in the backcountry evaporated. It wasn't fair. She'd been gone for all of ten minutes, and now Jo was reprimanding her like she had at the beginning of the summer. "I have a lot of jobs. I managed breakfast, sent you all off with lunch and started prepping dinner. The dishes are done, and I can have a snack out in a matter of minutes."

"You know what I mean," Jo snapped.

Daisy was poised to ask Jo to explain exactly how she'd let her down this time when Dave came jogging into camp. "Oh! You found her!"

"You sent your friends out looking for me?"

"Camp was empty! There was no sign of you, and you couldn't hear us hollering when you were by the river."

Dave's face flushed. "Oh. You were by the river." He eyed her wet hair and then turned away.

Jo's face flushed pomegranate red and she wouldn't meet Daisy's eyes, either. They were both thinking about her naked. Their discomfort made her stand taller. "I'll get the snacks together," she said to break the awkward silence. As the others trickled in, she apologized for the worry she had caused in her quest to be clean.

"Since we finally found Earl, we forgive you," Terry ribbed.

"It's the altitude that got me winded," Earl said.

"You could do with more walking to take off some of that beer belly."

Thus, he effectively routed the conversation back to their friendly banter leaving Daisy to prepare dinner. She kept her eye on Jo who studiously avoided looking in the direction of the kitchen. Daisy wasn't about to try to engage her in front of her friends. Later, she thought. After everyone went to bed, she would explain. Nothing had happened to the camp. Such a minor thing couldn't ruin the night, could it?

As the time to turn out the stock approached, Daisy held on to the chance that Jo would invite her to help again. Worse than not being invited, on her way to the picket line, Jo pointedly hoisted her bedroll onto her shoulder eliminating the possibility of sleeping together.

On the night that Daisy had been seriously thinking about seducing her.

She was crushed that Jo would move her bedroll without even talking to Daisy about it. Rattled by her thoughts, Daisy had difficulty timing dinner which left her scrambling to get everything hot at the same time while all the guests milled about. Though Jo wasn't even there, and none of her friends said a word, she felt incompetent, Jo's beginning-of-the-summer criticisms ringing in her ears. After the kiss they'd shared…

When Jo came through the kitchen with her dinner plate, Daisy had paused waiting for Jo to meet her eyes. Had she been wrong about Jo being attracted to her? It had sure seemed like she was interested in more before the stock had interrupted them. She wanted to ask, if only non-verbally, but Jo barely glanced at her before extending her plate.

Daisy answered by thwacking down mashed potatoes, stabbing the darkest steak and dumping a spoonful of her garlic carrots and zucchini on top of it. Daisy could build her own wall to save herself from hurt. If this was the person Jo really was, maybe it was best that Dozer had returned her bag. She probably owed him a thank-you for saving her from humiliating herself by throwing herself at Jo. As she'd done on the first trip, she ate her own dinner in the kitchen and worked on getting water warming for her dinner dishes so she could jump on the task as the guests returned their plates.

"Daisy! Daisy!" Earl's voice broke through her sulking. "We need your help over here for a minute."

She laid her rinsed plate on the table and dried her hands.

Jo looked worried when Daisy reached the campfire. "This better not be…"

"Ethan, you got it?" Terry asked, pulling a lit stick from the fire.

"Right here!" Ethan said, emerging from the dark with a small tin stuffed with candles.

"Oh, no!" Jo said.

"Get 'em lit quick!" Terry ordered Ethan.

Ethan lit one candle from the stick he held and quickly lit the others in the tin. "We couldn't fit twenty-nine candles on, so we did fifteen. Each one counts for two years."

"So one to grow on," Terry added. "Ready to sing!"

Daisy contributed to a properly horrible rendition of "Happy Birthday," surprised by the name her friends used.

"Josephine?" she said after Jo blew out the candles.

"Erase that from your head. Not even Takeisha knows what Jo is short for." She glared around the circle of her friends. "I told you guys I don't celebrate my birthday."

"You go right ahead and don't celebrate. You leave that to us!" Ethan pulled something from behind his back and passed it to Jo saying, "We all planned to celebrate with this."

"Pappy Van Winkle! Are you guys crazy? This is what? A hundred bucks minimum, and you risked putting it on a freaking mule?"

"You put it on the mule," Ethan said. "And got it here. Now are you going to see if you can pack it out without breaking it or are we going to try it?"

"I wouldn't have put this on a mule for the trip down. We're taking it out in our bellies!"

"Bust it open!" Earl whooped.

Daisy led the way to the kitchen, handing out the freshly washed mugs and slicing up pound cake for dessert.

"I wish I'd known it was your birthday before the trip," Daisy said before Jo returned to the fire.

"Like I said. I don't usually celebrate it," Jo said.

"It would have been nice to be able to…give you something." She looked woefully at her small mummy bag. "Guess it's too late for that now."

Jo looked in the direction of the picket line where she'd moved her bedroll. *Back where she belonged*, Daisy heard. That took a little of the sting out of Jo's emotional one-eighty. She fanned her irritation, preferring it to the hurt.

"Happy birthday," she said, so Jo could join her friends. "I hope you get what you wished for."

CHAPTER TWENTY-FOUR

Jo had spent years enjoying being alone with her thoughts. Now she would do anything to escape them. Unfortunately, once the challenge of loading the gear onto the mules for the trip back was finished, she had nothing to distract her from Daisy.

Daisy's every look asking whether Jo had enjoyed waking up in her arms.

Daisy's hand in hers, the would-be kiss following them.

Daisy refusing to let Jo escape without first delivering the softest kisses Jo had ever experienced.

Daisy's look when she had moved her bedroll to the picket line.

Daisy saying she wished she could help Jo celebrate her birthday, disappointment clouding her expression.

She'd been disappointed too. First that her friends kept her up long enough that Daisy had fallen asleep and then that Dozer had brought back that daggum sleeping bag.

She'd spent the whole day trying to remember a better start to a birthday and couldn't recall a single one. Daisy's kisses had previewed the promise of so much more, and Jo had given her thoughts free rein to imagine the both of them back in her bedroll with fewer clothes and plenty of time to explore Daisy's beautiful hills and valleys.

It had been hard enough to keep her arms and lips to herself at the picket line after Goldie had insolently interrupted their morning kiss. She needed time to put professional distance between them again, so her friends wouldn't know anything had happened.

She'd kept that mask in place during breakfast and happily spent the day lost in her thoughts only to return to an empty camp. It was like being punched in the stomach seeing Dozer there looking for her or Daisy. The embarrassment of covering for Daisy with Dozer quickly turned to worry after he left and Daisy failed to answer her shouts.

She had not liked the image it brought to mind of her mother searching through a house that she knew was empty, unwilling to accept that her latest boyfriend had left.

And then she'd seen Daisy's bronze body glowing in the sun.

She'd been so relieved. And then aroused. The sight of her naked on the granite had knocked the wind out of her. An alternate scenario played out in her mind. Her walking toward Daisy, hugging her, expressing her worry, accepting Daisy's apology. Daisy finding her concern sweet and smoothing the lines on her forehead first with a finger, then with her lips. Jo losing herself again in Daisy's kisses.

But she'd had her friends all searching for Daisy and had to return to camp where that gosh darn purple bag sat in the kitchen. Mountain water doused the desire she'd fanned all day long. She'd had no choice but to move her bedroll back to the picket line where she lay awake thinking about Daisy in her own sleeping bag by the kitchen.

It hadn't felt right. As Takeisha had predicted, she had easily become accustomed to having Daisy next to her in bed. She cursed her friend both for leaving and for being right. She missed Takeisha and the uncomplicated months of hauling gear around the backcountry. Uncomplicated small talk and uncomplicated sleep that led to the quiet days in the saddle that she loved. One hand on the reins, the other on her hip holding the lead rope to her lazy-eared mules and miles and miles of wide, open space to soak in.

Daisy had been soaking in those rays, every soft curve exposed. No matter how hard she tried to lead her thoughts away from yesterday, they kept returning to Daisy like a barn-sour pony.

She would have tasted like the river after her bath. When she had wished Jo a happy birthday, Jo had caught a hint of lavender the same as she had the day they'd met. She imagined brushing her damp hair away from her neck to search for the source of that subtle and lovely scent. What would it smell like under her waterfall of hair, between her shoulders, in the crook of her elbow? She might have had the answer had she followed Daisy to bed after they'd turned out the stock. If her friends hadn't stayed up late, if her bedroll hadn't been a mere stone's throw away from them, she might have succumbed to that flare of desire.

Desire that was inevitably extinguished, she scolded herself. She'd watched enough men leave her mother to know that it takes more than attraction to sustain a relationship. She would not make the same mistake her mother made again and again of relinquishing herself to the heat of desire only to be burned again. For Daisy, packing was a summer job. In a month, she would put her cowgirl experience behind her and return to her old life, whatever that was. Better for everyone involved that Dozer had brought the bag allowing them to keep their distance.

She tapped Tuxedo with her heels and kept the whole string traveling out, Cody zigzagging across the trail in front of her. When Cody had chosen to stay with Daisy in the kitchen after dinner last night, Jo had been sorely tempted to ask Daisy if she'd prefer to share the bedroll again. But at that point, she hadn't been ready to let go of how angry she was about finding camp empty.

Because she'd been frightened. It didn't make sense to be frightened. Angry, yes. Daisy should have been in camp. She had made an irresponsible decision. But Jo hadn't been angry at first. Her reaction was rooted in finding Daisy gone. Not having a girlfriend in her life meant that Jo was in control over whether she was alone or not, and that's the way she was going to keep it.

Suddenly Cody took off like a bolt. They were nearing the granite, and Jo wasn't surprised. This was where she liked to pass the riders. When she approached the small wooded area before the granite pass, she found her group lunching happily and Cody splayed belly-up at Daisy's feet.

"We were wondering how far back you were, and then he ran up." Daisy smiled at Jo as she rubbed Cody's belly.

Jo started to smile back and remembered, barely in time, that she was angry. She kept her face neutral. "Gotta keep these guys going so they don't get all boogered up. See you back at the Lodge!" she said crisply.

When Cody didn't run ahead, Jo was forced to look back. He was standing but lingered for a few more pats.

"C'mon Cody!" Jo called.

He jumped into action, bounding up to pass her and Tuxedo and shooting her a clear look of disapproval.

"Should I be worried about that?" she asked. "Don't be thinking you're staying with her again tonight. That was because of the bears, and we only bunked together because of her bag. It's just me and you. If we're lucky, Takeisha's mom won't need her help anymore, and we'll get our routine back."

A few hours later, they approached the yard. Jo closed her eyes and chanted *please, please, please let Takeisha be back.*

Her prayers were answered by a joyful "Cody!"

She opened her eyes to see him covering Takeisha with kisses. "Girl, did we miss you!" Jo hollered. Takeisha smiled back, and when Jo reached them, she swung off Tuxedo and opened her arms for a hug.

Takeisha stared at her. "What's wrong?"

"What do you mean? I'm happy to see you!"

"Nuh-uh. What is wrong with you?"

Jo threw her arms around Takeisha anyway. "You have no idea how much I missed you."

Takeisha leaned away from her, a wary expression on her face. "You feeling okay?"

"So much better now." Jo stepped away and handed her lead mule to Takeisha so she could tie Tuxedo by the saddle shed. "Please say your dad is fine and you'll be here for the rest of our trips."

"It went that bad with Daisy? I was kinda hoping when you got back in, you'd be all 'girl, I got myself a new cook. Have fun leading punk kids on day rides!'"

Jo threw a quick slipknot and returned for her mules. "You're kidding, right? Nobody could replace you!" She was doing what she always did. Now that Takeisha was back, the summer would fall back in place, and she'd be fine.

Takeisha studied her. She didn't hand over the lead rope. "What happened?"

"Nothing happened." Jo held out her hand.

"Liar."

"Give me my mules. I've got work to do. The riders will be here any minute."

"Something's going on, and you know I'm going to find out. You might as well get it over with right now."

Since Takeisha wouldn't give up the lead, she untied her third mule and led the tail of her string up to the pack dock. It wasn't the order that she usually did things, but there was no way she was going to answer Takeisha. She left Skeeter tied to Blaze and moved Dumbo to the second post. "Looks like your lucky day, Dumbo! Let's get this load off."

Takeisha joined her on the other side of Dumbo having parked the two mules she'd been holding at the saddle shed. "And you're talking to mules now? Did you hit your head out there?"

Jo did her work, loosening the lash rope and tossing it to Takeisha. "You never told me about your dad."

Takeisha said nothing as she matched Jo's movements untying the hitch and removing the load from the mule. Her eyes remained on Jo, though, slowly turning up the heat on Jo's discomfort.

Jo straddled a pannier quickly, chucking its contents into piles: trash, camp gear, sleeping bags. She paused on Daisy's purple sleeping bag, stared at it and then looked up to find Takeisha watching her. The trail was clear and Cody was resting. She had a few minutes. "Here's the skinny. This," she held up the bag, "didn't make it to camp, so Daisy and I bunked together."

Takeisha's jaw dropped. "Get. Out. What happened?"

Jo tried to hide her blush by moving to Skeeter's pack.

"Everything," Takeisha said. "Spill it all right now before they get back."

"There's not that much to say. Yesterday morning we kissed. In the afternoon, Dozer brought the bag by. We didn't sleep together."

Takeisha looked confused. "Why not?"

"I told you. Dozer brought her bag."

"But you wanted to sleep with her. You're attracted to her."

Jo didn't respond. She told herself not to look at Takeisha.

"How far did the kiss go? What are we talking? A little 'I'm interested' peck? Or did it go far enough you were starting to think about her clothes coming off?"

"Stop!" Now was not the time for Jo to start thinking about Daisy naked.

"Didn't you…"

"Drop it, okay? Her bag came back and…"

Takeisha held up her hands in surrender. "Okay. Okay. I get it now."

"Good." Jo sighed with relief that Takeisha agreed to stop talking about it.

"Mmm hmm." Takeisha pulled the kitchen box from the metal rack.

Jo removed the matching box on her side doing her best to ignore Takeisha who kept nodding and repeating, "Makes sense."

By the time they had untied Blaze's load, Jo couldn't take it anymore. "What makes sense?"

"What?" Takeisha feigned surprise.

"Say what you need to say."

Takeisha made her wait, pulling the tables from the top load of the next mule. Finally, she said, "Until the bag came back, you and Daisy had a reason to be sharing your bed. You wanted to sleep with her, but you couldn't come out and say that."

Jo wasn't going to respond. She hid behind her bedroll, self-consciously carrying it to the dock.

"You wanted to, but because you couldn't, you spent the whole day making a list of all the reasons you shouldn't have. Now that I'm back, you think you can avoid it." She shook her head. "That's messed up, you know?"

Cody rose to his feet.

"The riders are coming in," Jo said.

Takeisha frowned. "You should talk to her, you know."

"Nothing to talk about!" Jo said. "We've got the Yosemite trip."

"Work, work, work. I told you before that life's not all about work! Seize the moment! You've got two nights here! Do not tell me you're going to waste them thinking about work." She glanced over at the riders dismounting and moved closer to Jo. "You have an opportunity here. Don't go messing it up."

CHAPTER TWENTY-FIVE

Daisy's heart sank when she rode into the yard and saw Takeisha helping Jo with the mules. She'd spent the day thinking about how she and Jo might spend their nights where they had privacy and a real bed where she would convince Jo that there was no need to bring along her sleeping bag on their next trip.

Now there would be no next trip, no reason to be close to Jo. She slipped out of the saddle and mechanically took each of the horses from her guests, barely hearing the compliments they paid her about her cooking. Earl was flirting with Takeisha, saying he was going to tag along to Yosemite with her and Jo. He assured Daisy that her cooking was good, but he'd missed Takeisha's pulled pork.

They meant to make her feel included, she knew, but she'd never felt as much an outsider as she did then. Jo's friends sorted out their gear on the dock, and a new pang rushed through Daisy. Takeisha would take back her kitchen. Once she removed her duffel and stupid purple sleeping bag, she'd no longer be a part of Jo's team. She'd be staying at the pack station in the café or on day rides. Demoted.

She was embarrassed to feel tears threatening and turned to her own work of unsaddling the horses. The familiarity of the steps soothed her, and she gave no thought as she carried the thirty pounds of sweat-dampened saddle blankets plus the saddle and heaved them onto the racks in the shed.

"Hey there, cowgirl!" A voice she'd missed rang across the yard. Heather swung her right leg up over her horse's neck and jumped off even as he continued to walk. Her mount joined Daisy's by the employee shed, and Daisy met Heather by the last group of riders finishing their ride to Rainbow Falls. Heather gave her a quick hug. "Missed you!"

Daisy smiled. As good as that made her feel, the sting of losing her cooking position did not dissipate.

"I can't wait to hear all about your trip! I already feel like we don't have enough time before you go back out!"

"What do you mean back out?" They walked two horses to the tie rail.

"How long have you been back? You haven't met Wendy yet?"

Daisy's head spun. "We just rode in. Who's Wendy?"

Heather looked like she wasn't sure she should say what was rushing through her thoughts, but it was too much for her to hold in. "Wendy was a backcountry cook here a while back. She wants to do a trip down at Iva Belle for her wedding anniversary, and Leo had assumed that she'd be happy to be dropped off without staff like any spot trip we do. They're not keeping stock down there or anything."

The story was interrupted by their helping more riders from their horses.

"I don't see why they'd need me," Daisy said.

"They don't want to guard the food. Leo wasn't going to send anyone with her, but then Takeisha came back, and he said it'd be perfect for you because Wendy can show you what she knows about trail cooking."

"I did better this trip," Daisy said defensively.

"I'm sure you did, but Wendy's a real chef, and dude! What a sweet deal. You get to go to the hot springs, eat amazing food prepared by a chef, and all you have to do is keep bears from getting into the kitchen."

"When does it leave?"

"Tomorrow. That's why we need to catch up! Wendy's been putting together her kitchen all day. I'll introduce you after we unsaddle the horses. Course, now that you're a cook, maybe that's beneath you."

"I'd never think that! Besides, now that Takeisha's back, I may be part of the day-ride crew again."

Heather said she doubted that would happen, and she and Daisy collected the rest of the animals and began unsaddling. Heather was a great distraction with her day-ride horror stories, the gaggle of camp kids that came for a ride to Rainbow Falls and how she ran out of little stirrups and had to figure out how to fit them all to their saddles. She'd also been flummoxed when a rider had called out that there was something wrong with her horse's bridle. When she discovered that the entire headstall had fallen apart, she was forced to lead the horse home holding its lead rope.

"No tip from her, of course," Heather groused. "But the worst was this guy who would not let up on Homey's mouth. I kept telling him 'give that horse his head! Give that horse his head!' Did he listen?"

"No," Daisy said with Heather. They snickered. Daisy's eyes slipped over to the dock where Jo and her friends were lingering by their gear while Takeisha loaded her kitchen into a truck. Earl was helping her, which made Daisy smile. She hoped he'd ask for her number this year. His friends had egged him on about it the whole trip.

"So we're on our way up from Lower Falls, and he keeps pulling on Homey. I can see Homey's front end getting light, and then the son of a bitch pulled Homey right over."

"What?" Daisy tried to pull her attention away from the pack dock and Jo who stood quietly at the edge of the group.

When she wasn't around, did the guys razz Jo about her? Her sharing Jo's bedroll would have given them a lot of material.

"Aren't you listening? The rider on Homey flipped him over backward! And it gets better! When Homey was trying to get up? Stepped right on the guy's family jewels!"

Jo looked at Daisy, catching her watching. A swirl of attraction rushed through Daisy despite the fact that Jo's expression didn't change. After holding Daisy's gaze a moment, she seemed to tune back easily into her friends' banter.

"They complained to Leo and said I should be fired, so today is my last day."

"Wait, someone got fired?"

Heather smacked her. "You're not listening to me at all! What's so interesting over there, anyway? Got your eye on one of Jo's friends? Takeisha's spent two summers flirting with Earl. I kinda wonder if she made it back before he left on purpose. Who else is single? That one who is triangle perfect?"

Daisy was so confused. "What?"

"The one holding his hat. He's got those broad shoulders and the tiny hips." She made an inverted triangle with her thumbs and index fingers that she swung his way as if she was sighting him through a scope. "Yummy," she said when she'd fixed him in the imaginary crosshair.

Daisy smacked her hands down. "Stop that!"

"Hey, a girl can have some fun, can't she? C'mon. I'll introduce you to Wendy while the stock cools down." Without waiting for Daisy to agree, she set off for the kitchen breezing by Jo and her friends. Daisy envied her uncomplicated navigation past Jo's group. She didn't seem to suffer the *look? don't look?* inner dialogue that Daisy did.

"I found Daisy for you!" Heather announced when they reached the storage room.

Daisy smiled at the woman who stepped over her in-progress boxes and bags to shake her hand. She frowned at her palm and wiped it on her T-shirt. "I forgot how dirty everything is here!" Her short, curly brown hair was pulled back in a bandana, and she smiled warmly. "I'm Wendy. This is my wife, Kat."

Kat pushed off the counter where she'd been sitting. She wore her long, blond hair in two braids over her shoulders. In flip-flops, capri jeans, and a loose pink blouse, she looked more like she was going to the beach than the backcountry. "I'm so glad you'll be able to join us. Wendy barely convinced me to do this trip at all, and when Leo was saying we'd have to sleep by the food to keep bears away? I did not sign up for that!"

Daisy wanted to say she hadn't signed up for bear duty, either, but if she'd learned anything over the course of the summer, being employed by the Lodge meant she had signed up for it all.

"Is it true that you saw a pack string in the Rose Parade and decided you had to do it yourself?" Kat asked.

"Sounds crazy, I know," Daisy said.

Wendy laughed. "Not to me. A million years ago, I did some trail cooking. A guest of mine worked on a cruise line and convinced me to apply. It was a great adventure. Not without some problems, but such a good experience."

"Can I help? I wish I could say I'd done it before, but I've only restocked a kitchen that Takeisha had already put together," Daisy said. She smiled remembering how much easier it had been once Jo turned it into a game of Tetris. Then she remembered what a very good kisser Jo was and how much she'd wanted to learn more about that on the last night of her trip. The sound of boots on the wood floor sent a rush through Daisy with the possibility that they would deliver Jo and the opportunity for them to talk.

Her heart sank when Pete appeared in the doorway. "Hey, Daisy." He wore no cowboy hat and had his shoulder-length hair pulled back in a ponytail. "Good trip?"

"Not long enough," Daisy said, her thoughts on what she might have been able to do with an extra night or two.

"So you're not mad that we're making you turn right around and go back out tomorrow?" Wendy asked.

"No." Knowing that Jo and Takeisha were headed out on another trip, Daisy had no desire to stay at the pack station, but she dreaded the hours of time alone to regret her choice to walk away from her camp for ten minutes and take that dip in the stream.

Pete surveyed the room nervously before resting his gaze on Daisy. He inclined his head toward the store. "Got a minute?"

Not really, Daisy wanted to say. Heather poked her in the ribs. "Sure," Daisy said.

"I've got this if you have things to do," Wendy said.

Daisy waved off the offer. "I'll be right back."

Pete stood by the freezer peering at the selection of ice cream bars.

"What's up?"

"With your quick turnaround, I thought you might want a lift up the mountain to do your laundry. We could grab pizza or something?"

"That's sweet of you, Pete," Daisy said. "But I don't have a whole lot. I can use the washer here, so I can help get this kitchen together."

He nodded quickly. "Sure. Got it." He glanced back toward the storage room, hooking his thumbs in his pockets. She realized that his shirt and jeans were clean. He'd already banked on her saying yes. "Guess I should let you go. Hopefully, you'll be able to hang out a while after we feed. Throw the rope or…"

"I'm not sure how long this will take. Wendy has to put together a full kitchen from scratch."

"I thought she said she could handle it."

"But I want to learn." She realized how much easier it would be to tell him she wasn't interested in spending time with him, but she didn't want to explain, not when everything with Jo was in such a tangle.

"Okay." She could hear the disappointment in his voice. "You know where to find me if it turns out you have time."

Daisy watched him walk away, mentally fitting him to Heather's wide-shoulders-to-narrow-hips triangle. He fit the description, but she did not long to spend more time in his company. She had not given any thought to the evening activities that had been her staple before she'd taken Takeisha's place. From her position in the store, she could see Takeisha sitting on the dock next to Jo, her head leaning against Jo's shoulder.

When Jo put her arm around Takeisha's shoulders, jealousy surged through her. If Takeisha hadn't come back, that could have been her sitting next to Jo. Maybe if Dozer hadn't brought her sleeping bag to camp. Too many ifs. She sighed.

"I'm more than happy to get the kitchen all together."

Daisy yelped and jumped at Wendy's voice.

"Whoa!" she said, placing her hands on Daisy's arm and shoulder like she was a skittish horse. "You okay there?"

"Fine. I was on my way back to help."

"Daisy, if you'd rather go out tonight, please go! I feel bad making you turn right back around, but not bad enough to have your boyfriend be the one staying down there to guard the kitchen."

"Pete? Oh, he's not my boyfriend." Willing herself not to look out the window at Jo and Takeisha again, she walked back into the storage room.

"He wishes he was!" Heather said. "I'm going to put the stock out. Coming?"

"I'm going to stay here and help with the kitchen. I want to learn stuff from Wendy in case Leo sends me out again."

"You still haven't told me about your trip." Heather sounded disappointed.

"Later, I promise," Daisy said.

A half hour later, Wendy and Daisy were nearly through the list of kitchen essentials when Takeisha hauled in one of her kitchen boxes. "I'm not working on these tonight. I'll park them under the counter. Once I get the food put up, I'll be out of your way."

"There's plenty of room if you want to join our party." Wendy thumbed in Daisy's direction. "This one has some great stories!"

"Not many," Takeisha replied. "We've barely seen each other this summer with me on overnight trips and then off taking care of a family emergency. Daisy, thank you again, for taking over like that."

Jo entered the room with another one of the kitchen boxes, Cody trotting at her heels.

"I'm sure your next group will be glad you made it back," Daisy said.

Jo set the box down and started to walk back out.

"Jo said you did great. And now you get to pick up cooking tips from a real chef! I'm jealous. I'm Takeisha, by the way," she said to Wendy and Kat. In talking about Jo and introducing herself, Takeisha forced Jo to stop and introduce herself as well. This was followed by an awkward silence. Daisy would not look at Jo. She could feel how uncomfortable Jo was and wished she would excuse herself to get back to her work at the corrals.

"Did I hear that you guys are doing the Yosemite trip next?" Wendy asked.

"Day after tomorrow." Takeisha pulled tag-end boxes of crackers and pancake mix from a box.

"I love that trip. That last drop into the valley is breathtaking," Wendy said. "But I couldn't convince Kat to do that much riding."

"You're lucky I agreed to do this at all," Kat said. "These hot springs better be all you promised."

"Oh, the hot springs are so beautiful," Takeisha said. "I've never been able to camp there. I've only been able to pop over a few times when I've been at the Sharktooth camp. This valley doesn't have the crowds we see in Yosemite either and the bears are so much worse in the park! I sure miss Cody when we go to Yosemite." Hearing his name, Cody thumped his tail. "Dogs aren't allowed in the state park," she explained to Daisy. Then she turned to Jo. "Who's watching Cody while we're away?"

Something passed between Takeisha and Jo, a slight widening of Takeisha's eyes and tip of her head. She looked at Jo who was still pointedly not looking at her. Jo rolled her eyes and crossed her arms over her chest.

"You should have Daisy watch him. That way she has help protecting her kitchen!" Takeisha said.

Jo looked down at the dog who seemed to smile back up at her. "I don't know. He usually stays here with Heather, and it's really the guests' call."

Wendy jumped in without missing a beat. "We'd love to have him along if you think he'd stay with us!"

They all looked at Kat who held up her hands. "I'm literally along for the ride here. As long as I get my hot springs, I'm happy."

"That's all you want?" Wendy feigned hurt, and her words brought a bright blush to Kat's face.

"Having the dog along is fine with me," Kat said.

Daisy could feel Kat studying her.

Jo finally looked at Daisy, stirring up her insides. She was still mad as hell at Jo for overreacting about the camp and for refusing to talk about the sleeping arrangements on their last night, but that was her intellectual self trying to override the undeniable physical pull.

"Would you mind keeping an eye on him?" Jo asked.

"Happy to."

"Appreciate it," Jo mumbled. "I'll pack up his food for you tonight."

"Okay," Daisy said.

"You want the coolers by the kitchen?" Jo asked Takeisha.

"That'd be perfect, thanks!" Takeisha wore a satisfied smile as she efficiently placed food on the shelves.

Now it was Wendy and Kat's turn to communicate silently. Once again Daisy was left out. She thought maybe she should leave.

"Okay ladies! Have fun with it," Takeisha said.

Daisy was about to say she should start her laundry when Kat said, "Holy flirting war, Batman! Did that happen to you when you worked here, Wendy?"

"Ha!" Wendy rolled her eyes. "With a bunch of the cowboys, sure. But there wasn't anyone like Jo on staff."

"Lucky for me, or you would have ridden off with her!" Kat fanned herself.

"She is pretty hot. Your type?" Wendy pulled Daisy back into their conversation.

"Or Pete? He's no ogre!" Kat quickly inserted.

Daisy buried her head in her hands.

"Sorry, we didn't mean to make you uncomfortable," Kat said. "If you're straight."

"Or gay," Wendy offered.

Daisy uncovered her eyes to twin expressions of worry on Kat's and Wendy's faces.

"You don't have to answer. We're being super nosy," Kat apologized.

"It's okay." Daisy sat down heavily on a pack box. "I've dated guys and girls, but never an asshole."

Wendy flipped over an empty pack box and sat down, an eager smile on her face. "Which one's the asshole?"

Kat followed Wendy's lead, grabbing her own box to sit on. "Start at the beginning!"

CHAPTER TWENTY-SIX

Jo sat in the open doorway of her cabin, Cody curled at her feet. The yard was clean and the animals fed. Unlike the evening when Gabe had brought chairs over to share a drink, the day-ride crew was nowhere in sight. Not that she was looking for anyone. She hung her head. Idiot. Why hadn't she hidden Daisy's sleeping bag or at least asked if she was happy to have it back?

Because relationships made people stupid. She didn't need any of it.

Relationship? Why would she think that? *Because if it's not a relationship, it's a fling. Is that where you are?*

Jo didn't know where she was. All she knew was that tomorrow Daisy left for her Hot Springs base camp with Wendy and Kat, and the day after she and Takeisha left for Yosemite. If Leo decided to keep sending her into the backcountry, it was entirely possible for the remainder of the summer to go by without her even seeing Daisy again. She ran her fingertip over a chip in her thumbnail. Until Daisy, she'd never kept track of who was at the pack station when she was. She pulled her knife from the sheath on her belt and snapped it open, gently paring the nail with the sharp blade. She could step inside and find her nail clippers, but she didn't. She followed the arc of the nail as best she could before raising it to her lip to see if she'd left any sharp angles.

Daisy was standing over at her cabin, her hand on the doorknob, but her gaze directed at Jo. She was too far away to read her expression, but she continued to stand there without opening her door. Jo's breath went shallow. Was her mind spinning on how they might have spent the previous night as well? She was leaving tomorrow. What was the point of thinking about yesterday?

Jo shaved a bit of the next nail with her sharp blade. When Cody raised his head, she knew without looking up that Daisy hadn't gone into her cabin. His tail began to thump, lazily at first and with more fervor as Daisy closed the distance between them. Jo's own heart rate accelerated but she kept her eyes focused on her nail and the blade. Finally, when Cody stood to meet Daisy, Jo looked up.

When her eyes met Daisy's, her whole body tightened. Daisy didn't look away as she reached down to pat Cody. "Did you break it to him that he's stuck with me for the next few days?"

Jo deflated like a popped balloon. The dog. Daisy had come over to talk about Cody, not about the previous night. "He's easy." She reached out to pat her dog.

"Unlike his mom." Daisy covered Jo's hand with her own.

Jo's mouth went dry. She had no idea how to respond to that. Daisy ran the pad of her thumb along the edge of Jo's fingernail. Soot from the pots and pans was lodged around her nail. Jo turned her hand and ran her own thumb over the black in the fine cracks on Daisy's fingers. "You have cook's hands now."

"They may never be the same," Daisy said. She pulled her hand away, straightening to hold out both hands in front of her. She took a deep breath and turned her body, and for a moment Jo was afraid she was leaving. Instead, she lowered herself next to Jo, wedging her hips between Jo and the doorway. Their bodies touched hip to shoulder. "I'm mad at you."

"I'm mad at me too."

Daisy opened her mouth to say something but then snapped it shut. Her brows furrowed. "You're mad at you?"

"Takeisha said I'm an idiot. I hate to agree with her, but…" She took a deep breath. "Last night didn't go the way I wished it had."

"Huh." Daisy stretched out next to her in the doorway, her arms straight back, elbows locked and her legs in front of her.

"That's all you have to say?"

"You caught me off guard. I came over to talk to the Jo who hauled her comfy bedroll up to the damn picket line without saying a word to me, and instead I get a totally unfamiliar apologetic Jo."

"Oh."

"Why'd you haul your bed off?"

"You had your sleeping bag," Jo said matter-of-factly.

"Are there rules about using everything a mule carries in or something?"

"No."

"I'd been thinking about you all day, and then you bailed on me."

Had Daisy forgotten about the river and how she'd been more upset about finding the camp empty than having the sleeping bag show up? She didn't want to admit that she'd been scared to find Daisy gone. The silence was lengthening, and Jo knew she had to respond, but she didn't know what to say. Daisy was leaving tomorrow. It seemed like a moot point.

She'd been quiet so long that Daisy spoke again, more quietly this time. "Was I the only one thinking about how we could have used our time last night if we'd bunked together?"

"No." Jo could say that. She glanced at Daisy, the way she reclined accentuating her lovely breasts. She pulled her eyes away from Daisy's chest and met twinkling eyes.

"There's tonight." Daisy tipped her head coquettishly.

Jo looked back out at the corrals.

Daisy let out a growl that brought Cody to his feet, searching for the threat. She reached out to soothe him and said, "You're still mad about that stupid bath I took."

How could Jo explain that at the same time seeing Daisy's naked body made her burn inside, her leaving camp had thrown a bucket of cold water on that flame?

"I could understand you being mad at me if something happened, but camp was fine."

"You're right," she said to Daisy, though the conversation with Takeisha echoed in her mind. On the way home from Second Crossing, she'd found plenty of reasons it would be better not to sleep with Daisy, most importantly that she couldn't miss something she'd never had.

Daisy laughed. "If I'm right, then why aren't we in bed right now?" She leaned back and looked into Jo's cabin. When she leaned forward again she raised her eyebrows and bumped against Jo's side.

Jo tried to remember something from the list she'd created but came up blank. Her stomach tightened, and her breath quickened. Her palms started to tingle. Daisy reached out and traced the veins on the back of her hand.

"You have the sexiest hands. I couldn't take my eyes off them that first day when you untied my horse and yelled at me about not knowing a decent slipknot. I've spent so many hours on the trail thinking about what those hands would feel like on my body."

Daisy's fingers traipsed up Jo's forearm, but the touch reached much further inside. "I spent a fair amount of time imagining what that would feel like."

"So?" Daisy tipped her head toward the interior of the cabin.

"We can't just jump in bed!"

"Says who? All the chores are done. And I leave in the morning."

"And then what?"

A slow smile spread across Daisy's face. "We'll have a hell of a lot to think about on the trail?" Her eyes searched Jo's face.

Jo's mouth was too dry to say anything. Her body was saying *get up, take her hand. Take her inside. Make the most of Daisy's offer.* Daisy stood, her eyes on Jo. Jo swallowed and scanned the yard for any of their coworkers. Daisy maneuvered through the door, shrugging her coat from her shoulders. Cody trotted in after her.

A strange sound, a thwack, snapped Jo's attention inside. Daisy had unfolded the bedroll Jo had tossed onto the floor of the cabin. "What are you doing?"

"What I should have done last night." Sitting on the edge of Jo's regular mattress, Daisy pulled off her boots. She tucked her socks in one boot and unbuckled her belt. Eyes on Jo, she stood to shuck off her jeans. In her shirt and panties, she folded back the canvas, blanket, and top sheet and slipped into the bedroll. Jo watched from the door as Daisy slowly unbuttoned her plaid shirt and tossed it onto the bed. "Are joining me or what?"

Jo swiveled in the doorway, so her back rested against the doorjamb. "I didn't want to interrupt you."

Daisy raised her eyebrows. "You're not interested in helping out?"

"It looks like you know what you're doing," Jo said, regretting how critical of Daisy she had been, and not only about slipknots. Daisy had done so much to prove herself over the course of the summer.

Daisy laughed at her again. "You try to intimidate all the girls, tough stuff?"

"Just the pretty ones."

"Where is the logic in that?"

"Take that off, and I'll tell you."

Daisy's chest rose and fell more rapidly. She wet her lips before she reached behind her back and released her bra. Jo's gaze was drawn to Daisy's exposed breasts. Under her gaze, Daisy's nipples hardened. Jo finally stood up and shut the door. With the sun almost down, her cabin was quite dark. She took two steps and sat down on her bed. Daisy scooted down and turned on her side, propping herself on her elbow.

"I didn't think you belonged here. I thought you'd figure that out and leave. Your not knowing anything, being a hopeless hoo haw, gave me a reason to tell myself not to like you."

"But I stayed."

"And you learned, and that made you harder to resist."

"Is that so?"

"So much harder to resist."

"And yet you're sitting over there with all your clothes on. You're still holding back."

"It's hard to forget that you're leaving tomorrow, and I'm leaving the next day going in the opposite direction."

"That is true," Daisy said, lying back. She wriggled under the covers. "Maybe these will make you forget that for a while?" She hooked the elastic of her panties over her thumb and shot them at Jo, hitting her in the chest.

Jo's hands moved to her boots, quickly unlacing them and pulling them off. Next, they flew to the buttons on her shirt.

"Come here," Daisy said, her voice low with desire.

"What?" Jo was finished with the buttons and was about to push her shirt off her shoulders.

"I want to show you how good I am with buckles."

Daisy pushed the covers aside and sat up, once again exposing her bare chest. Jo wanted to rip off her clothes and get her hands on Daisy's beautiful body, but she reined herself in. With seductive slowness, she pulled her arms from her shirt and pulled off her tight tank undershirt. Only then did she kneel in front of Daisy on the bedroll. When Daisy's hands went to her belt buckle, Jo couldn't wait any longer. She leaned forward and kissed her way across Daisy's collarbone and up along the curve of her jaw.

"You're making my job harder," Daisy breathed, her hands fumbling down Jo's button fly.

"You could let me."

Daisy tipped her head back, exposing more skin. "No. I want your hands on me."

Jo worried about her hands feeling rough against the soft skin at Daisy's hips, but Daisy leaned in to her touch. She ran her hands up to Daisy's generous breasts. Her thumbs brushed against Daisy's nipples, eliciting a low moan from Daisy. The sound drew Jo's attention to her mouth. Wrapping her arms around Daisy, she brought their naked chests together at the same moment their mouths met. Moan turned to gasp, and Jo immediately took advantage, slipping her tongue into Daisy's mouth.

Daisy answered with her own tongue, dueling for control. They kissed until they were out of air and had to break to hungrily fill their lungs. Daisy seemed to melt in Jo's arms. She feebly tried to tug Jo's jeans and briefs down. Jo smiled and nipped at Daisy's lips. "Run into trouble there, cowgirl?"

With more strength than Jo had anticipated, Daisy pivoted Jo onto her back on the narrow cushion of the bedroll. She straddled Jo's hips, pinning her in place. Her hands were free, though, and she ran them up Daisy's sides and around her shoulders to pull her in for another kiss. She felt herself rushing hard and fast into Daisy like two streams merging and crashing over a waterfall. She happily followed every twist and turn of their kissing. When Daisy pulled away, Jo followed, unwilling to let the kiss end. Defeated, her head fell back to the pillow.

Chest heaving, Daisy said, "You stay put. This is my show."

"Is it?" Jo gently raked her nails down Daisy's back and a shudder followed.

"Trust me. I know exactly what I'm doing." Taking hold of both waistbands, she scooched them down, exposing Jo fully.

Jo tucked an arm behind her head watching Daisy's eyes flit across her body. Her skin blossomed along the trail of Daisy's gaze, and she wanted Daisy to know how wet she was and how much she needed to be touched.

"I want everything at once." Daisy caught Jo's gaze while her fingers traced the possible destinations, starting at her breasts and trailing down past her hip, frustratingly passing the ache between her legs. Slow as molasses, Daisy lowered herself aligning their centers, their breasts, their lips without contact.

Again, Jo stretched up to capture Daisy's mouth. She wrapped her arms around Daisy and tried to pull her body into contact. Laughing, she surrendered and rested on the mattress. "God, you're strong!"

"I'm glad you finally noticed," Daisy said, lowering herself into full contact. Now her deep kisses were accompanied by her grinding deliciously against Jo's center. Jo dug her nails into

Daisy's ass pulling her closer, closer, so close she thought she would orgasm from the contact alone.

"Whoa there," Daisy said. "There are so many things I want to do, so many places I want to touch you." She moved down to take one of Jo's small breasts in her mouth. Jo hissed with pleasure and pushed Daisy's hand toward her crotch. Daisy evaded the move, settling her hand on Jo's other breast. "You taste like the mountains."

"Mountains?" Jo breathed.

"Grass and sunshine." Again her tongue grazed Jo's breast. "Sweet, sweet pines."

"Touch me," Jo pleaded.

With Daisy's tongue sending shivers from her sensitive breasts to her clit, Daisy reached between Jo's legs. Tired of the teasing and aching for release, Jo raised her hips and pulled Daisy deep. They moaned in unison as Daisy touched her exactly where she wanted. She thrust against Daisy as much as her position would allow, digging in her heels to push against Daisy, to feel her deep, deep into her core. Daisy increased the speed of her thrusts, matching Jo's rhythm, stroking her until her entire body began to shudder. The orgasm burst through her and flooded her limbs. She once again allowed her body to rest against the bed, holding tight to Daisy who slowly coaxed the waves to continue sweeping through her body.

When Jo's body finally stilled, Daisy lay next to her, one hand between her breasts. Jo's heart leapt, her chest knocking against Daisy's hand for more attention. Daisy drew lazy circles with her tongue on Jo's neck. "Were you trying to buck me off?"

Jo laughed. "I never finish on my back."

"Hmmm. Never, huh? Guess that means I know what I'm doing!" She blew on her fingernails and polished them on her bare chest.

Jo took advantage of her distraction and flipped her over. She traced Daisy's face, her thumb resting in the slight cleft of her chin before she kissed her softly. "Come to my bed." She started to back out of her sleeping roll, tugging Daisy gently.

"No way."

Jo paused, confused. "But I have a thing or two to show you."

"Show me here. You're going to be gone for a week. Every night, when you crawl into your bedroll, I want you to remember having me right here."

"My bed already smells like you. Like lavender. It kept me up all last night thinking about you."

"I hope you were thinking about doing this." Daisy took hold of Jo's hand and guided her to the hot space between her legs.

"Already? But I…"

"Now! You can show me other stuff later. Right now I need you. I need you inside."

The musky scent of Daisy's desire made arguing impossible. Lowering herself back to Daisy's soft curves, Jo kissed Daisy once on the lips, then gently nipped her breast before she slipped inside. Each stroke through the silky cavern made right the wrong of the night her tantrum had caused them to spend alone.

"There," Daisy gasped. "More."

Each word stoked Jo's own desire. Daisy pulled Jo's head down to her breast, pressing herself against Jo. Jo happily accepted the offering, pulling and sucking. How had she missed how self-possessed Daisy was? She had done her best to avoid putting herself on a trail that led to Daisy, to anyone really. And now here she was with Daisy climbing toward release, pushing like the last stretch of steep trail. Feeling Daisy reach the peak was almost as rewarding as being there herself.

She nuzzled Daisy's neck as she crested, pushed deeper, held her close as she trembled. As the tremors eased, Daisy continued to rock against Jo's hand. Jo drank in the lovely landscape of Daisy's body bathed in the barest hint of moonlight. Daisy's eyes fluttered open. "Okay?" Jo asked.

"If you have to ask, you'll have to try again."

"I thought I'd let you catch your breath. The altitude seems to have you panting a bit." She caught Daisy's gasp with her mouth as she pulled her fingers free and shifted to straddle her. "You are so beautiful." She wove her hands into the thick brown curls fanned out against her pillow.

"It took you long enough to notice."

Jo kissed her hungrily until they were both short of breath. "Too long. Let me make up for it?"

"I don't know. It's getting pretty late." Daisy reached for her phone.

"Get back here smartass!"

"Who? Me?"

A pang of regret hit Jo, for all the weeks they could have played like this. But she was also ashamed of how much she was responsible for knocking Daisy's confidence. "I'm sorry," she whispered. She kissed Daisy gently.

"We have the whole night for you to show me," Daisy said.

So Jo did.

CHAPTER TWENTY-SEVEN

Dawn crept in the east-facing window. Daisy lay behind Jo, their night and early morning hours replaying in her mind. The images combined with the contact her breasts, hips, and thighs enjoyed and sent another flood of desire through her body. She pressed closer and was delighted to hear and feel Jo moan.

"My body hurts all over."

Daisy laughed. "That's how I felt the day after you hauled me out to clear the Red Cones trail. I was ready to quit the morning after that."

Jo turned in Daisy's arms. "Why'd you stay?"

"To prove you wrong."

"I thought it was to get into my bedroll."

"That too," Daisy said. She kissed Jo wishing she could disguise the fact that the window was growing brighter by the minute.

"The next time we do this, we've got to use the bedroll for its real purpose. We should be waking up watching the sky turn light above us."

"I was hoping you didn't notice that it was getting light."

Jo threaded her fingers through Daisy's hair. "You have to go."

"If I shut my eyes, then the day won't start and we can stay here. One night was so not enough."

"No. It wasn't. I wish there was a way I could pack you down there or someone else could do that trip, and you could…"

Silence hung between them. Part of Daisy wanted for Jo to march over to Takeisha's cabin and tell her to pack her bags for Iva Belle. They would have a whole week together. But she thought of the guests too. "I can't cook for the Yosemite trip. I'm a lot better, but it wouldn't be right to send me out when Takeisha is so much better than I am."

"You did a really good job at the base camp with the guys."

"Thanks," Daisy said softly. "You know, it's probably for the best. If I went on that trip, I'd be so damn distracted."

Jo propped herself on her elbow and traced a finger down Daisy's middle sending electric sparks all over Daisy's body. "Distracted? By what? The new scenery?"

Daisy shoved Jo's shoulder playfully. "Don't you dare say that it would be easy to bring me firewood and not stop to kiss me."

"I wouldn't dare kiss you in the middle of the day."

Daisy cocked her head in question.

"I wouldn't be able to stop."

Daisy leaned forward to kiss her, but Jo stopped her with a finger to her lips. "It's already late."

"It's still morning. Nowhere near the middle of the day."

"I wouldn't be able to stop." She ducked her head to kiss Daisy's collarbone before pushing back the canvas. With new appreciation, Daisy stayed where she was, admiring Jo's toned body. She knew by touch how solid Jo's muscles were and longed to run her hands over her defined biceps again.

"People are going to talk," she said, slipping into briefs and jeans.

Daisy heard the day-ride crew in the horse corral. "They already are. Heather knows I didn't sleep in our cabin last night."

"Good point." Fully dressed now, Jo sat on her bed to work on her boots. She picked up Daisy's panties and shot them at their owner.

Daisy caught them and begrudgingly sat up, stretching kinks from her back. When she bent to put on her panties, she noticed that Jo wasn't lacing her boots. Her eyes were fixed on Daisy. "What?"

"I'm going to miss you."

"You want to hang on to these?" She stretched the elastic of her panties as if to shoot them back at Jo.

Cody barked by the cabin door. Jo finished tying her boots and stood to let him out, grumbling, "I know, so inappropriate!" loudly enough for Daisy to hear. She stood with her hand on the doorknob. "If you tell me what horses you want, I'll get them caught up for you."

"Don't you have your own work?"

Jo shrugged. "I've got all day."

Daisy wanted Jo to stay with her, but the morning chores were inevitable. "Churchill and Trinket."

"Who else?"

"You pick. Kat said she's hardly ridden at all, so I'm giving her Churchill. He's taken good care of me this summer."

"And you'll ride whoever I pick?"

Daisy pulled her shirt over her head. "I trust you."

Her words hung between them feeling weightier than Daisy had expected. "You got it." Jo smiled and ducked out of the cabin.

Once she finished dressing, Daisy took a deep breath, steeling herself for some morning-after teasing down at the corrals. She stopped by the bathroom before she headed to the grain shed where she splashed feed into a bucket.

Jo approached with the guest horses, and Churchill nickered as he strode to the feed trough. "Now to pick somebody for you!" Her eyes scanned Daisy, sizing her up. She knew it was for a horse, but her body fluttered with the memory of Jo's touch.

"Nothing too exciting! I want to get to camp in one piece!" Daisy said.

"I'll take good care of you." Jo winked.

Daisy told herself not to stare as Jo walked away even though it took all her willpower not to. As she brushed the horses, she debated whether she would wait for Jo and walk to breakfast with her.

"Morning sleepyhead!" Heather said, grabbing her own bucket of grain to feed the horses she'd caught for the morning ride to Rainbow Falls.

"Morning! Need this?" She extended the brush she'd been using.

"What I need is the scoop on you and Jo! You promised to tell me what happened on your trip, and then you never came home. I'm guessing that more went down on that trip than I expected! And now you're leaving and I'll have to wait two and a half days to get the details! How much can you tell me on the walk to breakfast?"

"Zilch. Jo's grabbing me a new ride, and I want to go see."

"You sure she's not catching her own stock?"

"Pretty sure. Why?"

"She's grooming a mule over at the employee shed. I thought she was saddling her own mount." She whistled a long note and said, "Oh boy, this sounds more serious!" She held up her fingers and thumbs in her inverted triangle and settled them in Jo's direction. Her voice held a touch of hurt when she said, "You should have told me you were into Jo."

"I wasn't sure it mattered whether I was or not," Daisy said.

"She's a tough one to read. I get that."

"I'm going to go check out my new ride."

"And your babe." Heather held the triangle up again.

"Stop!" Daisy called over her shoulder, though she was smiling. A mule! Would she be able to ride a mule? Sure enough, at the tie rail stood a sorrel mule chasing grain in the trough. "You picked a mule?"

"You can't go through the summer without trying out a riding mule. This is Butterscotch, and she's great. She'll take even better care of you than Churchill."

Across the yard, Wendy unloaded her kitchen boxes on the dock.

"I need to grab my gear," Daisy said.

"Make sure your sleeping bag makes it this time."

Daisy bumped her shoulder. "Smartass."

"I call a smart ass a mule."

"You would."

"I'll get the stock saddled while you grab your stuff and get breakfast." Jo disappeared in the shed and returned with a saddle.

Daisy took the blankets from her and arranged them on Butterscotch. "You don't want to get breakfast together?"

Jo pulled the girth around and busied herself tying the latigo.

"Is something wrong?"

Fingers that had pulled all sorts of pleasures from Daisy's body now danced from buckle to buckle making all sorts of adjustments. The last one secured, Jo tugged on the saddle horn.

"Whose saddle is that, anyway?"

"Mine."

Daisy growled with frustration, finally grasping Jo's attention. "I'm confused. You're acting like you care about me, but then you're not talking to me. If you weren't sending me off with your gear, I'd think you were brushing me off."

"I'm not." Jo released her frustration with a puff of air. "I'm sorry. I suck at goodbyes, and I didn't expect after one night for this to be so hard."

"Oh." Daisy hadn't expected that. She smiled.

"What? It's not hard for you?"

"I wasn't expecting you to say that. Kind of like I wasn't expecting you to say you were mad at yourself either. You say exactly what's in your heart. I like that." She squeezed Jo's shoulder. "I don't want to say goodbye either. I want to spend every minute I can naked with you, and I have to wait a whole week." She was pleased with the blush that colored Jo's cheeks. "I'll be thinking about you. Remembering what I like and making plans for next time."

"That sounds good. Take Cody to breakfast with you. I have a red duffel with his food. Keep it in the kitchen and put a cup out for him with breakfast and dinner."

Daisy's throat constricted with emotion. It was hard to accept that she wouldn't see Jo for a week. "One hug for the road?" she asked.

Jo nodded, so Daisy stepped forward, wrapping her arms around Jo's strong frame. She took a deep breath, memorizing the sweet scent that was all Jo. "Miss you already," she whispered.

With a tight squeeze, Jo released her. "Have a good trip."

An hour later, well on her way to Iva Belle hot springs, Daisy closed her eyes to bring back the feel of Jo's arms around her. She shouldn't have shut her eyes. The rocking motion of Butterscotch's even stride pulled her toward the sleep her body craved. She'd prioritized touching Jo as much as she could over sleep.

"Announcement! Announcement! Announcement!" Kat sang, drawing out the last repetition with four syllables. She nearly startled Daisy from the saddle.

"My ass is on fire! With all the padding I have, how can it be hurting!"

"You don't have a big ass," Wendy called from the rear.

"I do so. And I've been thinking for months that finally, I would have an advantage over your skinny ass, and you're not complaining at all."

"It's too beautiful to complain."

"You went through this at the beginning of the summer, right Daisy? How long until it doesn't hurt?"

Daisy was glad Kat couldn't see her face. It had taken weeks for her knees and hips and ass to stop hurting. "A week."

Kat made such real sobbing sounds that Daisy glanced over her shoulder, relieved to find that she was faking. "Did you learn that announcement thing at camp?"

"Absolutely! I went to church camp every summer."

"Do you know 'Honey You Can't Love One'?"

Kat immediately launched into the song, and Daisy joined her thinking about how she'd driven Jo mad with her singing at the beginning of the summer. She wasn't even paying attention to the lyrics until Kat started laughing. "Can't love eight and still be straight…oh my god! I sang that song my whole childhood and never thought about what it was saying!"

"What in the world did you think it meant?" Wendy asked.

"I don't know, like being sober? Following the straight path?"

"If I didn't know better, I'd think you grew up under a rock!"

Daisy liked Wendy's laugh and enjoyed the way they interacted. "How many years is this for you?" she asked, thinking they must have been together for more than a dozen years, at least.

"This is our first anniversary!" Kat announced.

Daisy whipped around. "First?"

"It took me a whole lot of lives to figure myself out," Kat said.

"But you did. That's all that matters."

"What about you?" Kat asked. "Did you figure out whether Jo's really an asshole?"

"She seemed distracted this morning saddling our horses," Wendy said.

"She did?" Daisy asked in what she hoped was a light, conversational tone.

"It was like reality TV. Pete was asking Jo for help with one of the mules he was trying to load and she didn't give him the time of day. Check one in the 'asshole' column," Kat said.

"But she was saddling our horses, and Heather said she never saddles dude horses. That means she was doing something nice for you, doesn't it?" Wendy asked.

Cody looked over his shoulder as he trotted ahead of her. His tongue lolled out making it look like he was laughing at her as she tried to decide how to answer their question.

"She was. She did a lot of nice things this morning including catching up my stock and setting me up with her old saddle on this nice mule. I'm surprised at how different her gait is. It actually is more comfortable than a horse!"

"You two slept together, didn't you?" Kat squealed. "That's why she was ignoring Pete so hard? This is way better than reality TV!"

"How do you jump from saddling horses to them sleeping together? That's a pretty big leap," Wendy argued.

"It seems like it would be the cowgirl equivalent of breakfast in bed," Kat said. "Am I right? Am I right?"

"I don't think I should be divulging something like that to my guests," Daisy said.

Kat chortled. "I was right! I was right! I would fist bump you if I could reach. And if my ASS DIDN'T HURT SO BAD!"

"Hey, Daisy! There should be a meadow coming up on the right," said Wendy. "Look for a narrow footpath about halfway past it. Let's pull over for a spell."

In the quiet shade of the forest, Kat took the opportunity to probe for more information. "What happens now? Will she be there when we go back on Sunday?"

The lead that sat in Daisy's belly sat heavier. "No. She has a seven-day trip that leaves tomorrow."

"That seriously stinks!" Kat said.

"And while she's away, Pete is going to make an attempt to win your heart. This week on Backcountry Heartbreak!" Wendy said.

"You can't call the show Backcountry Heartbreak. There's supposed to be a happy ending. It could be called Backcountry Babe Hookup," Kat suggested.

"That's not happily ever after. That's a fling. Is this a fling kind of thing?" Wendy asked.

"If it was a fling, she wouldn't be riding in Jo's saddle, would she?" Kat answered.

Daisy was relieved that they didn't seem to need her contributions anymore. They happily debated whether the contestants would be looking for lasting love on the reality show they continued to create.

The forest trail ended abruptly, spilling them into a sunny meadow filled with dancing coral California poppies, sweet purple lupine and vermillion Indian paintbrush. The sun felt wonderful on her back. Had she not been watching for it, she would not have seen the tiny break in the foliage. "Is this the trail you meant?"

Wendy steered Trinket from the main trail to have a look. "I'm pretty sure. If we ride through this, there should be a trail that drops down to Pond Lily. It's pretty steep, so we'll stretch our legs and let the horses rest."

All three turned from the narrow dirt trail and pushed through the wild grasses that reached their stirrups. The hoofbeats were muted, the swish of their mounts' bodies parting the grass louder. Daisy worried for her guests when they reached a steep drop. They all dismounted—Daisy fluidly and both Kat and Wendy with much groaning and gimping.

"Wendy, are you sure this is a good idea? What if we can't get back up the hill?" Kat looked dubious.

"I've only seen Pond Lily once. Hardly anyone ever goes because it's so hard to get to. But it's beyond beautiful. It'll be worth it. And when we get back up here, you'll be happy to get back in the saddle."

Groaning dramatically with every step, Kat followed Wendy down the narrow trail. Daisy led the stock to a stand of saplings at the edge of the meadow. She tied them and tilted her head to the sun. She was bone tired, and the warmth was lulling her to sleep. A few steps away, she spotted a log. She eyed the stock. The knots were secure. She knew that. She looked back to the log and debated resting for one short minute. She checked the knots one more time before sitting with her back against the log. She scooted down until her shoulders rested against the bark. She had to remove her Zorro hat to lean back fully, so she rested it on her face and promptly fell into a deep sleep.

She had no clue as to how much time had passed when a fury of whinnies erupted in stereo, call and response from her three tied nearby and a string on the trail. Daisy jumped to her feet, snatching her hat from where it had fallen. She brushed it off as she strode across the meadow.

"Lose your riders?" Pete called from the trail.

"They went on a short hike."

He looked around. "Where?"

"There's a pond nearby that Wendy wanted to show Kat. They'll be back soon, and we'll be on our way again."

"Catching up on sleep?"

Daisy mentally cursed that he'd been able to tell. She quickly discovered how he'd known, the drool stain above her right breast a dead giveaway.

"Quick turnaround, and I didn't sleep well on that last trip."

"Huh."

"What's that mean?"

"Just something I heard about you sharing Jo's bedroll."

"Where'd you hear that?"

"Jo's shoeing buddies were talking about how you were more interested in Jo than any of them."

"Come on! Like I had any other option at all? I wasn't about to jump in a sleeping bag with a stranger."

"I defended you."

"What do you mean, you defended me."

"I told them you weren't gay."

"How is that your business?"

He looked past her, and she turned around to see Kat and Wendy returned from their hike.

"Keep them moving. I can't head back with your stock until you get them to the site. If you lollygag, I'll be riding in the dark." He spurred his horse and disappeared with the short string in a cloud of dust.

Gritting her teeth, Daisy marched back to the animals and prepared them for the next leg of the trip.

"I wish we had time for you to run down the hill. It is truly stunning," Kat said when she reluctantly accepted her horse from Daisy and noisily settled back into the saddle.

"Pete's in a rush for us to get to the campsite. The good news is that if we get moving, it's actually easier on your body."

"Tell that to the raw insides of my knees," Kat replied.

Thumbing her nose at Pete's rush, Daisy spent some time lengthening the stirrups on Kat's saddle. "See if that helps. If not, I can adjust them again."

Wendy rode up next to Kat and rested her hand on Kat's knee. "I hope you'll remember more than your chafed knees."

Kat squeezed her hand and said, "You've already given me many lovely things to remember."

While Daisy was thrilled that they were so freely enjoying each other, it stung to have a reminder of what she wanted that instant displayed before her and out of reach. They hit the trail again, every step taking her further away from Jo.

CHAPTER TWENTY-EIGHT

"Ain't this the shits," Jo grumbled. "I busted my ass to get camp packed up only to sit waiting for more than an hour."

"You can hear the stock truck a mile out. Sit down. I didn't think it was possible to be any more worn out, but watching you pace sure isn't helping," Takeisha complained from the tree she leaned on in the shade. The seven-day travel trip to Yosemite's Tuolumne Meadow wouldn't be complete until Leo and Sol arrived with a stock truck and van to haul horses and guests back to the Lodge. There, the two families, eight guests in all who had been pleasant enough, would reclaim their bags and tents.

"He's never been this late."

"You realize that you're making all the guests anxious?" Takeisha asked.

A scuffle broke out where the horses were tied. The hot parking lot had sparse room for livestock. "The stock's all on top of each other. Are you going to blame their being anxious on me, too?"

Takeisha's droll look clued Jo in on the fact that she didn't buy Jo's argument. Jo walked to the drinking fountain for something to do. Everyone around her was excited to be in the beautiful Sierra Nevada Mountains, but she felt none of it. Like Takeisha, she was tired from the long trip, and though she was always antsy to get back to Cody, knowing that she might be losing precious time to see Daisy put Jo on the edge of coming unglued. She checked her watch. "On top of everything, we're going to miss dinner."

"Like you've ever cared about that." With a dramatic sigh, Takeisha hauled herself up and rooted around in her kitchen boxes. "Aha!" she finally said victoriously, holding up a colorful bag. "Work your jaws on these."

Jo caught the bag of Starburst. "I guess I should say thank you."

Takeisha guffawed. She walked closer to Jo and said softly, "For the distraction, or are you finally ready to admit that I was right about Daisy?"

Popping an orange square in her mouth gave Jo a few minutes to prepare her answer. "I'm not sure I should thank you. The way my luck's been running, she's probably going to be in the backcountry already on an overnighter."

"Or she's there, and you have a few nights before we go out again."

Jo worked the candy, and soon it was gone. She peeked in the bag. Four left. She wanted an unlimited number of days with Daisy, the way a kid wants a full bag of candy. Takeisha would easily replenish the stash of Starburst she packed especially for Jo. If only it were that easy to stock up on extra days. She unwrapped a pink square and chewed it slowly, savoring it. "Do you know how big the trip to Holcomb is? You think there's any argument we can give the boss man to get him to send Daisy out with us?"

"Well there's an interesting idea," Takeisha said. "It made sense that he sent her with Wendy to pick up some cooking skills, so we can't say she's going to shadow me."

"How about we argue she's going to shadow me and learn some packing. She's learned nearly everything else this summer."

Takeisha frowned.

"What?"

"You think this place needs another lady packer?"

"I don't know what you're talking about. The Lodge doesn't have any lady packers I know about."

Takeisha started to laugh but then paused, a faraway look on her face. She threw her arms up in a victory stance. "Hear that? The truck is coming!"

"Hallelujah! We're going home!" Jo's stomach danced around as much as the mules and horses, anxious to get loaded into the stock truck. She was nervous to see Daisy again after a full week. Did her skin burn like hers did at the mere thought of being alone with each other again? In a little more than an hour, she'd have her answer.

Jo was no less anxious when they finally rattled into the yard at the Lodge. She'd ridden with surly Sol who was bent so severely with age that Jo often wondered how he managed to see over the steering wheel. Though he moved slowly, he got a good amount of work done. Still, with a full truck of stock to unload, Jo wished she had someone like Gabe or Dozer to lend a hand.

She lit up inside like the Fourth of July when she saw Daisy standing at the bottom of the ramp. Hands perched on her hips, she wore the work of the day on her clothes, her thighs and breasts highlighted with dust from the trail and oil and dirt of the gear. "Care for some help?"

Jo would have very much liked to help her out of her dirty work clothes. Reluctantly, she pushed the thought aside. "I'd appreciate it!" she said, tossing the horse's lead to Daisy. It was hard to take her eyes off Daisy's rear as she headed toward the tie rail. *Focus*! she told herself forcing her hands to move to untie the next lead rope in line when what she really wanted to do was run them down Daisy's body.

After she led the next dude horse down the ramp, Sol gimped up saying he would send the rest down to her, so he didn't have to walk. She crossed paths with Daisy as she led the horse to the tie rail. "How's it been around here?"

"Like did I miss you?" Daisy asked.

Jo waited for her to answer, but she kept walking. Not wanting to be caught staring, Jo started to turn back around but then caught Daisy wiggling her ass. Was she flirting or mocking?

Again they passed, this time with Daisy leading two horses. "Well? Did you?" Jo asked quietly.

"I don't know. Did you miss me?"

She kept walking, the wide smile that used to irk Jo now making her heart flutter. When Jo had the next two horses in tow, she walked straight toward Daisy, forcing her to stop. She handed her the lead ropes and caught her wrist before Daisy could turn again. "I want to show you how much I missed you."

"I look forward to that," Daisy said. "But you're falling behind."

Jo, too, heard the next animal clomping down the ramp. This time, it was one of her mules, which she led to the lower corral. With all the dude stock unloaded, Daisy had stayed by the saddle shed to unsaddle them. It made sense but being so near yet unable to touch or kiss Daisy was driving Jo mad. She put mental blinders on herself and focused on getting all the mules out of the stock truck. Last to unload was Tuxedo who she led to the employee tie rail.

As she approached the rail, Daisy pulled a saddle off one of the dude horses, balancing it on her hip while she pulled the cinch over the seat so it wouldn't drag. Jo smiled remembering how she had used those muscles to keep Jo pinned beneath her. God, she wanted Daisy again.

Daisy caught her eye as she walked back from the shed. Her expression mirrored Jo's desire. "Need some help there, cowgirl?"

"I do. What do you do with this thing?" She held up the rope. "Wind it around this rail a bunch of times?"

Ducking under the troughs they used to grain the animals, Daisy popped up next to Jo. She took the lead from her hands. "I know some knots. I could show you."

"Please." Jo hadn't meant to sound so much like she had when she had begged Daisy to touch her, but they both heard it now.

"I think there's a spare rope in the shed."

Jo scanned the yard. With all the animals unloaded, Sol had driven off in the stock truck leaving them alone. "I'll help you look."

Daisy quickly tied Tuxedo to the rail and led the way to the saddle shed. It was a small building with a dozen racks to hold saddles and hooks for other equipment. Bridles, feed sacks, and bells for the bell mares hung from the walls. There was no electricity and it was dark, but Jo didn't need any light. She kicked the door shut behind them and pulled Daisy to her for a searing kiss.

They fought for control, Jo chasing Daisy's tongue with her own, moaning when they collided and danced. Jo swept her arms up Daisy's back and started to tug the fabric up in an attempt to get her hands on Daisy's smooth skin.

Daisy broke the kiss. "We can't fool around in here," she gasped, moving her kisses to Jo's neck.

"Why not?" Jo asked, her fingers nimble on Daisy's buttons.

"Someone might come in."

Jo reached behind her and locked the door, returning immediately to the now-open shirt. She fanned her hands out and ran them up Daisy's flat tummy, trying to reach her breasts. The shirt was form-fitting and made it too difficult. "You look great in this shirt, but I can't work around it." Her hands now on top of the fabric, she swept up all the way to Daisy's breasts smiling when Daisy pushed into her hands. "I'm getting the impression that you did miss me."

"You haven't tested that very thoroughly," Daisy teased.

Jo responded by pinching Daisy's nipples through the fabric, and she yipped in surprise. Jo pressed one finger against Daisy's lips. Daisy responded by opening her mouth and grasping her fingertip in her teeth. Jo used the leverage to pull Daisy's mouth back to hers, freeing her fingers to find and unfasten Daisy's buckle and fly. Kissing her slowly, teasing and savoring, she eased one hand past the loosened jeans and found all the proof she needed pooled and ready for her fingers.

Daisy groaned, driving Jo's desire. Holding Daisy's shoulder tightly with one hand, she slid the other further into Daisy's jeans, pushing her finger deep into Daisy. She responded, grinding her clit against Jo's palm. "I missed you," she said, her voice low and so sexy.

Jo lost herself in Daisy, in the lavender that clung to the skin of her neck, in her full-body embrace, but especially in those words. She had been missed, and it made her head spin. She pumped her fingers and listened for the change in Daisy's breath, the hitch that came right before her body trembled and squeezed Jo from the inside. She held on tight, Daisy's heart pounding against her chest.

"That was unexpected," Daisy said. "I've never…I'm so…I can't feel my legs."

Gingerly, Jo freed her hand and swept around to cup Daisy's ass. "Better?"

Daisy hmmed against Jo's neck. "A little. My legs are noodles. They haven't felt like this since the first week."

"I had a little hitch in my giddyup after we messed around last week."

"That would have been fun to watch."

"C'mon, you. The stock's waiting on us."

"But what about you?"

Jo could hear her tugging her jeans and tucking in her shirt. She ran her fingers up Daisy's arms. "I don't leave for a few days. I was hoping I could convince you to bunk with me again tonight. Ready?"

"Not quite. I need one more kiss."

"One," Jo said sternly. "And no tongue. The kids are waiting."

Daisy located Jo's face with both hands. She ran her fingers along Jo's jawline. They were so still and so quiet. Jo waited expectantly to hear what Daisy was thinking, wishing she could see her face and read her expression. Then Daisy's grip tightened and she planted a firm kiss on Jo's lips. "Okay, Boss. Ready."

Shadows stretched long in the evening light when they stepped out of the tack shed and found the yard empty. Jo's thoughts were far from the latigos she loosened to release the mules from their work.

"Do you know where Pond Lily is?" Daisy stripped a light sawbuck saddle from one of Jo's mules.

"I've seen it on a postcard in the store. That's it. On the way to Fish Creek, I think."

"That's the one."

"Why?"

"I had an idea that I was hoping might get me one night under the stars with you."

Two saddles stowed, they stood between the tie rail and the shed for pack saddles. "I was brainstorming the same thing with Takeisha."

Daisy looked disappointed. "You already knew about the blocked trail?"

"Blocked trail?"

"Down near Pond Lily. Kat and Wendy walked down when we were on our way to Iva Belle. She said there are three trees like pickup sticks blocking the trail. I remembered how you're an expert with a two-man saw and thought maybe you'd be able to convince Leo to let us team up to take them out."

She wasn't the bossy-in-bed Daisy, but she wasn't the know-nothing that Jo had tried to scare away when she'd volunteered her to help. "You're pretty handy with a two-man saw yourself."

Daisy beamed. "You think he might send us out and let us stay overnight? It's three trees which would take three times as long to clear, right?"

"Doesn't hurt to ask him. We've got a few days before the Holcomb trip. I'll ask him at dinner. Speaking of…seems late, doesn't it?" Standing in the evening breeze, Jo could feel how late in the season it was. It brought with it the sadness she felt when she was forced to leave the mountains.

As she approached the last tacked mule, Jo looked over the saddle to see Takeisha and the rest of the crew exiting the store and unwrapping frozen treats. "I think we missed dinner."

"How…"

"See, I told you they were working," Takeisha said as they approached.

Saucily, Heather said, "I said we'd probably hear the two of you thumping around in the tack shed!"

Jo would not look at Daisy. She absolutely would not look at Daisy. She untied the latigo with fingers that had been stroking

Daisy to climax a half hour ago. How had they missed the dinner bell?

"But I know you better," Takeisha said. She rubbed Blaze's forehead until her long blond ears swayed apart. "You never put anything before taking care of your animals."

"Guilty," Jo said. She pulled the saddle and pads from the mule and walked them to the shed. The last empty spot was on top. As she swung the saddle above her shoulders, she caught Daisy's scent. She touched her fingers to her nose and had to bite her lip sharply to keep from smiling. Her gaze caught on Daisy's for an instant, just long enough to see her erase her look of surprise.

"Cook set aside a few plates. It's your favorite, fried rice. You want to head over? I'll turn the stock loose for you," Takeisha said.

"Don't you want help feeding?" Daisy asked.

Heather bumped against her shoulder as she headed to the first corral. "Nah, you lovebirds go have a nice dinner together."

Daisy looked to Jo who shrugged and tilted her head toward the café. A few steps away from the group, Daisy jabbed Jo with her elbow.

"Ouch! What was that for?"

"You're smelling your hand? They're making jokes about us screwing around, and you're smelling your hand?"

Jo raised her hand again, and Daisy smacked it midair. "Stop it!"

"I can't help it."

"Try harder," Daisy said, holding the door open for Jo. "Focus here. I'd really like to have a night away with you."

"Yes, ma'am."

CHAPTER TWENTY-NINE

"This is what I wanted." Daisy lay with her head on Jo's shoulder, her arm and leg sprawled over Jo. She nudged closer taking a deep breath to savor everything right about the moment—the smell of them together and the scent of the lilies and pines carried by the gentle night breeze.

"For your entire body to hurt?"

"You didn't complain back when we worked on that first log together," Daisy said.

"I didn't complain to you but ask Takeisha. It took days for my arms to feel the same. I hate trail maintenance!"

"The things you'll do to get more time with me."

Jo squeezed her body, but Daisy felt it all the way to her heart. She was exactly where she needed to be, a place she hadn't even known about a few short months ago.

"To be with you under this amazing blanket of stars," Jo said huskily. Daisy's head lifted as Jo filled her lungs deeply and slowly let the breath back out again.

"Yeah," she said. They gazed up at the night sky together for a long while, and then Jo whispered, "I miss these stars so much when I sleep inside. I miss waking up as the sunrise chases them away."

"That's what I saw in your eyes."

The moon provided enough light for Daisy to make out Jo's expression of confusion.

"When you rode in the parade…You had this look in your eyes that I didn't know. It was like you were seeing something nobody else could see. I wanted to chase after you and ask what it was."

"And look at you. You did it!" Her arms tightened around Daisy.

Daisy laughed. "Maybe in tracking you down at the Lodge, but after that, it was more trying not to get chased off."

"I thought maybe you'd forgotten about that."

"We haven't had enough nights like this for me to forget about that. But get me out in the backcountry again and I might reconsider."

"Think you'll come back next year?"

"That depends." Daisy drew a line with her finger from the hollow at Jo's throat down to the curls between her legs. "Are you?"

"Every year."

"Then count me in."

Jo ran her fingers through Daisy's hair, lulling her to sleep. The strokes didn't alter at all when she said, "What are you doing for the off-season? Think you'll go back to your coffee shop?"

"I don't know. Wendy was telling me about college agriculture programs, but Heather said if I want to spend my summers out here, I should teach. That way, I'd always have the summer off."

"You were talking to her about coming back?"

"You're probably going to laugh at me, but…I feel like the mountains have been calling me my whole life, only I never heard them until they sent you and the mules out for me."

"That sounds about right."

"It does?"

"It's a way better explanation for why I ended up in that awful city. I've never seen traffic like that in my whole life. And the dang garbage! Has no one ever taught those mother truckers how to pick up after themselves? If I never go back to Pasadena, it will be too soon!"

Part of Daisy agreed with Jo about her native city, but at the same time, her parents still lived there, and she loved that they loved the parade. They spent the whole year anticipating it the way Jo anticipated her months in the backcountry. "The parade is crazy. But Pasadena is a lovely town."

"Pasadena is a city. Sebastopol is a town."

"Well there are lots of people who think Pasadena is a lovely *city*," Daisy said.

Jo hmphed and then barked with surprise when Daisy nipped her shoulder. "Hey, I was *about* to say that it at least turned out lovely residents. Now I'm not so sure!"

Daisy kissed the spot she had just bitten. "You're such a baby. It's hard to see why I spent so much of the summer scared of you. When I started, Heather told me not to worry about it because you'd usually be in the backcountry. Now…" Daisy had to swallow to keep Jo from hearing how her throat was closing up.

"You're not counting the days until I leave anymore?"

"I am, but for a different reason. I'm calculating every minute I can get you to myself."

"I used to hate coming back in. I don't like thinking about how every trip brings me closer to the end of the season when I have to leave the mountains. But this last trip, I couldn't get back fast enough."

"How many more trips do you have?"

"Takeisha and I have two more until she has to go back and get ready for the next school year. You could talk to her about how she likes teaching during the off-season."

"Two more."

"And then the season slows to almost nothing. Leo might give me a few more spot trips, but I also have to think about getting back to my clients. I have horses to shoe."

Daisy moved to her back. She rested her arm on her forehead trying to keep herself from worrying about what would happen with the end of the season. She should probably investigate teaching or agriculture programs, which would thrill her parents, but would she check out the community college in Pasadena? Or was there maybe a college near Sebastopol? How far away was Sebastopol, anyway? Her parents were surprised enough with her spending the summer in the mountains. What would they say if she followed Jo to Sebastopol?

"You got quiet over there." Jo turned on her side placing her warm palm on Daisy's tummy.

"It's going to be so hard to leave," Daisy whispered.

"Let's think about the time we have right now and what we could be doing with it." Jo lowered herself, touching her lips to Daisy's.

Daisy threw her arms around Jo and pulled until she had Jo on top of her. She swept her arms down Jo's back and pressed up against her. "I've got a few ideas."

It would be difficult to get up in the morning and break camp. She would have to pinch herself to keep from falling asleep in the saddle. But she wouldn't regret a second of how she and Jo had kept each other warm through the night.

Daisy would never forget the way the sun sparkled on the broad lily pads at Pond Lily. She understood perfectly why Wendy had insisted that she and Kat detour on their way to Iva Belle. After they had climbed the steep hill that met with the main trail, Daisy itched to point her horse to the right and follow the trail on to First Crossing. They of course turned left and made what now seemed like a quick ride back to the Lodge, her mind flitting through the mental photo album of her summer. She had tried taking some actual pictures on her phone, but none of them fully captured the majesty of the High Sierras.

As she followed Jo's lead, with an intimate eye she viewed her strong shoulders. She hadn't even noticed how today had contrasted with their first trail-clearing challenge until Jo turned and said, "No soundtrack this time?"

"At the beginning of the summer, all this space intimidated me. I felt like it was going to swallow me. I don't feel like that anymore."

Jo nodded, and they returned to their quiet ride, Daisy doing her best not to think about how lonely it would feel when Jo and Cody left on their next trip

When they reached the yard, Takeisha was at the employee tie rail tightening the cinch on Tubby.

"Where are you going?" Daisy asked, leading Butterscotch and Tuxedo to the employee rail.

"Red Cones. The second half-day already left, and this family was stuck on the bus. I said I'd take them."

"You want me to take them?" Daisy didn't understand the confusion her question brought to Takeisha's face.

"I figured you'd need time to get laundry done before tomorrow."

"Did Leo book another trip?" Daisy asked.

"Were you two too busy making out to talk about the Holcomb trip?" She looped Tubby's lead rope through her belt and mounted. "Jo asked me to get you on as extra help. She didn't tell you?"

Daisy spun around and looked across the yard, finding Jo at the loading dock near the workshop. Their eyes met, and Daisy put her arms up in a "what gives?" shape. She wanted to run over and leap into Jo's arms. She had Jo for the night at the Lodge, and now she would have her in the backcountry for five more. Jo gave her a simple thumb's up and returned to her work. Daisy followed suit, stripping both her mule and Jo's. She then walked over to Jo loosening the girths on the first of the two mules they had taken for their brief overnight stay.

"Takeisha seemed pretty surprised that you hadn't talked to me about Holcomb."

A sneaky smile played at the corner of Jo's mouth. "I told her she could ask for help if she needed it."

"Because you don't."

"I guess if she runs out of things for you to do, I could find some odd jobs for you."

"It's going to be hard to keep my hands off you."

"Harder than waiting for me to come back from the trip?"

"I'll manage."

Jo nodded. "Morning is going to start early catching up the mules."

"Then I vote for early bedtime. Unless you had other plans?"

All Jo had to do was slide her gaze down Daisy's figure, and Daisy could clearly see what she had planned. One poorly tied pack, one lost sleeping bag and her whole life had shifted to a place where watching Jo's fingers at the buckles and latches of the pack saddles brought her mind to Jo's hands on her belt in the shed. As Jo ran her hands over the mule's neck and down her shoulder to pick up a foot, a shiver went up her spine in anticipation of the next time those strong hands would be caressing her. Jo worked her way around all the mule's hooves, flicking out the dirt. On the last one, she looked up and found Daisy watching her.

"What?" Jo said, pulling Daisy from her thoughts.

"I love watching you work."

"I love the company."

The seriousness of Jo's tone gave Daisy such pause, she hoisted herself up to perch on the edge of the feeding trough. "I can't tell if you're serious."

Jo walked to Daisy and nestled herself between Daisy's knees. "I don't say things I don't mean."

Could she lean over for a brief kiss? Daisy wanted so badly to kiss Jo, but they were at work. She told herself to be professional. "I like that about you."

With the barest squeeze to Daisy's thighs, Jo moved to check the next mule's shoes. "I've got time to put on a new set of sneakers, but these guys are fine. Want to grab the riding mules and come help me scope out hooves in the pasture? If I don't find some work to do, I'm likely to get myself into trouble."

"I don't want to get you in trouble." Daisy popped off the feeder and grabbed the two mules. She caught up to Jo at the mule corral, unsnapping Tuxedo's and Butterscotch's leads. They trotted toward the other mules in the corral, shaking their heads, seeing who they could boss around. "You find work. I'm going to put in a load of laundry, but I won't be long."

She returned to the yard with cold sodas, one of which she delivered to Jo at the shoeing shed before helping Heather unload the last Rainbow Falls ride. Heather shared the highlights of her day, though Daisy knew she was dying to grill her on the night she'd spent with Jo down at Pond Lily. While they let the horses cool down, they sat at the edge of the shed that held all sizes of horseshoes and watched Jo trim and file each hoof before fitting the mule with new shoes. As the half-day rides rolled in, more people gathered, telling stories while Jo worked.

As Jo led the newly shod mule back to the corral, Takeisha leaned close to Daisy. "I'm glad you're coming on this next trip. You're good for Jo. She never would have put up with all this chattering. You're making her relax a little."

Daisy now strode around the pack station with confidence. She no longer felt like she needed to prove herself. She was undoubtedly part of the team. She knew what she was doing, and nobody questioned her.

The next morning, she and Jo dressed side by side as if they'd been doing it for years. They caught stock and moved fluidly from one task to the next with little communication.

One reason Daisy was accompanying them on the Holcomb trip was that the number of guests created eight mule loads. In addition to helping Takeisha in the kitchen, Daisy would also lead a short string of mules, three that she'd seen Jo pack all summer, and Jo would round out her string with stock unfamiliar to Daisy.

Pete helped Jo with the first loads of gear as Daisy helped the guests who would be riding horses instead of hiking in. A half hour or so after Takeisha had left the yard, Jo was tying off a box hitch that pulled the pack boxes away from the mule's side. Jo had walked Daisy through the steps, saying that you could pack almost anything with the simple hitch. Remembering the fit she'd thrown about the separation of duties when she'd taken over for Takeisha, Daisy was happy to learn. The weight of the loaded panniers surprised her, and she stepped back on the dock to catch her breath. Her boot hit something.

Her stomach lurched. "Is there another trip going out today?"

"No. Why?" Jo grunted as she tugged slack from the rope.

Daisy pointed to a pile of saddlebags. They held everyone's lunches.

Brows furrowed, Jo strode toward Daisy. "Why are those here?"

"They didn't get onto the saddles."

"Obviously."

Daisy recoiled at the one word, more from the tone than the word. She dreaded what she knew came next.

"Poop on a stick! How did that happen?"

Daisy had helped the guests onto their horses. She should have slung a saddlebag over the horn of every rider's saddle. She'd been distracted, wanting to get back over to where Jo was sorting out the mule loads. "It's my fault. I..."

Jo cut her off. "Doesn't matter." She looked at the sky and then over to the mules. There were still three left to load. "Pete! Would you teach Daisy how to put together her string? She's taking Dumbo, Ladybird, and Goldie in that order."

"I'm sorry..." Daisy started.

"If we wait until both strings are ready, Takeisha will be stopping for lunch with no food. If you go now, you'll catch them pretty quick. You remember how we got to Beck Lakes, right? Cross the bridge, go along the ridge where you can see Devil's Postpile before you head up the mountain?"

Daisy thought she remembered, but her breath was coming fast and she felt lightheaded. She'd already messed up, and it was only the first morning.

"Look, you're going to catch them in the next hour. By the time you get the lunches sorted out, I'll be gaining on you. There's good signage up there, and if you get confused, you can wait. The three I'm sending with you won't get into trouble if they have to stand still a bit. Got it?"

Daisy nodded. She took a deep breath. She could do this. At least she'd been on this trail. That was better than when she had to find Jo and Takeisha's camp on her own before they left for the morning. Jo squeezed her shoulder, bringing back some of the warmth Daisy had so quickly grown used to.

"You'll be fine. This is an easy fix."

She watched as Pete measured out the lead from one mule to the next. He was telling her something about the amount of room they needed. Too much better than too little. Breathe. He handed Ladybird's lead to her, and she tied it around Dumbo's neck.

"You need anything else?"

"I'm okay."

"You have your lunch?" Daisy narrowed her eyes and he threw his hands in the air. "Kidding! This is going to be a sweet trip. Relax."

"Thanks. Hold them while I get Butterscotch?"

"You got it."

She told herself that if Jo trusted her, she'd be fine. She checked the cinch on Butterscotch. Jo believed in her ability to ride something more than a dude horse. She could do this. She looped the lead rope through her belt and mounted. She settled into the saddle that Jo had lent her instead of continuing to use one of the pack station's. She belonged here. She straightened her back and held out her hand. Pete handed her Dumbo's lead and tipped his hat before he went to help Jo with the next pack.

Jo acknowledged her leaving with a raised hand, but by the time Daisy tapped Butterscotch with her heels and pointed her toward the trail that led to the bridge crossing, she had already returned to her work.

Every hoofbeat made her more certain that she was going to be fine. Daisy turned and watched her three mules fall into line behind her. Jo had told her to watch the packs to make sure the saddle always rocked back to center. Each one did. All the long mule ears swung lazily in time to their steady stride. Daisy turned back around and, between the tall ears in front of her, took in the view of the trail.

She turned off the trail to take her past the small grove of aspens and to the bridge that crossed the San Joaquin. Heather had said that she didn't want anything to do with the long trips, but Daisy was so relieved that she wasn't headed down the crowded trail to Rainbow Falls for the umpteenth time this summer.

At the bridge, Butterscotch's hooves echoed against the thick wood. Suddenly the lead rope turned hot as it pulled quickly under her hand. She yelped in surprise and barely caught the end before she lost it. Heart hammering, she looked back to see Dumbo with his neck outstretched and hooves rooted to the dirt of the trail.

"C'mon mule!" Daisy dallied the lead around the horn like Jo had taught her and kicked Butterscotch, holding tightly to her rope as she pulled Dumbo. He didn't budge. "You've got to be kidding me! You've been across this bridge before. Why are you messing with me?"

What to do. What to do. Maybe if he watched the other mules crossing in front of him, he would follow their lead. She carefully dismounted, tied her mount to the bridge and figured out how to rearrange the mules with Dumbo at the end. Goldie kicked at Dumbo, making Daisy question herself. She tied Dumbo to a tree. Maybe if she took the other animals across the bridge, Dumbo would want to follow to stay with the herd. No luck. As she led the mule to the bridge, he rooted himself once again.

Daisy felt like she was going to throw up. If this took much longer, Jo was going to catch up to her and see that she was incompetent. She couldn't let that happen. She brought all the animals back over the bridge and strung them in the order Pete had. She mounted Butterscotch and sat by the bridge. She looked at Dumbo. She looked at the bridge. She looked at the river. Hadn't Jo said the river had a crossing downstream from the bridge? She pointed Butterscotch back the way they came and looked for a trail leading to the river. She found a break in the trees.

Maybe? Her heart rate increased. Should she risk it? Or should she wait for Jo? No. She did not want Jo to see that she had failed to do something as simple as cross the stupid bridge. She gave Butterscotch an enthusiastic kick and pointed her toward the river. The mule balked at the edge, but Daisy leaned back and kicked again. She looped Dumbo's lead around the horn. If she dropped the lead in the river, she would be so screwed.

Butterscotch eased into the river. It was so loud, and the water seemed to be going so fast. She gulped. The river was about as wide as six mules lined up tail to muzzle. Not that far. She looked back to see Dumbo walk into the river.

"Look, dad! There are mules in the river!"

Above on the bridge, she now had the audience of a father and son. *This better be a river crossing*, she told herself. Ladybird followed Dumbo. She held her breath waiting to see if Goldie would make it. Now in the middle of the river, Daisy could feel Butterscotch bracing against the flow of the river with every step. She tripped, and Daisy's foot submerged in icy snowmelt. She held tight to the bridle and sat as still as possible as the mule scrambled to regain her footing. Behind her, Goldie leapt into the river.

"This is so exciting!" the boy above called.

With all of them now in the river, Daisy urged Butterscotch forward, hauling the mules, those stupid mules! She assessed the riverbank on the other side for the least steep place to exit. She gripped the saddle horn and prayed that she'd picked a good place. Butterscotch lurched out of the water and bounded up the hill. Daisy was sure it didn't look pretty, but she stayed on! Behind her, Dumbo! Ladybird! Then Goldie, her pack lurching dangerously to one side, followed her up the hill.

The hiker and his son clapped from the bridge and continued on.

With shaky legs, Daisy dismounted. She tied her mount and ran back to Goldie. Standing on the right side of the mule, she grabbed hold of the ropes holding the pack and lifted her feet as she'd once seen Jo do. Hanging from the bag, she added her full weight to one side of the load, pulling it back to center. Not trusting the pack to stay balanced, she grabbed a rock and shoved it in the bag, hoping the few pounds would keep it rocking evenly.

Her mouth dry with panic, she mounted again and gave a big kick to get Butterscotch moving. She had to get going if she had any hope of staying ahead of Jo and her string. Her stomach hurt. She looked behind them. One, two, three sets of ears; one, two, three packs rocking gently back and forth. They'd made it. They were on their way, and they were fine. Her stomach started to unclench. She thought of the view from the bridge. It must have been something to see them in the water and then bursting out the other side. And she'd done it! Herself! "We did it, girls!" she crowed. "I am such a cowgirl!"

Finally relaxed, she enjoyed the scenery and the compliments she got from the hikers along the way. Her spirits rose along with the trail as it climbed the switchbacks carrying her and the mules up and out of the deep valley. Soon the trail leveled out, and she rode in and out of forest and open meadow with a gentle stream meandering though. She was thrilled to hear voices and found Takeisha and the guests stretching by a stand of trees.

"See? I knew they'd notice our oopsie," Takeisha said easily. She approached Daisy and the mules. "Boy am I glad to see you!" she said more quietly.

Daisy beamed. She'd done it, fixed her mistake of loading up the guests but not their lunches. She'd caught them before Jo had caught up to her. "You wouldn't believe what it took to get here!" She sat down to tell Takeisha about Dumbo and the bridge. She was relaxed, in her element, believing her day could only get better from there.

CHAPTER THIRTY

"Come over here and help me, would you? You're supposed to be assistant packer, you know?" Jo ribbed Daisy who stood facing the lake below the Minarets.

"How can you work?" she said.

"Camp won't set itself up," Jo said, loosening the knot of the first pack.

Daisy jogged over, Jo thought to get to work, but instead she threw her arms around Jo. "Stop. Everything will get done, but for one minute before Takeisha gets here with the guests, I want to pretend that it's just you and me here in this amazing place."

Jo allowed Daisy to pull her away from Blaze and her pack, doing her best to repress a smile. Daisy stopped at the water's edge. Across an expanse of crystal blue water stood the massive jagged rock face that made up the Minarets.

Daisy threw her arms wide. "I have never seen anything like this. Doesn't it make you feel small but at the same time so…I don't know…" She turned to Jo. "Full."

Jo struggled to remain composed in the face of such excitement. She wrapped an arm around Daisy's shoulders and suddenly found Daisy burrowed in her arms.

"I feel so thankful to be here with you. You brought me here. In so many ways."

The sky was reflected in her eyes bringing out the blue, and Jo allowed herself that moment appreciating the High Sierras through those wondrous eyes. She scanned the trail and, finding it empty, placed a kiss on Daisy's lips. "Now are you ready?"

Daisy turned toward the mountain range once more. She closed her eyes and took a deep breath. Cody barked. "Okay, okay!" she laughed. "I'm ready."

She had observed Jo at work enough to know to take the tarp and spread it away from the mules so they could stack the tents, duffels, and sleeping bags on it. She carried chairs to the fire pit and placed the tables and kitchen boxes closer to the trees. She wound lash ropes, tied them off and hung them from a branch. "You do the picket, and I'll set up the privy?"

"You don't mind?"

"I'm pretty handy with a shovel, and I know how to string up the tarp on the lash rope for privacy."

"Whoever finishes first comes to help the other?" Jo asked.

"Deal."

"The privy needs to be on the other side of the picket. Why don't you grab your string, and we'll walk over?"

"Where does the stream come in? I'll grab some water while you get the first picket up."

Jo explained where she got water and where she found wood, and they spent the rest of the day in complete synchrony, checking off the camp chores well before sunset. Between dinner and dessert, Jo signaled to Daisy that it was time to turn out the stock. She grabbed the bell for their mare, and when she untied her from the picket and hopped aboard, Daisy started to release the animals from the picket. They fell into line behind her, and she was pleased to see Daisy hop onto the back of the shortest dude horse to bring up the rear.

She led them away from the lake to a lush mountain meadow where she dismounted and slipped the halter from the mare. She let it drop from her hands and took the halter Daisy held, so she could wrap her arms around her. The sharp intake of breath betrayed Daisy's surprise.

"I don't want you to feel like you always have to be the hugger."

Daisy softened in her arms. "I like that."

Jo kissed her softly and turned her around, molding her front to Daisy's back. "How do you like the view now?"

"I didn't think it could get any better but look at that! That's what they mean in the song when they say 'purple mountain majesties,' isn't it?"

Jo's heart swelled. She knew Daisy thought that she worked too hard to notice their gorgeous surroundings, but she was quite attuned and had timed turning out the stock to coincide with the late evening sun lighting up the Minarets. "Absolutely."

"Thank you for showing me."

"Thank you for doing so much to set up camp," she said. Though they needed to get back for dessert, Jo took one more moment with Daisy, hooking her chin over her shoulder and enjoying the sunset.

Daisy turned in her arm. "Just doin' my job."

"That plus half. You're amazing."

"I learned from the best." Daisy leaned in and kissed Jo, teasing her lips apart.

Their day was not yet over, but Jo couldn't help but accept and reciprocate the sweet kiss Daisy offered.

"When's bedtime?" Daisy whispered when she broke away.

"Not soon enough," Jo responded. She leaned over and picked up the halters, looping the lead ropes and slinging them over her shoulder.

Jo always liked the first day of a trip when the guests were so exhausted they disappeared from the fire pit immediately after dessert. Daisy gathered empty mugs and took them to the washbasin.

"Sit! You already did the dinner dishes. I'll get those," Takeisha said.

"You sure?" Daisy asked.

"I got 'em." Takeisha stood stiffly. "Amazing how sore I am after not riding every day!"

"We were in the saddle a lot of hours," Daisy said. "I feel it, too. I'm going to go brush and turn in."

"I'll be over in a few," Jo said.

"Goodnight," Takeisha called, turning her attention to the washbasin.

"You want to keep Cody tonight?"

"Of course. It's not fair for you to have Daisy and Cody." Takeisha smiled at Jo. "She's amazing, isn't she? Or is she knocking herself out to impress me?"

"She's a helluva hard worker, that's for sure."

"You should marry that girl."

Jo froze. What was she supposed to say to a statement like that? "We've only…"

"Relax! I'm just saying I like her, and I like who you are with her. You were talking to the guests tonight! It's nice. Here you thought she was going to be a useless disaster at the beginning of the season, remember? And she turned out to be way more kick-ass than that. Man, that bridge thing? I for one would have given up on the mules and waited for you to sort them out, but she didn't."

"What bridge thing?"

"Oh, my bad. I thought she would have told you about it. Guess the two of you don't have a whole lot of time for talking?" She gave Jo a coy smile.

"She didn't mention it. What happened with the mules?"

"Dumbo wouldn't cross the bridge?" Takeisha seemed uncertain about sharing Daisy's story.

"What do you mean Dumbo wouldn't cross the bridge."

"She said he planted his feet and no matter what she tried, he refused to cross."

Jo was stumped. The mule had crossed the bridge without complaint more times than she could count. "So how did she get across?"

"She used the river crossing."

Jo must not have heard her correctly. Only a daggum fool would take a string of mules clear across the San Joaquin. Her whole body felt as cold as if she'd been dunked in the water.

"Jo? Are you okay?"

She nodded numbly. "Thanks for telling me. You need anything else tonight?"

"Just Cody. You sure you're okay?"

"I'm beat. The altitude, you know?"

"You're not upset about the marriage comment, are you? I don't want for you to be offended."

"I'm not. We're good. See you in the morning."

It's a normal evening, Jo told herself walking over to the picket line where she'd set up her bedroll. Only it wasn't because there sat Daisy, holding a flashlight and jotting in a notebook resting on her lap. So many emotions coursed through her that she couldn't even put one name to how she was feeling. She grabbed her toiletries and continued to the privy to prepare for bed.

She couldn't get into bed before she sorted herself out, and the time it took to brush her teeth and use the toilet wasn't nearly enough. When she was finished, she walked back to Daisy. "Bears are bad up here. I'm going to put the toothpaste back at the kitchen since we don't have Cody."

"Okay!" Daisy said brightly.

Jo walked back over to camp, making a bunch of noise so Takeisha would hear her coming. She was standing by the kitchen brushing her teeth.

"Forget something?" she asked with a mouth full of toothpaste.

"Toothpaste." She lifted a tarp and tucked it into one of the boxes. Cody thumped his tail, so she squatted to pat him. She could feel Takeisha watching, her mouthful of toothbrush keeping her from pelting her with questions. "Night you two," she said before Takeisha finished.

For once in her life, she wished one of the guests had lingered at the fire to give her an excuse to stay at the fire a little longer.

"Flashlight on or off?" Daisy asked after Jo had shed her boots next to the bedroll.

"Off is good." In the darkness, she undressed, folding her clothes neatly and tucking them under the canvas. As she lowered herself onto the foam mattress, Daisy scooted close and enfolded her in a warm embrace. Jo sighed, appreciating that comfort and trying to keep her mind on that instead of letting it keep spinning on the image of Daisy hauling three mules across the San Joaquin. Though she was right there, safe and sound next to her, Jo vividly imagined a different scenario where water tipped over the edge of a pannier. It wouldn't take long for the water to weigh Dumbo down. The river would be flowing too fast to double back and cut Ladybird free.

"You're quiet tonight." Daisy peppered Jo's neck with kisses.

"I wore myself out trying to keep up with you."

The kisses stopped.

"It feels so good to stop moving. Would it be okay if I'm not up for more?"

Daisy lifted Jo's arm and nestled in tighter. "Of course."

Jo put her other arm under her head and stared out at the stars, trying to locate constellations. She would not let her brain feed her the image of the mules being pulled into the current, scrambling, desperately trying to regain their footing. She squeezed her eyes shut tight trying to find something else to think about. Maybe she should kiss Daisy, run her hands across her skin to see if indulging in physical pleasure would shut down the mental unrest.

Too late. Her mind was already projecting the image of a panicked Daisy struggling to hold the mules. If she didn't let go of Dumbo's lead rope, he would pull Butterscotch in as well. She would have had only seconds to decide whether to hold on or let go. Why hadn't she waited for Jo to help her? Her thoughts made her stomach churn. She turned to her side, and Daisy turned with her.

Daisy spooned Jo and sighed. "Funny how once you stop, you do feel how exhausted you are."

Within minutes, her breath became deep and rhythmic and her arm relaxed in sleep. Jo envied the ignorance that allowed Daisy to drift off so easily. She was awake deep into the night.

* * *

"Guess you were tired," Jo said the next morning when Daisy joined her at the picket, rubbing the sleep out of her eyes.

"Why didn't you wake me up?"

Why hadn't she? As the sun came up, Jo had watched Daisy's features, waiting for the light to bring her to awareness. It was a test of sorts. Was she relying on Jo to wake up and start the day, or was she in tune with what the job demanded? She had easily slept through Jo dressing, even when she rustled around in her duffel for a sweatshirt.

"Mouse came in early for her grain." Jo had already haltered all the horses. Daisy secured a few of the mules. The silence wasn't comfortable.

"I didn't even hear the bell."

Jo shrugged. "You could see how Takeisha's doing with breakfast. I haven't been down to the kitchen yet."

She'd grabbed a brush and was already at work whisking it over the saddle area of the riding stock. Now wasn't the time to talk. They would need to, but Jo still hadn't figured out how to say what she needed to say. The more she'd thought last night, the angrier she'd become with Daisy's decision. She knew better than to talk when she was angry. Daisy surprised her by walking toward her instead of going to the kitchen.

"Good morning." She placed a light kiss on Jo's lips, smiled, and then left Jo alone with her thoughts.

Jo kept her thoughts on a tight rein, paying close attention to the fit of each saddle. She took the time to adjust cinches on the horses that had dropped weight over the course of the summer, pulling the rings of the latigo closer together than they needed to be. She rotated the thick newer pads to a few of the horses who were getting rubbed raw by their saddles.

Only when she was certain breakfast would be ready did she head over to the kitchen for her first cup of coffee. She greeted Cody and grabbed one of the blue enamel mugs, filling it from the kettle hanging on the arm she'd designed.

She blew on it and took a sip. Perfection. "Does anything beat a good cup of coffee?"

"Everyone's been raving about it," said Takeisha. "I'll have to ask Daisy what her trick is."

Jo nodded to show she'd heard. She was sure Daisy had said something about it when they were at Second Crossing.

"Tell me when you're ready for food because the eggs are something else too. She said Wendy puts a little powdered sugar in them. I was skeptical, but all the plates are coming back clean."

"She already ate?" Jo asked.

"Like me, she snacked and tested while we cooked. She said she wasn't hungry enough for a plate."

Jo didn't see Daisy by the guest fire. "Thanks for finding stuff for her to do over here."

"I was pretty surprised you sent her over. I sure thought she'd be helping you with the stock. Not that I'm complaining! Like I said yesterday, she's amazing. I didn't even have to ask her if she'd grab water for dishes. I hadn't even thought it, and she was already gone with the bucket."

In the crisp morning air, the coffee cooled quickly. Jo downed half the cup and grabbed a plate from the table.

"Some of everything?" Takeisha lifted the lid from the skillet. When Jo nodded, she heaped eggs, bacon, and French toast onto the plate.

"Thanks," Jo said. "Could you hit me with more coffee, too?"

Any other trip, she would have sat on a cooler and eaten her breakfast in peace while Takeisha made lunches, but she wasn't ready to talk to Daisy. With her due to return with water any second, Jo took her plate and settled in at the guest fire and steeled herself for the chitchat that would sap her dry.

The end of the day found her back at the fire, poking the remaining logs apart to ensure no sparks would find their way out of the circle during the night. She stayed there facing the lake, the moon's light dancing on the water.

Takeisha walked over from the kitchen when she was finished bear-proofing the kitchen. "You should be in bed."

She'd been telling herself the same thing.

"Are you mad at Daisy?"

Jo crossed her arms over her chest. "Mad isn't the right word."

"She knows, and she's hurt that something's bothering you and you won't talk to her about it."

"She told you that?"

"Not in so many words. But she asked if I knew what was up with you. I said I thought it was something I said before you went off to bed last night. Wouldn't it be better to get it off your chest than lugging it around the whole trip?"

"I can't stop thinking about Eddie."

Takeisha didn't say anything for a few minutes. "He left midseason, didn't he?"

"After he lost his string up at Thousand Island."

"Oh. This is about Daisy crossing the river."

"Yup."

Takeisha pulled air through her teeth. "You have to talk to her. She deserves to know why you pulled away all of a sudden."

Jo rubbed her hands over her face and kept her palms pressed to her cheeks for a moment. Then she dropped her hands to her sides. "You're right."

"Good luck." Takeisha squeezed her shoulder and returned to the kitchen. Jo patted Cody goodnight and sent him after Takeisha before picking her way back to her bedroll.

Following the light of Daisy's lantern, Jo felt a pang of guilt when she was met by a tired smile. Without undressing she lowered herself to the edge of the bed, her arms wrapped around her legs. "I should have told you what was on my mind last night. I thought I could sleep it off, but…" Her throat was tight and she paused to swallow.

Daisy sat up and ran her hand in a gentle circle on Jo's back.

"A few years ago, a packer named Eddie had a string of mules up at Thousand Island. Have you been up there this summer?" She turned to look at Daisy who shook her head.

"We drop people at The Pond, a pool that's cut off by one of the bigger islands. I learned from Sol to go down to the bridge and then back up the peninsula. It takes a while, but he never trusted the sandbar that cuts right across from the main trail to the camp. It cut nearly an hour off the ride, though, so Eddie always did it. His last trip, one of the mules slid off the sandbar. Tripped or something, and the bags filled with water. Eddie jumped off his horse and managed to cut his second mule clear of the first, but the last one had already pulled the second one off balance. He got them cut apart and tried his best to cut the loads off the animals, so they could get up. Get out. But the loads were so heavy, and the mules were too terrified to let him close. Both of them drowned."

"That's awful," Daisy said. She scooted closer to Jo and tucked her arms under Jo's to pull her close.

"Last night when Takeisha told me about you crossing the San Joaquin… I couldn't get those mules Eddie lost out of my mind. He couldn't, either. Left that night, and nobody ever heard from him again."

"That is so sad." Daisy held her tight. "And so scary."

The longer Daisy held Jo, the more she softened. Eventually, she rested her head against Daisy's shoulder. Takeisha was right. She felt better for having talked. Now Daisy understood how dangerous her stunt had been.

She didn't stop Daisy when her fingers found and unfastened the buttons on her shirt. As Jo shed her boots and jeans, Daisy pulled off the long T-shirt she wore to bed, and when her warm, sure hands pulled Jo into the bed next to her, river crossings were swept from her mind. By the light of the moon, she covered Jo with kisses of apology. They still ignited a fire between her legs, but it was not the quick flash of a blaze started with lighter fluid. Daisy built it as carefully as a one-match fire from scratch. The brush of her hair tinder for the match she struck with her delicate fingers. The heat intensified until Jo was ready for Daisy to add the full weight of her body.

When she did finally give her whole body to Jo, expertly stoking the fire with her mouth, her breath, Jo's body approached climax in a wholly new way. Before, she chased the rush of pleasure, out of breath and completely spent by the time she climaxed. This time, Daisy lovingly coaxed her body until she gently tipped into ecstasy.

When the waves of pleasure ceased, Jo did her best to offer the same to Daisy, wordlessly communicating how grateful she was that Daisy was safe in her arms.

CHAPTER THIRTY-ONE

Daisy awoke the next morning to Jo's hands gliding over her soft curves. Already enjoying the warmth of Jo's athletic body pressed against her back and thighs, Daisy felt a deeper ardor taking hold. Jo's arm stretched up, nestling between her breasts. Her nipples tightened in memory of how thoroughly Jo had worshipped her body the night before. As her fingers touched Daisy's chin, Jo leaned over her shoulder. Daisy stretched to accept the day's first kiss.

"It's still dark," Daisy whispered when Jo sat up and pulled on her jeans.

"Travel day," Jo explained. "And if we catch up the stock now, you'll see the sunrise on the Minarets. You don't want to miss it."

Like she had yesterday, Daisy thought. She would much rather wake up and get dressed in the soft darkness of pre-dawn than wake to an empty bedroll. She shivered as she pulled on clean but cold undies and jeans. Jo pulled on only a sweatshirt, but Daisy wore three layers to ward off the chill that came with the hour and the altitude. And the season? She looked forward to a time when she could read the morning temperature and recognize the shift from the peak of summer to the fade toward fall.

She carefully followed Jo, impressed with her ability to navigate the unfamiliar terrain. Within minutes, she heard the gentle clang of Mouse's bell. As they approached the meadow, Jo handed the mare's halter to Daisy. "You want to be the Pied Piper this morning?"

"Absolutely!"

Mouse raised her head on their approach and walked toward them eager to enjoy a few mouthfuls of grain from Jo's sack. Once she'd secured the halter, Daisy accepted a leg up from Jo. The other animals jostled around them, trying to get a bite of grain, but Jo held them off for a moment, resting her hand on Daisy's thigh. The intimate squeeze before she haltered one of the other dude horses went straight to her heart.

Like a drum major leading a band, she guided all the stock back to camp. Once they'd secured them to the picket, the first hint of blue touched the sky. "I'll brush down the stock," Jo said. "You can see the sunrise from the kitchen if you don't mind helping Takeisha for a bit."

"I wish we could see it together."

"We should be able to pull that off tomorrow at Emily. We'll be able to see Banner Peak from the picket."

Daisy kissed Jo lightly. "I look forward to it!"

Takeisha was still in her sleeping bag when Daisy got to the kitchen. Daisy mounded the coals from the previous night's fire and added kindling, smiling privately as she remembered Jo holding her and describing the fire Daisy had built within her. This morning, Daisy cheated, spraying lighter fluid on the teepee of branches she'd built. One match and the fire whooshed to life. She instantly saw the difference, how this fire burned hot and fast where one built with careful tending built more slowly. Was that the difference between sex and making love?

An elongated "Whyyyyyyy?" came from inside Takeisha's sleeping bag interrupting her musings.

"Jo said it's a travel day. I'm going for water."

She grabbed the bucket and gazed up at the Minarets. Sunlight graced their very tips, lighting them like icing. Her trip to the spring took her away from the view, and when she came back, light had drizzled down the mountain. She set down the bucket before she returned to camp. This was her moment alone. She savored it knowing how hard she had worked to get there.

"Someone's in a good mood." Takeisha had rolled up her bed and was slicing cantaloupe for the early risers. "I take it Jo talked to you?"

"She did. What a relief. Did you know about that packer?"

"Only when she reminded me."

"Such a terrible story." Daisy pulled the slushy orange juice from the cooler and mixed it. "Would you have gone through the river?"

"It wouldn't have occurred to me," Takeisha said.

Daisy thought about that. What had given her the idea in the first place? "Heather and Pete and I asked about it earlier this summer." She searched the memory for more details. All she could remember was Jo saying in her usual curt manner that she used the bridge.

"Now you've got a story for them."

"I'll have so many stories from this trip. Two days in, and I already have so many."

"Like getting laid in the mountains."

"Hey!" Daisy blushed hard.

"Thanks for confirming that for me."

"Like how gorgeous the sunrise was. It was worth getting up early."

They turned their attention to breakfast, and when Jo came down, they shared the briefest of glances, which would hold Daisy over until they were alone again. She vowed to be professional and also careful, not that an occasion like Dumbo refusing to cross the bridge was likely to come up again. She loved being on a trip with Takeisha and Jo, loved being able to help out with both the cooking and the stock. The rest of the trip passed with the three of them working in perfect harmony.

* * *

"Hey, stranger!" Heather hollered, jumping up from the dinner table back at the Lodge. "How was the trip?"

"Not long enough," Daisy said.

"You always say that."

"It's always true! I don't know how I'm going to be able to return to civilization when the season ends."

"Come sit next to me. You haven't had dinner, have you? You're not going up the hill, are you? We have so much to talk about!"

The other employees shifted on the bench, making a spot for Daisy. "Pour me some of that juice, would you?" she asked Pete.

"Sure thing." He reached for the pitcher and a clean cup.

"You must be hungry," Heather said.

Daisy happily accepted the juice, gulping down almost all of it. "More thirsty than hungry. What's new around here?"

Pete had a funny story about coming home from a spot trip to Noname Lake. "Before I set my horse to autopilot on the way home, I checked the mules to make sure all the bags were hanging fine and everything. One, two, three, four, five sets of ears swaying."

Though she'd only had three sets of ears to count, Daisy knew exactly what he was describing.

"So I get down to the main trail and glance back again. "One, two, three. That's it! I'm missing two mules."

Everyone laughed as he continued to explain how he tied the three, hoping they would stay put, and galloped back to find the last two still tied together and grazing in a small meadow.

When he finished his story, Daisy said, "That day we went out, I had to cross the river with my three."

"Why?" Heather asked.

"Dumbo refused to cross the bridge!" Takeisha and Jo entered the café and grabbed seats across from Daisy.

Daisy dramatically explained how Dumbo nearly pulled her out of the saddle when he planted himself in the dirt before the bridge. "First I tried moving him to the end of the string. Goldie's so much bigger, I thought she could pull him, but she wouldn't stop kicking at him…"

Jo had been reaching for the mashed potatoes and paused. Daisy couldn't remember if Jo had heard all the things she tried before going through the water, so she described how she thought peer pressure might help get the mule across.

"Then I remembered Jo telling us that there was a river crossing. A hiker and his son watched the whole thing." Leaning back from the table the same way she'd leaned in the saddle, she continued, "The mules had to slide on their haunches down to the river. In the water, Butterscotch tripped, and my feet got soaked! The water was so cold!" Something had shifted in Jo's demeanor, and she almost cut her story short.

But Heather nudged her. "And the pack mules crossed fine?"

"They went right through, but one of the packs started tipping over. I had to get off and pull it back to center and find a rock to make it balance again." The look on Jo's face made Daisy feel like she'd swallowed a rock.

"That's amazing," Heather said.

"You're a real cowgirl now," Pete agreed.

Their praise made Daisy smile, and she sat up tall and proud. She felt what she had tried to describe to Jo when they had stood at the base of the Minarets.

Jo exploded. "It wasn't flippin' amazing! It was completely unwarranted and dangerous to boot. The last thing this outfit needs is a bunch of empty-headed fools encouraging that kind of stupidity, and with a full string of livestock!"

The once boisterous table went silent.

Daisy wanted to disappear.

"Can any of you imagine what would have happened if the river had been a half-inch higher? That would have been three mules downriver faster than you could blink. And then what do you do? Do either of you jackasses know how to decide whether to hold 'em or let 'em go?"

Someone down the table whispered, "Damn, I've never heard that many words come out of her mouth at once."

"She's got a bunch when she's really pissed," Heather answered quietly.

Daisy's ears burned and her head spun. "But they didn't," she said very quietly.

"No because you got lucky. We talked about how dangerous that stunt was and how much it could have cost me. It's irresponsible for you to sell it like some kind of heroic maneuver."

"I get it," Daisy said.

"Do you? I'm not talking about a float breaking down during the Rose Parade where you get a tow and fix it up for the next year. One wrong move…"

"And mules die. I know, you told me." Sweat moistened her back, and she knew her face burned.

"Why are we talking about mules dying?" Leo strode toward the table, his hat in one hand and the other patting down his thinning hair.

"Daisy's boasting about crossing the San Joaquin instead of using the bridge."

"There's no water crossing there." Leo turned to Daisy. "Why would you do that?"

Leo's question magnified tenfold the helplessness Daisy had experienced when she didn't want Jo to find her stuck at the bridge. She had not wanted Jo to see her incompetence. Now everyone did. She knew it in the way they looked away.

Daisy didn't want to speak, but she knew she had to and that she must not let her voice quaver. Searching for the confidence she'd felt on the other side of the river, she explained the predicament she'd faced at the bridge, including the part about hearing there was once a water crossing there.

"Rivers change year to year. Earlier in the season or after a winter with more snow melt, those mules would have been dead for sure. Good experienced mule like that is worth at least five grand. Crossing a river the size of the San Joaquin is a real gamble," Leo said.

Daisy had been riding a mule as well. She had made the equivalent of a twenty-thousand-dollar wager when she'd urged her mount into the water. She felt ill.

"Better to leave a choice like that to the experienced staff. We clear on that?"

Daisy nodded, not trusting her voice.

"Next trip out is smaller anyway. I'm sure the day-ride crew could use you here." Without another look her way, Leo tucked his hat under his chair, sat and poured himself a glass of juice. Others at the table started passing dishes to him, so he could load his plate.

Daisy didn't know how she could eat. Something had broken inside of her. "I'm not hungry," she said to Heather. "I'll catch up with you…" she almost said at feeding time, but she already knew there was no way in hell she'd be feeding with the crew tonight. Tears threatened, but she glued her tongue to the roof of her mouth. She would not get emotional. She would not cry.

"Are you okay?" Heather asked. She was the only one Daisy could look at.

"Fine," she lied. "See you."

She walked past Jo and Takeisha, and neither of them reached out for her. Had she really expected them to? It wasn't Takeisha's place, but Jo? Well, it was clear to Daisy now that what mattered the most in the world to Jo were her precious mules. Here she had been stupid enough to hear Jo's story about Eddie and think that she'd been concerned about her. Stupid. She'd been angry about how Daisy had taken the mules through the river.

At the end of the pack dock sat her lone bag. Jo had said she had two more trips. Fat chance Leo would agree to sending Daisy out with her again. She tried to imagine spending the last weeks of the summer in the yard while Jo was away. For that matter, she tried to imagine looking at anyone after what had been said at the dinner table. Jo had said Eddie up and disappeared after his mules had died. Daisy understood. She imagined being back on day rides. Without a taste of the backcountry, she might have been content with what she'd learned, but being back when Jo was away? She'd be seeing her mistake mirrored in her coworkers' eyes every single day. All the work she'd invested be damned. She couldn't do it.

Shouldering her bag, she strode to her cabin and grabbed her car keys. How long had it been since she'd driven her car? She clicked the doors open with the remote and threw in her filthy duffel. The rest of her things, the sheets and blankets on her mattress, her clothes, she grabbed by the fistful and chucked in on top of the duffel.

Her hands shook, and soon all her things were in the car. She was going to miss the sparse wooden cabin. A few tears tumbled down her cheeks. She swiped them away angrily. There was no time for tears. No time to say goodbye to Churchill or Butterscotch. No time to say goodbye to Cody. Takeisha. She wouldn't even allow herself to consider seeing Jo again before she left. What she had said had shattered her and still hurt so badly.

She had to get out of there. She sagged into the driver's seat remembering how Heather had teased her for driving a foreign-made two-door sporty car. Once dust covered it, she and the others had moved on. Dirt had hidden the stupid city girl but was easily wiped away. She engaged the wipers and watched the trees emerge through the windshield as she sprayed the glass.

Knocking at the passenger-side window scared a yelp out of her. She used the button on her door to roll it down.

"What gives?" Heather said.

"I have to go."

"That was pretty shitty of Jo to call you out like that in front of everyone."

"I can't look at her right now."

"I get that. But it'll blow over."

"I don't think so," Daisy said.

Heather frowned. "You're going to town?"

She'd be going much further than that, but she wasn't going to tell Heather. She opened the glovebox and pulled out an old receipt. She jotted down her number. "Stay in touch, okay?"

As the window hummed back up, Daisy turned away from the confusion on Heather's face. She threw the car in reverse and inched onto the dirt wagon road. This she followed slowly to the paved road where she floored it, happy that the first stretch out of the pack station was a straight shot. She'd have to slow down for the curves, but that would be after she was long out of sight.

As the pack station disappeared from view, she rolled down the window and held up her middle finger. Satisfied she'd made her point, she clicked on her stereo. For an instant, she heard Jo criticizing the bouncy pop tune that poured from the speakers. No more worrying about what she thinks, she reminded herself. She cranked up the music in an attempt to drown out the realization that Jo had succeeded in chasing her from the backcountry. For the first time in her life, she'd thought she'd found a calling. Every mile she drove, it became harder and harder to hear.

* * *

Daisy felt trapped. Once again she was bunking with her parents and dodging the questions from them about what she was going to do with the rest of her life. She traded her cowgirl outfit for the slacks and tees that were her uniform at Temptation.

Every morning, a new cowboy coffee joke on the chalkboard listing the specials greeted her. She walked inside, away from the trees and birds and sunshine into the air-conditioned shop. No longer accustomed to the small space behind the counter, she could feel herself pinning back imaginary ears to send an angry message to her colleagues when they bumped her. She envisioned kicking them to re-establish her place in the pecking order. She even got mad at her own body when she held up cups to measure syrups or steam coffee milk and caught sight of the persistent farmer tan.

She might have been able to reset to her life if she didn't walk down Colorado Boulevard every morning on her way to Temptation. It was impossible to forget how Jo had looked leading her string in the Rose Parade. That look in her eyes. Now when Daisy looked at the San Gabriel mountains, she couldn't stop comparing them to the massive stretch of the Minarets.

Worst was the music that her colleagues played. When she had shared the story of working with the woman she'd seen in the parade, she'd used Jo's full name to avoid confusion that might have come with the masculine nickname. Someone on staff thought it was funny that Brandi Carlile had a song titled "Josephine" and made sure it played at least once during Daisy's shift, unaware of the effect the song had on her.

The melody haunted Daisy and the lyrics propelled her to the nights she'd memorized Jo's body by the light of the moon. She could not help but remember how blessed she felt when the sun graced them with another day together. Every time the ballad came on, Daisy's wound opened fresh to uncover the twin humiliation of her early-summer ignorance and late-summer irresponsibility. The way Jo had talked to her that day in the café absolutely made her wonder how she'd ever loved Jo.

But she had loved Jo. It was easy to pluck out the best parts of the summer: Jo's sly peek over the first cup of perfect coffee Daisy had made, the first time that she thought maybe Jo liked her. When Jo had picked out a mule for her to ride, it had felt like Jo accepted her. Then when she'd given Daisy that look of pride when they cleared the trail to Pond Lily together, she'd felt like Jo valued her. She had loved being seen by Jo. When Jo had given herself to Daisy, she'd felt such a rush of power. In bed they were equals.

In the backcountry, she would never be Jo's equal. It didn't matter how adept she became, Jo would always see her as needing to be taught. That hurt, and the pain didn't fade. Not after the weekend where she thought about Jo heading out on another trip. Not after a week when she had to have been out and come back in again. She told herself she didn't need to date someone whose approval she desired.

The Dixie Chicks' "Wide Open Spaces" came on—music right in tune with her life. Daisy closed her eyes and thought of all her big mistakes. Was abandoning the Lodge one of them? Leaving Pasadena to strike out on her own had felt glorious. Now back again, standing in the fan of the air-conditioning, she longed for the breeze that lifted off the surface of a moonlit Lake Minaret.

CHAPTER THIRTY-TWO

Jo glanced at the dude corral again, though she could tell by how quietly the feeding was going that Daisy still hadn't shown up. She'd been upset when she left, and Jo thought it best to give her time to lick her wounds before she tried to talk to her again.

Daisy had never missed a feeding.

Jo rolled another bale of hay into the feeding trough. She cut the twine and willed Daisy to leave her cabin. Something seemed different, but Jo wasn't going to look again. She would do her work. Daisy knew where to find her when she was ready to talk.

Dozer had his mules in the backcountry, so it took her no time at all to spread the hay. She returned her hay hook and reluctantly walked up toward Daisy's cabin. Pete, Heather, and Takeisha sat on hay bales next to the corral, all staring at her. She should have walked around the other side of the dude corral and straight to her cabin, but it was too late. Besides, she didn't want more of the evening to pass without being next to Daisy.

These were the hours she savored most when the work was finished, and she and Daisy had time for each other.

A few steps away from the cabin, she realized what was missing.

She stopped. Swallowed. Turned toward the crew. "Where's Daisy's car?"

Pete looked away. Heather looked at Takeisha. Takeisha frowned before she stood, inclining her head toward Jo's cabin.

Jo did not want to follow. She didn't want to hear what Takeisha had to say. But she wasn't going to stand there being gawked at.

They walked in silence, Cody at her heels. Maybe Daisy had gone to town to do laundry her hopeful self offered. Reason asked why she hadn't taken Heather along.

In front of her cabin, Jo stopped. Takeisha surprised her by opening the door and motioning Jo inside. "You probably want to sit."

Jo stood. "Just tell me."

"Daisy left."

Jo clenched her jaws together so tightly she thought her teeth might pop. She reached for her keys that hung on a nail by the door.

"Heather said she cleared out her stuff. She's not stopping in Mammoth. She went home." Takeisha shrugged apologetically.

Jo's hand returned to her side. She felt like she'd been kicked by a mule double barrel in the stomach. She sat and stroked dust from Cody's coat. "Daggummit…"

"Do you want company?" Takeisha asked.

Only Daisy's. And she'd left? Jo had seen that she was upset, but Daisy had weathered what had seemed like so much more over the course of the summer that Jo was having trouble making sense of her departure. She wanted to talk to Daisy. She wanted to explain that she hadn't meant for Daisy to leave. The details Daisy had shared at the table had shaken her badly, and she'd planned on talking to her about it, but not at the table. Now she had no way do that. She didn't even have her phone number. She hung her head. "Do you know her phone number?"

"She gave it to Heather on her way out."

"You're going to make me talk to Heather, aren't you?"

"I'm not making you do anything."

"Maybe she'll come back. After everything that happened this summer…" She shut her eyes so she wouldn't look at her bedroll. How could Daisy have left after all the nights they had held each other?

It hurt like hell to think that Daisy could walk away from what they'd shared, without a second thought. Surely she'd get lonely on the long two-lane highway and realize her mistake. Jo went to sleep confident that Daisy would be back in the morning.

But she wasn't.

Jo sat through breakfast thankful that nobody expected her to talk. She heard their thoughts loudly enough. Everyone blamed her. Leo frowned when Heather told him Daisy wouldn't be helping with the two-hour ride. He shook his head and mumbled, "Well now, that's too bad. I thought she had more grit than that. But not everyone is suited for the backcountry."

Jo thought she'd be able to push her disappointment aside on the next trip, but Takeisha pointed out a dozen things a day that had been easier with Daisy's help, even after Jo had reminded her that Leo wouldn't have sent the extra pair of hands on such a small trip.

"That's what she is now?" Takeisha had asked. "An extra pair of hands?"

"You know she's more than that," Jo said.

"Does she? Have you tried calling her?"

"She left, and she's stayed gone. I don't know how to fix that."

"Do you want to?" Takeisha asked.

"Of course I do."

"Yeah, I can tell." Her sarcasm stung like a wasp.

"You know what tomorrow is?" Takeisha asked, dropping into the camp chair next to Jo.

Jo did not like this game, knowing that Takeisha had something to share about Daisy. She could avoid it by going to bed as she had been the last two weeks, but her bedroll still smelled like Daisy and sex. She could change the sheets, but she didn't want that either. All she wanted was to have Daisy back next to her.

"Scrambled egg day. I hate cracking eggs in the morning. Did you know that's my least favorite thing to do? Daisy knew, and after she found out, she told me she'd be happy to crack them and she did. Man, I miss that girl."

They were on their way to Yosemite again, the last trip of the season. Jo knew how much Daisy would have loved to add Tuolumne Meadows to the list of destinations she had visited over the course of the summer. She and Takeisha both knew it was entirely Jo's fault Daisy wasn't there with them. Takeisha never let a chance go by where she could point out how something was easier or more fun with Daisy around.

"You remember how flighty Tuxedo was at the beginning of the season? You said he wasn't practical, but you still put a ton of work into him. You see how good he is now? The same goes for Daisy. She was as green as they come, but just like that mule of yours, she learned. You gave him plenty of time and encouragement, way more than you ever gave Daisy. Talk about a daggum fool!"

As if Jo needed a reminder. What Takeisha pointed out wasn't half as painful as the memories that were hers and Daisy's alone. Holding her as morning crept across the sky at Pond Lily. Kissing her as the horses clomped into their Second Crossing camp. Having her in the saddle shed. She was so much more than a pair of hands. If only she hadn't shared that story of the river crossing…

"We had already talked about how dangerous that river crossing was," Jo said, not for the first time. "And then she's sharing it like she hadn't put her neck on the line?"

"So you point out how you don't want anyone else to try such a dangerous move. You don't chew her out in front of all her friends. Have you even tried to apologize?"

"Heather gave me her number after the last trip."

"That doesn't answer my question."

"It always goes to voice mail, and she doesn't return my calls and stopped answering my texts."

"Bummer." They sat in silence staring at the fire. "You really fucked up."

"Why do you keep saying that?" Jo was frustrated. "I'm not the one who crossed the dang river and nearly killed the mules."

"Enough about the fucking mules, okay? Can you even hear yourself? You said that you told her about Eddie. Did that little chat include how she was an irresponsible idiot?"

"I didn't call her an idiot."

"Jo."

Jo put her elbows on her knees and rested her chin in her hands.

"All that girl ever did was try to earn your respect. Did you ever consider that? So put yourself in her position. If she stays stuck at the bridge and you ride up, she loses your respect."

"I would have helped her."

"And she would have felt like a failure. No matter which way you did it, she would have felt like she let you down. You always made that quite clear. You never gave her any safe place to be with you when she'd done something wrong. Or didn't meet your expectations. It was important to her that she show you she could handle herself out here, and what did she get? Her ass handed to her. In front of her friends."

"You already said that part."

"I don't know if you hear half the things I say. What did you say that night that made the two of you think you were square in such different ways?"

"I didn't know about the stuff she tried before she went through the river."

"So? Why does that matter?"

Jo did not want to say it again. It had been hard enough to say it on the message she'd left for Daisy. But Takeisha kept sitting there, the fire crackling in front of them. "I lost a mule once. When I was learning how to pack." She got up and fussed with the fire, using a long stick to rearrange the large chunks of wood. "There was a little mule who always drug on me like a sled. One of the old-timers told me to put him second in line, so the lead mule would set the pace. I strung them up like he'd said. I hadn't even left the yard when my lead mule started kicking the hell out of the little mule. Broke a rib and punctured a lung. He died right there in the yard."

"Shit."

Jo poked at the logs, unwilling to look at Takeisha.

"You left all that on a message?"

"Yep. And she texted that she was sorry."

"That's it?"

"She said I run hot and cold and she's never sure what will piss me off because I only share stuff with her after I'm mad."

"And you said?"

"I don't know what I'm supposed to share. Mules don't expect me to talk. That's why I get along with them better."

"First, I pray you didn't say that thing about the mules."

Jo absolutely had. It made sense to her, and she thought it helped explain who she was.

Takeisha rolled her eyes. "Second, you're full of shit. This isn't about talking. It's about paying attention. You're the one who says keep an eye on their ears, that they give a warning before they bite or kick. You're the one who figured out that Skeeter has to be tied to Blaze. They're important to you, so you figured it out. What you said doesn't make it sound like what Daisy needs is important to you."

"You're saying I fucked up."

Takeisha slapped her thighs and then clapped her hands. "Exactly!! Now what are you going to do about it?"

Long after Takeisha turned in, Jo sat by the dwindling fire. She slouched low in the chair and returned to the story she'd told Daisy. She remembered that Daisy had said Eddie's story was sad and scary. What Jo had said as a cautionary warning of how foolhardy crossing the river was, Daisy had felt emotionally. Eddie had lost his mules and with them his ability to enjoy all the backcountry that Jo knew Daisy had come to love. She remembered how emotional the sunset at Second Crossing had made Daisy. She had learned so much of what Jo knew, but she had also taught Jo about pausing to bask in the wonder of the backcountry. Jo thought about how Daisy had stuck with every punch Jo had thrown her way and then how she had started pushing back, slowly working her way past Jo's walls.

This wasn't about losing her mules. It was about losing Daisy. That was why the way they had shared themselves had felt so different. Loving Daisy made her feel vulnerable, but the way Daisy had loved her had made her feel whole. She was no longer whole without her.

She remembered the first time she was the solo packer, she had turned out stock in the mountains. She'd nearly thrown up with fear and worry when she caught up the stock in the morning and found that she was three horses short. As confused now as she had been standing in the middle of what looked like an empty pasture, she searched for a solution. In that situation, she solved the problem by saddling a horse and taking Cody out to search beyond the meadow.

"You think if we saddled up a few mules, we could find Daisy in Pasadena?" she asked, reaching down to rub the pup behind his ears. He thumped his tail.

By the time the Yosemite trip wrapped up, Jo had a Takeisha-approved plan. She stowed her kitchen for the last time and gave Jo a hug. She was done for the season, so Jo's plan didn't impact her at all. "Good luck, cowgirl. I hope she talks to you."

It was harder to go to Leo, but she knew she needed his help if she had any hope of convincing Daisy that she was sincere. He surprised her by sitting down to hash out details that she hadn't even taken into account.

She left at daybreak the next morning and called out a loud thank-you when she rolled into the employee parking of the Pasadena pet adoption a few blocks south of Colorado Boulevard that afternoon. Finding a place to park a truck and horse trailer in downtown Pasadena wasn't something she and Takeisha had included in their brainstorming, but Leo had.

She unloaded the stock and saddled, sweat dampening what had been a crisp blue button-down in the cool of the mountain morning. Twenty minutes later, her shirt was soaked. While

Daisy was right about her city being less crowded in August than January for the Rose Parade, the temperature made it feel like hell all the same. One that she had invited herself to, her inner self said. Time to cowgirl up. Foot to stirrup, she swung into the saddle and pointed Tuxedo for Colorado Boulevard.

The combination of movement and shade made riding up the northbound street almost tolerable. Then she turned onto the main drag. Sun blazed down on her directly. People stared. Traffic slowed even though she had decided to stick to the sidewalk. She caught a glimpse of herself reflected in the huge glass windows. Strangely, in the reflection she didn't look out of place as she had anticipated because the windows also reflected Daisy's San Gabriel Mountains.

When she caught sight of the sign for Temptation, she wished for the first time that she had saddlebags with a bottle of water. Her mouth was as dry as a desert. She stopped outside the store realizing that while she had thought through what she wanted to say, she had not planned how to get Daisy's attention. It didn't feel right to tie Tuxedo to the spindly tree outside her store. Butterscotch rode up on Tuxedo's rear end, and he kicked out. Their shoes rang out on the pavement as Jo swung him around.

She dismounted and put herself in between the two mules. Could she open the door and simply holler for Daisy? She felt like an idiot and had to chuckle realizing how that served her right. She reached for the door.

CHAPTER THIRTY-THREE

Daisy always dreaded the end of the lunch rush when her mind had time to mess with her. She hadn't even realized there was no longer a line to the register until she heard hoofbeats. How long would it take for her to get the sound out of her memory? Sighing heavily, she looked out the window. Were those mules?

The door opened.

Jo poked her head in.

Jo? Her heart did a double-take.

"Maybe she wants cowboy coffee," the barista next to her joked.

"I'm not just imagining a cowgirl with mules outside the store?" Daisy blinked a few times, willing the image to disappear.

"Nope," the bored teenager said. "Do you think she brought the campfire you'll need to make her coffee?"

Daisy crossed her arms.

"Daisy!" Jo sounded relieved and waited for her to respond.

How many times had she dreamed about Jo chasing after her? The first week she was away, Daisy had entertained the fantasy of running back into Jo's strong arms. The second week, she had marinated in the anger that Jo hadn't even bothered to run after her when she'd left the café at the Lodge. After three weeks, she found herself strangely neutral to the sight of Jo waiting on the other side of the glass door. Instead of walking to the door, Daisy turned and walked into the back where the staff lockers were. She released a frustrated growl and rested her head against the cool metal.

"What's wrong?" Her manager propelled herself from her office on her rolling chair. She liked Melanie, who was opposite of Leo in every sense. Not white, not old, not male and not slow. But she knew how much the short relationship with Jo had meant to Daisy and how angry and hurt she'd been when she returned to Pasadena.

"Jo's out front," Daisy said.

Melanie pushed off again, now rolling to the doorway where she would be able to see the front of the store. "I don't see any cowpokes out there."

"She's back on the street." Melanie stared at her long enough that she added "with two mules."

"You're going to let that poor girl cook out there?"

"I don't have anything to say to her."

Melanie released a puff of air with a dramatic eye roll that ended aimed at Daisy's boots. "Right."

Daisy frowned. "Just because I happened to wear jeans and boots today doesn't mean that I've been waiting for her to show up like this."

"That's not the point. She's come all this way to say something. So you listen. Then you can decide whether she's worth any more words."

Reluctantly, Daisy walked to the front door feeling every single eye on her. Outside, cars slowed to take in the random scene on the sidewalk. Though she had clearly made a huge effort to reach Daisy, Jo simply stood there. "Well?" Daisy prompted. "Did you take a wrong turn somewhere?"

Jo took off her hat, squinted at the sun, and put it back on. "You wouldn't return my calls."

"I don't need another explanation of how you were right, Jo. What you said at the Lodge made it clear that I don't fit in there. You won."

"You know that's not what I wanted."

"Do I? Come on. You bet Takeisha that I wouldn't last, and I didn't. But that's on you, not me."

"Why do you think I'm here?"

"I don't know. Maybe you want me to hold the mules, so you can go inside and humiliate me in front of my city friends too?"

"Daisy."

"You didn't even try to stop me from leaving. That message was clearer than any you left on my phone."

"I know. I didn't think you'd leave." Sweat ran down Jo's temple and Tuxedo butted her back with his muzzle.

"How could I have stayed? You actually think that's something I should have been able to brush off? That I wouldn't feel it the rest of the summer, at the evening feeding, saddling in the morning, leading a ride?"

"It was one mistake…"

Daisy cut her off. "You made me feel like *I* was the mistake. That Leo had made a mistake in letting me work at the corrals."

"I didn't mean it was you. Everyone's made mistakes. Even me. I told you that."

"You told my voice mail."

"Takeisha told me I fucked up."

A sharp breath escaped from Daisy.

"What?"

"You talk to Takeisha, but you don't talk to me. Don't you think that's a problem?"

"I'm here to talk to you now." Jo wound the lead rope in her hand, making even loops. "I know you're angry, but will you take a short ride with me? Please? The mules are hot."

"Get back on the horse?" Daisy made air quotes with her fingers. "That's the idea?"

"Butterscotch might have hurt feelings if you refuse."

Daisy softened. Jo had been smart to bring the mule. Daisy passed Jo and ran her hands down Butterscotch's neck. "Who has Cody?"

"Some friends of Leo's. They've got an animal shelter a few blocks away."

"By the park," Daisy said. When she closed her eyes, the mules and their gear brought the mountains back to her. There was no forgetting she'd left, though. She opened her eyes. There was no ignoring that Jo was there, either.

"Hold on a minute." Daisy ran her hand down Butterscotch's neck a few more times to keep herself from hugging Jo. Her body begged to be pressed up against Jo's, but her mind had not caught up yet.

Melanie was watching from the counter when she walked back in. "She wants me to take a ride."

"You want me to say 'no'?" She had the stature and frame to intimidate even Jo. It hadn't taken more than a stern look from her to make Daisy spill the details of why she was reluctant to talk to Jo again. Daisy could tell Melanie was poised to drop kick Jo all the way back to the mountains.

"I could tell her to hit the trail if I needed to," Daisy said.

"Just making sure. We'll be slow till closing if you want to be off the clock for the rest of the day. And I need to know ASAP if you're not coming in tomorrow."

"I wouldn't…"

Melanie interrupted her. "Pack all your things and be a mysterious no-show at your next shift? We both know you absolutely would."

Daisy started to apologize.

"Stop." Melanie held up her hand. "I knew this could happen when you came back. Don't take it the wrong way, but I can get someone else at the counter in a heartbeat. That's way easier than finding a cowgirl with an extra horse in tow."

"Mule."

"Whatever it is. Get your stuff. Get out of here. The suspense is killing me."

Daisy nodded and grabbed her bag from the break room. She slung it over her shoulder, hugged Melanie and walked out of Temptation trying her hardest not to smile when Jo's face lit up.

"I can tie your bag behind your saddle."

"I'm fine." Daisy slung the satchel across her chest, so it rested on her left thigh and reached for Butterscotch's lead rope.

Jo leaned like she was going to hug Daisy, but Daisy wasn't ready for that. She checked the girth and tightened it. She put her left hand on the saddle and raised the stirrup to check its length before she swung aboard.

"You look great, by the way. Not the same without your Zorro hat, but great."

Daisy flushed at her words. She was not going to give Jo the satisfaction of knowing how she looked like a dream standing there in front of her shop with Tuxedo. She imagined Jo stopping mid-parade and offering her the extra mule in her string. There was something about Jo that would have made Daisy follow her even then, even before she'd worked with her. She also remembered where she had led Jo and how much more she wanted to fuel the fire that still burned within.

As Jo scrambled to mount her own mule, Daisy took in the view from the saddle. Through the window, she could see everyone watching. She responded with a parade wave and gave Butterscotch a kick.

"Do you know where we're going?" Jo called from behind.

Daisy nodded and headed east on Colorado Boulevard. She scanned the streets from Jo's perspective, knowing it had taken a lot for her to return to the city. At the corner, she turned south for two blocks until she hit the park where they could ride side by side.

"Daisy," Jo said to bring her gaze to her.

"Were you worried we were going to get pulled over by the police?" There was no avoiding hearing what Jo had to say, yet Daisy didn't feel ready yet.

"Daisy," Jo said again.

For the last three weeks Daisy had been thinking about how Jo said her name, and hearing it again started to penetrate the armor she had built around her heart. She deflected again. "I guess you could have told them one of the mules lost a shoe in the Rose Parade and you came back to look for it."

"You know how you can only travel as fast as your slowest mule?"

Daisy reined in her mule, a familiar frustration with the way Jo held on to information flaring. "No. You never told me that."

"You can string up four of the fastest mules from the herd, but put a sled to your string, and that's how fast you can go."

Daisy frowned at her. "A sled?"

"A slow mule who pulls on you."

"You came all this way to tell me I'm a sled?"

"No, I came all this way to tell you I spent way too much of the summer treating you like the slowest mule, especially in how I reacted in front of your friends at dinner. All I could think about when you talked about re-stringing the mules…"

Daisy clenched her teeth. Time had not taken the sting out of the criticism. "Was the mule you lost. I know. You said that in your message."

Jo must have read her expression because she quickly added, "That's not what I'm saying. I mean, I am. I did say that on your machine, and I should have said it to your face. Partly I'm here to apologize for how I chewed you out. But also, I wanted to explain how I realized *I'm* the sled."

"You're the slow mule?" Daisy was doing her best to follow Jo's cowgirl explanations.

"All summer, I was the slowest mule. I did my best to slow you down. I'm not proud of it. And for a while I convinced myself that I was fairly testing the city girl to see if she could handle the challenge of the backcountry. The truth is, I was as stuck as Dumbo at that bridge trying my hardest not to fall in love with you."

Like the first hint of dawn, Jo's words peeked through the darkness Daisy had been holding on to. Love was not a word she'd expected to come out of Jo's mouth. Daisy wished she could search Jo's eyes to determine how sincere she was, but she'd tipped her head, hiding behind the brim of her hat.

"I was afraid of losing you. You can't lose something you don't have, see? I was the one who refused to own up to feeling anything for you because what would happen if I did, only to have you leave at the end of the summer? And then it was the end of the summer with a few small trips that meant weeks of not seeing you. I wasted so much of the summer fighting you when I could have been encouraging you. You are such a fast mule. Look at how much you learned over the summer. And how much you taught me."

Daisy had been so angry when Heather had told her about Jo's prediction that she would leave. And yet, how much had Jo's doubt kept her from giving up? Remembering the constant struggle it had been not to disappoint Jo, it was hard to believe Jo now. "I didn't teach you anything."

"You did. You taught me that cooking is a lot harder than I thought. You taught me that sharing the workload has benefits. And that maybe I do belong to the human herd. Even if I'm a stubborn asshole who spent way too much of the summer slowing you down. That wasn't right, and I'm really sorry."

"Sorry doesn't make it possible for me to go back there," Daisy said.

"Everyone was pissed at me after you left, even Leo."

"Leo was going to put me back on day rides."

"Only for the slow part of this season. He wants you back next summer. Why else would he help me with this whole plan?" She gestured to the animals. "I could not have gotten this crew down here without his help."

"For the café? Or for trips? I'm not going back to work at the café."

"On trips. With how much you learned, you're a valuable employee. You know a bunch of the trails. You can cook and you're learning to pack. It's like you completed Cowboy 101. Now you can move on to the next level."

"Cowgirl 101," Daisy corrected.

Jo nodded her agreement. She held Daisy's gaze and said, "I want you to come back."

"And Leo said yes."

"Yes! That's why he helped me get down here."

"He knows I want to be in the backcountry?"

"I told him I want us to be a team. We'd be working together."

That surprised Daisy. She sat with what Jo had said and how she'd said it. She hadn't said she wanted Daisy to cook for her trips. She'd said she wanted to work together. In the weeks since she'd left, she had fiercely missed the mountains and riding, but she thought she would have to find another way to enjoy them, another outfit or even as a guest. She had not once thought about returning to the Lodge. Her stomach clenched at the possibility.

"Will you come back next season?" Jo asked.

"I can't answer that," Daisy said honestly. "Next summer is a long way off. And right now, I'm not sure I'm ready."

"But you aced Cowgirl 101. Considering how much you didn't know at the beginning of the season, it was huge that you took on so much of the advanced stuff so quickly. But one summer doesn't make you an expert." She looped the reins around the horn of her saddle and untied a lariat that was hanging from the saddle and extended it to Daisy.

Daisy accepted the rope. "What's this for?"

"Every cowgirl needs a lariat. Nobody expects you to catch everything the first try. That's why you keep throwing another loop."

The waxy rope was not the least bit flexible her hands. "It's so stiff."

"A little bit like me." Jo smiled tentatively at her. "It takes a while to break in. Keep practicing, and it'll be supple by summer."

"You think I could catch the pink cow?"

"I know you can't catch anything if you don't throw a loop. Gabe taught me that, and it's why I'm here. This is me throwing a loop. I missed big time when I heard you talking about crossing the San Joaquin. Come back? I want another shot. It won't be the same without you."

Jo's question clanged in her ears. Why did it matter whether Jo thought she could learn to rope? She'd fallen right back into worrying about what Jo thought about her and knew exactly how vulnerable that had made her. She wasn't going to do that again. If she went back, it couldn't be to impress Jo. Jo would always have more experience in the backcountry, but that didn't have to prevent them from being equals. Holding the stiff lariat, Daisy remembered how many throws of the mental rope it had taken to engage Jo and how satisfying it was when she had. She couldn't hide her smile.

"What's that for?"

"I was thinking about how hard it was to catch your attention," she said. The way Jo held her in her gaze, Daisy knew she now had it completely. Her body warmed remembering how good it had felt when Jo used that attention to express her desire.

"Haven't you been listening to me? You caught my attention the second you stepped into the yard. What's hard was resisting you. What's harder is sitting here untethered to you, knowing that I'm the one who cut the rope. I miss being caught by you."

Tuxedo fidgeted under Jo, and she patiently worked him around again. "So, cowgirl..." She motioned to the rope in Daisy's hand. "You need a lariat?"

Daisy closed her eyes and weighed the question, even with the word "yes" pushing to escape her throat. Saying yes didn't just mean going back to the Lodge. It also meant trusting that Jo genuinely wanted to be a team. She needed to know that she had gained Jo's respect.

Butterscotch raised a hoof and stomped as if she were tired of waiting for Daisy's answer. She studied Jo, taking in the rings of sweat darkening her shirt. She had literally traveled hundreds of miles to a place she loathed to ask her question. She had made herself vulnerable, and unlike the mules, she waited patiently for Daisy's answer. Daisy studied Jo's eyes and could see mirrored in them how alone she'd felt since she had left.

"Leo said we could work together?"

"Yep. I'll teach you more about the packing side of things, and you can teach me more about being part of the people herd."

This finally made Daisy laugh, and Jo relaxed a little. "What if I have other stuff to teach you?"

"I'll try my hardest to not be a sled," Jo said.

Daisy nudged Butterscotch and circled around Jo and Tuxedo, so she could get close enough to reach out and bring the full coil of her new rope over Jo's head and shoulders. She pulled gently until Jo leaned over close enough to kiss.

Jo rested her hand on Daisy's hip and kissed her back, kissed Daisy all the way back to the other side of the San Joaquin where it was possible to find a new way across.

Tuxedo stepped away, forcing them to break apart.

"So you think you could love a city girl?" Daisy said, her heart in her throat.

Jo met her eyes and smiled. "I'm pretty sure I already do."

"I'm glad to hear that because I'm definitely in love with you, cowgirl," Daisy said. All around them, people were staring. She marveled at the picture they made. "What do we do now?"

"Take a ride in your city?"

"How far were you thinking?" Daisy asked.

"How about into today's sunset and as many more as you'll give me."

"Deal."

EPILOGUE

"All set!" Daisy called from the living room. "It feels like we've packed the entire place!"

Jo closed the cooler and scanned the refrigerator one more time to make sure she'd left it clean for her landlord's parents. They always spent the summer in the one-bedroom place right next door to their daughter and her family. They enjoyed being with their grandchildren and escaping the humidity in Virginia. She'd been thankful to find a place that worked so perfectly to allow her the summer in the backcountry without having to worry about subletting it or finding a house sitter. She'd worried that it would be too small for Daisy's taste, but she had found plenty of room to make herself at home.

Jo carried the cooler to the front door and surveyed what they needed to load before they made the drive to Mammoth for the start of the season. "What is this?" she exclaimed, pulling a tightly stuffed sleeping bag out of the pile.

"My sleeping bag."

"And when are you planning on using it?"

"You never know. I might end up needing it."

Jo took aim at Daisy and threw it, but Daisy easily dodged it. Cody jumped in circles barking up a storm. "You tell her, boy. She sleeps with us every night."

Daisy reached down and picked it up. "You think we'd be together if your packing job had gotten my bag to Second Crossing."

"Hey, I've never lost a single thing. Pete tied that load."

"I still think you chucked it on purpose because you couldn't think of any other way to get me into your bed."

Jo stepped over all their gear and wrapped her arms around Daisy. "If you hadn't spooned me, we would have shared that bedroll like roommates the entire time."

"But then you had your arms around me, remember? Deep in your subconscious, you knew we belonged together."

Daisy kissed her as she had that first time and lit the same fire she'd maintained through the winter. "Keep that up, and we'll lose another day of the season," she murmured, swaying against Daisy.

"You could have been there a week ago," Daisy said. "You didn't have to wait for me to finish the semester."

"It didn't feel right, not with the way you left." With her more flexible schedule, Jo had always arrived at the very beginning of the season every previous year. Daisy had encouraged her to do what she normally did, but Jo remembered how hard the last two weeks of the season had been without Daisy. She didn't want to feel that way again. Ever. "I don't want to be there without you, not even for a single day."

"Nobody's going to recognize you if you talk like that."

"You know me better than that. You're the only one who will ever hear those words, and don't for a second think that I'm going to be teaching some know-nothing hoo haw everything there is to being a cowgirl."

"There's one way to find out." Daisy grabbed a few bags and slung them over her shoulder to carry to the truck. She caught Jo watching and wiggled her tush.

"You lead and I'll follow," Jo said, though Daisy was already many steps ahead of her. She'd happily follow her wherever she went.

Bella Books, Inc.

Women. Books. Even Better Together.

P.O. Box 10543
Tallahassee, FL 32302

Phone: 800-729-4992
www.bellabooks.com